REDLINED

SHADOW CREW SERIES

CALA RILEY

Cover Photo and formatting by: Books and Moods
Editing by: My Brothers Editor

To Callie and the mountain yacht.
If you know, you know.

Love,

Cala

+

Riley

PROLOGUE

I've always loved the thrill of the race.

Engine purring, vibration rolling through me like adrenaline. The way it feels to have the full power of a beautiful machine at my mercy. Willing to whip whatever way I choose at a whim. My heart beating erratically with excitement and fear. It's exhilarating.

Focusing back on the road, I shift gears as I see the flash of silver in my peripheral.

He's gaining on me.

He won't win though.

I won't let him.

Gritting my teeth, I keep my pace, not caring about my opponent. Right now, it is me and the open road. Nothing to stop me.

I can see the finish line up ahead, made of random spectators standing around to witness the finale.

Only a couple hundred meters left. I can't help but smile.

Another race down.

My heart lodges in my throat as the car lurches forward, the sound of metal crunching against metal meets my ears.

"Fuck!" I yell as I clench my hands to try and maintain control, but the back of the car fishtails before I spin out. Then something hits the driver's door, pain radiating against my side.

The car begins to flip as I clench my eyes shut to avoid the dizziness threatening to settle in.

The car finally comes to a stop, but I'm hung upside down being held in only by the seat belt I'm grateful Ross forced me to wear.

I slowly peel my eyes open, my vision blurry. Taking a deep breath, I try to calm down and fight back nausea. My head is pounding, ears ringing. I blink several times until my eyes focus as much as possible. I make out several dark figures rushing my way.

Help is on the way.

He's coming to me.

Then the blackness creeps in, pulling me under.

CHAPTER ONE

Roxy

Standing outside of the looming house in front of me, I take a deep breath.

I don't want to be here. I want to be back home with my friends. Alas, I've been sent off like some petulant child who needs to be reformed.

I know that's not the truth, but it feels that way.

I'm twenty-five, for fuck's sake.

I can still remember the words he spoke when I woke up in the hospital.

It's not safe here for you anymore. You need to go while we figure this shit out.

It's a bullshit cop-out. I begged him to finally let me into their little club instead, but he refused. It doesn't matter that I've spent the last twelve years hanging around them, he never let me get closer than teaching me everything I know about cars and allowing me to race for them.

I'm not a moron. I know they do illegal shit. Other than the races which are not sanctioned, I think they run drugs or something. Ross has more money than a man at his age who has never had a real job should have.

Still, he has it in his head that if he keeps me at a distance then I'll finally fuck off and abandon them.

Not abandon them. He wants me to grab a better life for myself. Or so he would tell me every time I would harp on him to let me take a more active role. Sometimes they forget I'm an adult now and not the kid they took in. Everyone around Ross has the same tattoo with minor differences. I've heard some people talking about it before.

Soulless.

That's what people whisper as they walk by. They are something to be feared in Riviera. They aren't the only ones though.

He thinks I didn't notice, but everyone was tense at the last race. There were men there with different tattoos. It was obvious they were not overly welcome. When I asked a couple of spectators, they called them Hellions. Occasionally people from something called the Devil's Den come around too.

It's obviously some criminal enterprise.

Yet instead of letting me use my real skills, Ross made me go to college. He even paid for it. He kept telling me a degree would help him in the long run, so I went for business. What better way to help him out but to learn how to help him run his business?

I believed it at the time, but now I've graduated and he no longer has a reason to keep me out, but he does. Every time I take one step forward, he takes four steps back, making the line in the sand clear. If I was a weaker woman, I might think it was because I'm not good enough.

I know that's not the truth though. I'm the best driver he has. I would be a damn good addition to his team.

Still, he sent me here instead of keeping me under his protection.

Asshole.

That's how I found myself standing in some town I've never actually been to, seeking out a cousin I haven't talked to in years.

Letting out a deep sigh, I make my way up the steps to the house. It's nothing special. Just another cookie-cutter house in some boring suburban neighborhood.

I miss my little apartment in California. It wasn't much, but it was mine.

Taking a deep breath, I knock on the door. I shake off the feelings washing over me. I let the blank mask settle over my face.

A couple minutes go by before the door swings open.

The man standing before me is *not* my cousin. He's taller than my five foot six. If I had to guess, he's probably six foot. His slightly curly blond hair is sticking up like he just woke up. He's shirtless, showing off every ridge of his chest leading down to the V showing beneath the gray sweats he's wearing. This man is sex on a stick.

"Well, who do we have here? Babe, did you order a gorgeous present to join us?" he calls out over his shoulder.

There she is.

My cousin, Hannah, bounds up behind the man dressed only in a man's shirt, which I assume is the man standing before me.

"Shit. Roxanne, when did you get in?"

"Not too long ago. Sorry to rock up unannounced."

"Nonsense. I would have picked you up if you had called. Get in here," she says, waving me inside.

I brush past the man, but he doesn't give me an inch.

"Hey, Han, are you kissing cousins? I'm still down for a threesome."

"Shut up, Blaze," she snaps at him, but it only makes him laugh.

"Fine. I'm out then. Catch you later."

He grabs a set of keys and a phone off the table next to the door before stepping out the front door, shutting it behind him.

"I didn't mean to chase your boyfriend away," I tell Hannah, slightly confused by the whole interaction.

I mean, he's a sleazeball, but if that's what she's into, then I can't judge.

She scoffs. "He's not my boyfriend. Blaze is my best friend. Let me show you to your room."

"Oh. Okay."

"Don't look so frightened." She teases as I follow her down the hall.

I wipe my confusion off my face until my blank mask remains. "I'm not."

She rolls her eyes, stopping next to the first door we come to.

"Whatever. This is your room. The bathroom is there" —she points to a room down the hall— "it's the guest bath, but for the most part, you'll have it to yourself."

"Thanks." I take a step inside, looking at the bland room.

The walls are white without anything hanging on them. In the middle of the room is a bed and box springs sitting on the floor. The bed isn't even made. A comforter and sheets are piled on the end of the bed, not even folded. Other than that, the room is empty. No dresser. No knick-knacks.

"It's not much, but it's yours for as long as you want it. I just pulled the bedding from the laundry earlier, so it's clean. I didn't get around to making the bed."

I nod my appreciation. "Hopefully I'll be out of here quickly. I don't plan to stay long."

She gives me a small smile. "Meet me in the living room after you settle. I can give you the rundown around here."

I drop my bag inside the door.

"Lead the way."

She chuckles and starts walking down the hall. "No nonsense. I like that. You're not the girl I remember."

I scoff. "And you are?"

She purses her lips. "Not really."

She gestures to the couch, taking an armchair.

"So what's up?" I ask as I sit down, crossing my arms over my chest.

She shakes her head. "That attitude is likely to cause you more trouble than it's worth. Listen, I'm not your enemy here. I know you don't want to be here. You made as much clear when you called, but that was a choice you made. Don't take it out on me."

I take a deep breath, relaxing my arms. She's right but fuck if I'd admit it. I didn't want to call her, but Ross had already given her the heads up I was coming. I had to talk to her myself. Especially since I really had nowhere else to go.

"Understood." Then more calmly. "What do you need to tell me?"

She smirks. "I meant what I said. My home is your home. You can stay as long as you want. With that being said, I ask that you check with me before you bring any strangers into my home. It sounds controlling, but I have a very good reason to ask. Other than that, try and stay out of trouble. There are…" she trails off, thinking over her words. "Politics here that are at play. I don't want you to get mixed up in it."

I'm intrigued, but I don't ask questions. "Got it. Anything else?"

She reaches over, picking up a key that was sitting on the end table, handing it to me. "Eat whatever you want in the kitchen and welcome home."

"I'm going to get a job. I'll pay you rent and whatever else you want me to contribute."

Her eyes soften. "You don't have to. I know something happened and when you're ready, I'm happy to listen, but until then, take the time you need. Sort your shit out. Honestly, it will be nice to have you here. It gets too quiet sometimes. We might be different, but you're still like a sister to me. I'd like to get to know you again, if you do too."

I take a deep breath. I wasn't planning to get close to her again. I don't need any attachments holding me here when I'm finally ready to leave.

Still, the soft, hopeful look on her face keeps me from shooting her down right away. Part of me remembers the chubby-faced twelve-year-old who would eat cheese puffs until her fingers were orange then chase it with an energy drink. The same girl who would crawl into my bed at night so that we could whisper until we both fell asleep.

Maybe it's that nostalgia or maybe I need more sleep than the broken hours I manage to grab on the bus, but I find myself speaking before I consider my words.

"I'd love that, Hannah."

ROMAN

"Well, she's here," Blaze says as he walks into the office, sitting down across from me.

I toss my pen down on the desk and rub my eyes. "Who's here?"

"Hannah's cousin, Roxanne."

"Already?" I frown, grabbing my phone.

"Yeah."

"Damn," I say, looking at the date.

"Time flies when you're living your best life," Blaze quips.

"Is that all?" I ask as I pick the pen back up.

"Aren't you going to ask me what she looks like?" he asks, making himself comfortable.

"Why would I do that?" I sigh, knowing that work is a lost cause for right now.

"Because she's female and new to town," he says slowly.

"I already told you, stay away."

"But why?"

"Because last I checked, she was a Soulless on the run. We don't need to be pulled into her shit any more than we currently are."

"Okay."

"Just keep an eye on her. Ross said she wouldn't bring trouble to our doorstep but you never know."

"Whatever you say, boss."

"Now how about you get out of my office and go help Axel and Marco in the garage."

"You got it." He stands, walking away. "For the record, she's hot as fuck," he says over his shoulder.

I lean back in my chair and rub my face, exhaustion setting in. When Ross called, it caught me off guard. I had no idea that Hannah had ties to someone involved with Soulless.

"Hello," I answer.

"Hey Roman, it's Ross."

I frown as I lean back in my chair wondering why a Soulless would be calling. It's not like we communicate regularly.

"What can I do for you?"

"Remember that favor you owe me?"

Fuck. I knew him saving my ass the one time I ventured out to Cali would come back to bite me. It's the reason I haven't ventured into his territory in more than ten years.

"Yeah..."

"I need to call it in."

"What's up?" That sinking feeling in my stomach intensifies. Whatever he needs, it must be bad to call me in for it.

"My girl, Roxy, she needs a fresh start and I'm sending her your way."

His girl? I thought her name was Ashley, not Roxy.

"Why?"

"Her cousin Hannah lives in your town. I figured a fresh start with a familiar face would be in her best interest."

"What kind of trouble is she in?" I frown.

"She's not."

"Then why are you sending your girl away?"

"Look, Roxy is just a friend. Like a sister to me. She's not a member of my crew. She won't cause you any trouble. That's not her style." He pauses. "Unless someone gives her a car and she's on the line. Then all bets are off."

"She's your racer," I say as it dawns on me.

"She was." The sound of defeat in his tone piques my curiosity.

"Look, man, I don't know. I have enough shit going on with Devil's Den."

"I'm not asking you to bring her into the fold. I'm letting you know she's in your area as a courtesy. But as a favor, I'm asking you to make sure she doesn't do anything stupid."

"You just said she wouldn't be trouble."

He sighs. "She's spirited. She won't mean to cause trouble, but she also has a habit of turning up places she shouldn't be. If you keep an eye out for her, consider your debt paid."

I sit in silence for several minutes before finally responding.

"Okay, but only if Hannah is okay with it."

"I appreciate it, man. I'll check in when I can," he says before hanging up.

The sounds of tools dropping onto the cement floor in the garage pull me out of the memory. Call it a gut instinct, but I think she's going to stir shit up around here and that's the last thing I need.

Giving up on paperwork, I stand and make my way toward the garage. My hands itch to do anything but paperwork. Invoices and orders are the bane of my existence and the worst part of being a business owner, but someone has to do it. In order to make money, you have to finish jobs. In order to finish jobs, you have to have parts, and so on and so forth.

As I step into the garage, I instantly relax. "Shook Me All Night Long" plays on the radio as I grab a jumpsuit off the hook by the door to protect my clothes.

"You getting your hands dirty today?" Marco asks from under the hood of the car he's working on.

"If I don't then nothing will get done," I joke, making the guys scoff. "What are we working on today?" I ask as I approach Marco.

"General maintenance. Nothing I can't handle." He shrugs as he wipes his hands off with a rag. "So..."

"So?"

"Blaze came in here talking about Hannah's cousin."

"She hasn't even been here twenty-four hours and I'm already tired of hearing about her," I groan.

"Yeah, well, between Blaze and Hannah, I'm sure you'll hear her name so much your ears will bleed," he teases.

"That oil change still in the parking lot?" I ask as I glare at him.

"Yeah, there's one still out there."

"You good, man?" I ask as I really look at my best friend.

"I'm fine," he says with a weak smile.

"You know where to find me when you want to talk," I say as I take in the stress lines on his face.

For the past several weeks, he has been acting cagey. Marco has been my best friend for most of my life. I can tell when something is bothering him.

"Get to work, we got bills to pay," he jokes as he turns back toward the car.

I pause and watch him for a minute, wondering if I should let it go or push, but I choose to let it go and walk away. He will talk when he is ready.

I HIT THE button and watch as the garage door slides open. I take a deep breath as I pull the car into the garage and shut it off. Laying my head back against the headrest, I savor the moment of silence while my brain fires off a list of things I need to do before the others show.

Pull the meat out of the fridge for burgers.

Take a shower.

Make sure the bathroom is clean for Hannah.

I groan as I open the car door and slide out and make my way inside. Walking into the house, I kick my shoes off in the mudroom before stopping in the kitchen. I make my way to the fridge and grab a beer and pop the top. I close my eyes and savor the first taste as I relax. Pulling out my phone, I shoot off a text to Marco telling him to grab more beer before heading this way as I walk toward the shower.

Marco: 10-4

Placing my beer on the shelf in the shower, I turn the water on and let it heat up. First I set my phone on the counter and then I remove my wallet from my pocket before I strip down. Stepping into the shower, I reach for my beer as the water washes over me. By the time I'm done with my beer, I'm clean and relaxed.

As I step out of the shower and wrap a towel around my waist, I hear the door open.

"Honey, I'm home!" Marco yells, making me shake my head as I walk into my bedroom.

"Be out in a minute," I holler back.

By the time I'm dressed and have checked the spare bathroom to make sure it's still clean enough for Hannah to use, everyone is here.

"Hey." Hannah smiles as she sits at the island.

"How are you?" I ask as I head toward the fridge, pulling out another beer and the meat for dinner.

"I'm good."

"How's the new roommate?" Axel asks as he walks out of my pantry with a bag of chips.

"Make yourself at home, why don't you?" I mutter.

"Don't mind if I do." He smirks.

"Roxy's good, I think."

"What does that mean?" Axel frowns.

Out of the corner of my eye, I watch Hannah bite her lip. "Everything is fine. I promise. It's just been so long since I've seen or talked to her. When we were kids she was always laughing and smiling and now..." She shrugs. "She's closed off I guess. Guarded. It's almost as if they are two different people. And she kept saying how she would be out of my hair soon enough."

"If anyone can get through to her, it's you, Han," Blaze says as he comes up behind her, wrapping his arms around her as he kisses the top of her head.

"I know. It's just going to take more work than I thought it would," she says as she leans into him.

"Just be careful. Don't let your guard down," I warn her.

Hannah was ecstatic when she found out her cousin would be coming to stay with her. She has this wild idea that they will reconnect and be best friends again. I'm more skeptical.

"She's family," Hannah says adamantly.

"Is she though?" I raise my brow. "Last time I checked, family was there when you needed them. I've known you for how many years now and I didn't even know you had a cousin," I point out.

"Yeah but—" she says as I raise my hand, cutting her off.

"I'm not saying you shouldn't let her in, but just be cautious. Like you said, she's different now. I don't want to see you end up hurt because of some shit she does because she doesn't care. You don't know anything about this chick anymore."

"Enough," Blaze hisses as he squeezes Hannah, looking at me.

"How about we change the subject," Axel says as he pops another chip into his mouth.

"What did I miss?" Marco asks as he walks into the house from the back door.

"Where were you?" I ask.

"Starting the grill. I'm fucking starving."

"When are you not?" Hannah teases, making us chuckle.

Thankfully, the conversation moves on from the new girl and on to our day-to-day life. Looking around the kitchen, I take a drag of my beer. Watching my family move around as a well-oiled machine makes me feel content. Like everything I've gone through to get to this point has been worth it.

So why does it feel like there is a storm on the horizon?

CHAPTER TWO

Roxy

Groaning, I turn over, reaching for my phone.

Seeing Ross's name on the caller ID, I hit ignore. He doesn't get to check in on me anymore. He cast me out like unwanted trash all because of one little accident.

I know I'm being irrational. I know if I stopped and actually thought about the reasons why he sent me away, I would agree with them, but I'm so angry and hurt that I don't want to.

I'm not ready to forgive him yet.

If I focus on my anger, then I can push the hurt down. Maybe by the time I run out of anger, the hurt will be a distant memory.

Immediately a text comes through.

Ross: Let me know you made it safe.

I roll my eyes. He shouldn't even care anymore. Part of me wants to ignore him, but I know if I do, he is likely to make the fourteen-hour drive to come see for himself.

Me: I'm not your concern. Have a nice life.

I toss my phone on the bed, padding out into the kitchen. Fuck him and the rest of them. They were supposed to be my family, but now that Ross says so, they all dropped me.

That's what hurt me the most. Ross has always been my constant, but he wasn't the only one. His friends became my friends. His core group used to hang out at his house with me at all hours of the night. We would watch movies or play video games. They would take me to parties and help me get ready for the races. They were my family, but one word from Ross and they stopped responding.

I tried reaching out to each of them the first hour on the bus. By the sixth hour of no response, I realized it didn't matter if I ever went back. I had nothing to go back to.

Letting out a sigh, I focus on the present.

Opening the fridge, I take stock of my options.

I'll need to make a trip to the store, I think as I see nothing but water and orange juice.

Fuck, I'd kill for an energy drink about now.

"Oh, you're awake," Hannah says as she walks in, putting her earrings in.

"Unfortunately," I mutter.

"Still not a morning person, huh?" She smiles.

Hannah and I used to spend summers together when we were younger. My mom was usually chasing off after her next boyfriend, but Uncle Mike was happy to let me come stay. I stopped coming when I was thirteen. By then, Mom no longer felt it necessary to spend the bus ticket money to send me, so I ended up staying all alone in the neighborhood.

It was then I learned my love for cars and racing.

"Well, there is coffee in the cabinet and creamer in the fridge. Like I said last night, make yourself at home."

I grunt in response, moving to the cabinet to grab the coffee. It will have to do.

"I have to go to work today, but if you need a ride into town, let me know. I can arrange something."

"I will," I lie.

She smiles at me before leaving.

I plan to go to town, but I don't need her help. If it wasn't for the fact that I would be homeless, I wouldn't even be staying with her. Ross made that decision for me when he brought me to the bus station after my accident with my suitcase already packed. After refusing to leave on my own, he cast me away by force.

You don't belong here anymore. I've arranged for you to stay with your cousin, Hannah. Don't bother coming back here. You won't be welcome. It's for your own good.

I shiver at the thought. How he could act so unaffected by casting me aside.

I met Ross the first summer I stayed home. With Mom off with some guy, I would walk the streets. I grew up in Riviera my entire life, so it wasn't like I was scared. I knew there were shady things going on. I just wasn't afraid of them.

I was young, dumb, and fearless. I wasn't afraid because I knew if something bad happened to me, it meant that I'd either die and this life would be over or I'd be hurt enough that someone would take me to a hospital. Then at least someone would give me attention.

It was on one of those walks that I stumbled upon Ross. He was working on a car in front of his garage. I watched him for a moment as he was underneath it. His hand kept searching for tools blindly.

I don't know why, but I walked over and handed him the wrench.

When he rolled out from under the car, I knew I was in trouble.

I think I fell in love right then and there.

His dark brown eyes with the hair that was laying across his face, almost in his eyes. Grease was streaked across his face.

I was thirteen, but that didn't stop me from feeling the butterflies in my stomach when he smiled at me.

"What are you doing here?"

I shrug my shoulders.

"Where are your parents?"

"I don't know who my dad is and my mom's…"

I didn't want to finish my sentence. If I told him the truth, he might tell on me and get me taken away. I'd rather be alone than in the system.

He nods once. "Well, what do you know about cars?"

"Nothing."

That was the start of our friendship. He was five years older than me, but

I didn't care. He would let me hang out with him and teach me how to work on his car. He taught me to drive when I was sixteen and how to race when I was seventeen. He slowly introduced me to his crew, giving me the family I always hoped for. I would have done anything for them.

So when he asked me to go to college, I did. When he limited my exposure to their world, I accepted it.

He always insisted that I didn't really want to be a part of his business.

No matter how many times I tried, he would repeatedly tell me they weren't what I needed. That I deserved better.

Honestly, I'm not surprised he made me leave. He made it clear he never wanted me to be part of their group. I was some kid that hung around. I'm surprised he kept me around as long as he did. He could have sent me on my way at eighteen, but he didn't.

I can't regret my time with him though. Without him, I wouldn't have my love for cars and racing. Without him, I wouldn't know self-defense.

Still doesn't mean I'm ready to forgive him yet.

Finishing making my cup of coffee, I head back to my room. Picking up my phone, I see another text from Ross.

Ross: Don't be like this.

Shaking my head, I send one last response.

Me: I'm not welcome to the only place I called home. Go fuck yourself, Ross. You're officially blocked. Don't bother showing up here either.

Before he can respond, I block his number.

I blow out a breath. I know I should be the bigger person and put it behind me, but I am still so angry at him. I'm twenty-five years old. If I want to live in Riviera, I should be able to.

Logically, I know that I could go back if I really wanted. There is nothing stopping me from living in my apartment and continuing on with life except what kind of life would I have?

He put the decree out. If I go back now, I will be as alone as I feel here, only it will be worse because at least here I don't have to see the people I once thought of as family. I don't have to walk down the road and remember all the fun times we had. Besides that, he would never let me race again, which was my only source of income.

No. Here is better for now. At least here, I can cut my old life off cold turkey and start over anew.

One thing is for sure, I won't trust anyone like that ever again.

Taking a quick shower, I get ready to leave. It's a five mile walk to town, but I have nothing better to do.

The walk was uneventful. Cars passed me, but none stopped. Thank goodness. When I finally see the town, I smile. I've seen a bus pass a couple of times so I know that I'll have transportation. Now all I need is a job.

Walking through town, I take in the scenery. Even with this being area being unfamiliar, it's oddly comforting. As angry as I am about everything that went down, being here is relaxing. Like a weight has been lifted off my shoulders. Sure, I want to be back home, but there is something about a quaint small town that can settle your anxiety.

I've never been to Chita before. Hannah moved here after graduation from a couple towns over where my uncle still lives.

Technically, I suppose I could have gone and stayed with him, but Hannah had always been a feeling of safety for me. We were once close as children. Maybe we could be again.

Shaking my head, I banish the thought. Hannah and her family will have my back, but I'm not sure I'm looking for permanent roots again. Maybe I'll become transient. Floating from town to town. Taking small jobs. Maybe finding some races to compete in.

Yeah, that sounds like the life. Forget relying on anyone else. I can rely on myself. All I have to do is get a car.

I never needed one back home. Ross always let me use one of his. I'm regretting that now. I should have saved my money and bought a car. Instead, I spent all my extra money running around with the people who I thought were my friends. Smoking weed and drinking. Going to clubs and partying. That's all my life was and I loved every minute of it.

Looking back, I should have been preparing for this future. I always knew deep inside that Ross had no intentions of claiming me as Soulless. As long as I had known him he always managed to keep me at a distance. I knew one day he would tire of me and drop me. Why would he ever want to keep me when my own mother didn't?

As much as I'd like to say I hate the cunt for abandoning me, I can't.

That small little girl still inside wonders if she ever thinks about the child she left behind. Sure, she came home occasionally to make sure I was still alive, but do I honestly believe it had anything to do with me?

No.

She would pop in to remind me of the consequences of calling the authorities on her. How they would snatch me from my life and place me in a group home. She always made sure to tell me that they take the teens to a group home that is more like jail than anything else.

I was scared shitless of that.

Then I met Ross and any inkling of giving up my freedom vanished.

Still, what would I say to her if she were standing in front of me right now? Would I even recognize her? I haven't seen her in nine years. I know she wouldn't recognize me. Even if she did, would I want to hear what she had to say?

I don't realize how lost in my thoughts I am until I bump into someone hard enough to stumble. The hand on my arm steadies me as I look up.

"Sorry. Are you okay?" the man asks.

He's young. I'd even venture to say he's younger than me. He's cute but has that cocky arrogance that makes me want to punch a guy in the face. His dark hair is cut short, the color matching his dark brown eyes.

"I'm fine."

I stand straighter, pulling my arm from his.

"Good. I didn't mean to bump you."

I look down at the phone in his hands. It's obvious he was playing on it instead of watching where he was walking.

"Maybe next time keep an eye on the sidewalk. Walking and texting can be just as dangerous as texting and driving," I say, raising a brow.

He smiles wide. "That it can. You're not from around here."

He doesn't pose it as a question, but I can't help but snark back at him. "Wow. What gave me away? The fact that you haven't known me since kindergarten? Or was it the way I'm walking aimlessly around town? Oh I know, it's the tattoo on my forehead. Forgot all about that."

He snorts. "You're funny. My name's Jordan."

When he reaches out his hand, I stare at it for a moment before accepting. "Roxanne, but my friends call me Roxy."

He quirks an eyebrow. "Are we friends?"

"The jury's still out on that."

"Well, tell me, Roxanne, what would it take for me to earn the privilege of calling you Roxy?"

I shrug. "What's there to do for fun around here? Seems too boring for me."

"Yeah? Where are you from?"

"California."

"Ah. You need some hustle and bustle?"

"Something like that."

"How about this? You give me your phone number and I'll take you out and show you all the fun tomorrow night."

"Asking for my number? Bold, but I'm desperate. Fine, take me out tomorrow, but just so we are clear, if you try anything I do not agree with, I'll cut your balls off."

"Feisty. That's hot. No funny business. I promise. Not unless you beg," he quips.

I shake my head, a hint of a smile on my face. This guy is an asshole, but maybe he can help distract me for a little while since I'm stuck here. I might not need any attachments, but I never said anything about some good dick.

Holding out my hand, I wait until he places his unlocked phone in my palm. I enter my phone number with the name of *Badass Bitch.* Then I close his contacts before handing it back. If he can figure it out, then he can call me.

"I should go. Maybe I'll hear from you later." I wink, leaving him behind me.

"Oh, you will," he calls out to me.

When I turn the corner of the next block, I make a decision.

I might not be here because I want to be, but I can make the most of it. I made the choice to come here. I let Ross run me off with the innate need to obey his demands, but that doesn't mean I can't enjoy my life out here.

I'll make the best of my time here, starting with getting a job. Then I'll pay Hannah rent while saving up money to get a car. Once I have it, I'll leave this place and never look back.

As I continue to walk down the main strip of town, I window shop. So far everything is pretty generic to every small town. A small bookshop, a bakery, knick-knack shop, and a café. There's even a bank on the corner next to a small post office.

Then I see it.

Help Wanted.

The sign hangs in the window of Julio's, a Mexican restaurant.

I can serve. It's not like I haven't before. Sure, the races provided me money back home, but I did pick up odd jobs sometimes when things were slow or Ross wouldn't let me race.

Walking in, a lady in what appears to be in her mid-thirties smiles at me as she walks toward a table with food in her hands.

"We will be right with you."

I nod my head once. I watch as she moves effortlessly around the table, placing plates where they belong. Once she is done, she heads my way.

"Welcome to Julio's. How many?"

I shake my head. "I'm here for an application."

Her smile widens. "Wonderful. Come with me."

I follow her over to the bar area on the right as she pulls out a stool at the end.

"Have a seat. I'll go get the paperwork."

A man walks behind the bar and over to me once she leaves. "Hey there, I'm Julio. Can I get you anything to drink?"

I smile politely. "Oh, no thank you. I'm here for an application."

"How about a water while you wait?"

I give him a short nod. "Sure. A water would be great."

He walks away, coming back with a glass of water a moment later.

"Thanks."

"You're welcome. So why would you want to work in a place like this?"

I shrug. "I'm new in town. I need a job. I won't lie and say my end goal is to be a server or whatever position is open, but I don't mind working. I've done some serving in the past, so I figured why not."

"I see. Where did you move from?"

"California."

"That's a big move. Well, welcome to our little slice of heaven."

I smile brighter at him. "Thank you for the warm welcome."

There's something about Julio that makes me smile. He's an older man, in his fifties, but he has this playful youthfulness about him.

He nods as the woman comes back. "Oh, Julio. This young lady is filling out an application. I'm sorry I didn't even ask your name."

I smile at her. "Roxanne, but you can call me Roxy."

She smiles back. "Here is the paperwork and pen."

Julio jumps in, "Once she's done, give her a brief tour and introduce her to everyone and get her sizes. She'll start on Monday."

I gasp, looking back at the man. He winks at me.

"Seriously? Just like that?"

"You have a nice smile, you're polite, and you are honest. You'll fit right in."

"Thank you," I say sincerely.

Julio walks back around the bar, disappearing into the back.

"That's the owner. You get used to his quirkiness. I'll be back in a couple minutes."

I nod. I figured out who he was as soon as he told me his name.

I fill out the paperwork quickly, pulling out my ID and social security card as well so that she can make copies. When she comes back, she gives me a short tour, ending in the office where she makes copies of my cards before handing them back to me.

"So you'll start Monday morning. Be here at ten-thirty. Knock on the back door here and we will let you in. If all goes well next week, we will start adding you on the weekends as well."

"Sounds good."

"Welcome to the family."

CHAPTER THREE

Roxy

It didn't take long for Jordan to text me last night. He figured it out pretty quick, even going as far to tell me he wouldn't mind getting to know a badass bitch like me.

He's a tool for sure, but I have to admit he made me laugh. He has no shame, which is refreshing.

That's how I ended up in the passenger seat of his Mustang tonight. First we went to the café I saw yesterday for an early dinner. Now we are taking a walk down the street.

Both of us have fallen silent.

"So is this your idea of a romantic date?" I ask him after a while.

"I guess so. I wasn't sure what you would want to do. I won't lie, this place can be pretty boring."

"I'm going to miss home then. I'm used to parties, races, clubs, and overall debauchery every weekend. Fuck, sometimes during the week. I'm going to die of boredom here." I groan.

He laughs, looking down at his phone. "All that, huh? You want some debauchery?"

"I wouldn't say no to a little excitement."

He reaches down, grabbing my hand and starts pulling me back toward the car. "Alright then. Let's get going. We don't want to be late."

My blood starts to pump through my veins. The excitement of the unknown. I know I should be smarter, thinking about what this guy could have planned, but I'm not. I can feel in my bones whatever we are about to do is worth it.

Once in the car, he speeds off, making me laugh with joy.

"Faster," I yell to him over the music.

He smirks at me, downshifting to speed quicker. He flies around a curve, barely keeping the car on the road, but straightening out once around it.

My heart stutters in my chest. My hands ache to be on the wheel. To be the one manipulating this machine until it obeys my every command. I can't even deny the dampening of my panties. It has absolutely nothing to do with the man next to me and everything to do with the thrill of the race. The speed and the danger.

When he pulls up to a parking lot, my eyes widen. He brought me to some car meet-up. All around are people milling about. There are cars lined in the middle that are obviously the attraction while other older, boring cars are parked away from the crowds.

Jordan parks in a space closer to the middle.

I get out of the car as soon as he stops.

"So what do you think?" he asks as he rounds the hood of the car.

I smirk at Jordan. He thinks this would surprise me. He has no idea where I'm from.

I inhale deeply, loving the smell of asphalt, burnt rubber, and oil. This is home.

"I love it."

He chuckles, sliding an arm around me. "You keep getting better and better."

I let him, even though I know this guy couldn't handle me. He isn't thinking with anything but his dick. I won't be sucking his cock tonight, but if he's lucky, I won't shank him for getting handsy with me.

Jordan leads me around from group to group, introducing me to people who couldn't care any less about who I am.

That's not true. Some of the guys eye me like they would like to get to know me better, but the girls all turn their noses up at me.

I can see why. They are all dressed in short skirts and low-cut shirts, whereas I'm in jeans and a tight, black tank top. Add in my Chucks and, well, I do not belong with these girls.

Well, that and the fact that I'm not hanging off Jordan or standing back as the men talk. Instead, I'm peeking under the hoods of the cars surrounding the groups.

This is where I belong. What I love.

I might be angry at Ross, but I'm thankful that he gave me this. My love of cars.

As the night wears on, I get farther and farther away from Jordan as he continues to socialize.

Jordan's engaged in conversation with a group of guys with his back to me when I decide I'm ready to move on to the next car. Instead of interrupting, I turn and make my way down the line.

After fifteen minutes and several deflections from the horny male population, I make it to the end.

That's when I see it.

It's beautiful. The sleek deep blue paint reflects under the streetlights. Two white lines mark the center of the hood. Walking around the car, I peer inside.

It looks authentic. I can't pinpoint the exact year, but fuck, if it isn't a beauty. If I had to guess, I would say a sixty-nine, but it could be a seventy too. I've seen them in red, but this blue makes it sexier. More dangerous. Like the blue hides the true intentions of the car, whereas the red screams sex on a stick.

When I get back around to the hood, I peer inside. The engine is a sexy as fuck supercharger. It's clean as fuck. I know that as soon as this car starts up, the purr of the engine would entice anyone within a mile radius to come at its call.

I shiver. There is something innately sexy about this car. I want it. I want to drive it. Race it. Fuck on top of it.

The hair on the back of my neck prickles as if there are eyes on me. I straighten, looking around, but don't see anyone paying attention to me. I can't even see Jordan anymore. I suppose I walked too far away from him.

I turn back around, admiring the car for a moment before I turn to make my way back down the line where I last saw Jordan.

He meets me halfway.

"There you are. I thought you let someone else whisk you off."

I shake my head. "Not unless it's the owner of the sexy as fuck Chevelle down there. Man, what I wouldn't do to get behind the wheel of that car."

He chokes on the air. "The Chevelle? Fuck, you don't want to go there."

"What are you doing here?" I startle as Hannah pulls me away from Jordan before I can respond.

"What?" I ask.

"I told you to stay out of trouble. How the hell did you end up here?" she hisses as she pulls me farther away.

I rip my arm from her grip. "You're not my keeper. I didn't follow you here, if that's what you're implying. I'm here with a friend. Go mind your business and I'll mind mine."

So much for a friendship with my cousin. Seems she thinks she can control me. I had enough of that with Ross. I won't put up with it here too.

She huffs, but her eyes narrow as I feel an arm sling around my shoulder.

"They are about to leave for the races. You ready?"

I look over to Jordan and give him a small smile. I wonder if I can convince him to let me race his car. I bet Hannah would shit a fucking brick.

"Yep."

He smiles at Hannah.

"Keep your head low, Roxanne," she murmurs.

"Yeah, whatever." I roll my eyes at her.

As I let Jordan pull me away, he turns to whisper to me. "How do you know a Shadow?"

"A what?"

"Shadow. They run things around here. Should I be worried someone is going to slit my throat in the middle of the night?"

Sounds like Hannah has a few secrets she's keeping.

I chuckle. "Only if it's me. I handle my own business."

"So how does she know you? You said you just moved here."

If these Shadows are anything like Ross's Soulless, I know the rules. You keep your mouth shut. Don't answer any questions from anyone not in. I might not be in, but it sounds like Hannah is and I'm no rat. It's none of my business. Even if he's asking an innocent enough question.

Why are you loyal to a group you don't even know? The words filter in unbidden.

I shrug. "I make friends fast."

"I don't doubt that."

As he helps me into the car, I take notice of all the cars around us. The crowd is dispersing, everyone climbing into a vehicle. I notice one guy at the front of the line, checking cars as they go past.

When Jordan climbs in the driver's seat, I turn to him.

"Why are they checking cars?"

They never did this where I'm from. A race was a race. It didn't matter who you are.

"You have to have a ticket to play, baby. Don't worry about it. You're my plus-one tonight."

When it's our turn, a dark-haired man steps forward.

"Who's the fresh meat?" He asks looking at me.

I narrow my eyes at him, but Jordan answers before I can.

"A new friend."

"You vouching for her?" he asks as we stare at each other.

Jordan nods.

"Alright then."

When he pulls away, I look back and see the man's eyes on mine. He smirks at me, so I turn around, ignoring him.

"What was that about?" I ask Jordan.

"You're my responsibility. I'm vouching for you, so if you rat or do something stupid, it's on me. I'll face the consequences."

"Why would you do that? What if I am a narc?"

He smiles. "Well, you're one sexy narc and worth going down for."

I roll my eyes. "I'm no narc."

"I know."

"So, are you racing tonight?"

He smiles. "Not tonight."

Disappointing. Like I thought. All brawn, no brains. Definitely not the good dick I'm looking for.

"So you're just a spectator."

He shrugs. "Tonight I am. I'm not crazy enough to enter tonight. I know there's no chance I'll win."

"What's tonight?"

"Only the best of the best are racing tonight. It's a five thousand dollar buy-in. I'm an amateur compared to these guys. No way I would take a chance."

I feel that familiar competitive spirit inside me. Five thousand buy-in? That's the type of race Ross would have put me in back home. I almost never lost. Except the last time.

A shiver makes its way down my spine.

After several minutes, we pull up to a lone stretch of road. There are no streetlights and no houses. The area looks like an underdeveloped subdivision. Like someone started the renovations by paving the roads, but then ran out of the money to actually build the houses.

He pulls in next to another car on the side of the road, parking. He gets out of the car, rounding it to come to my side.

"Are you cold? I can find a jacket for you."

"No. I'm good."

"Okay, well, stay close. Shit can go down quick around here."

"Got it."

I let him walk me around to a group near the side of the road. As they talk, I take in the area around me.

This isn't like in California. Back in Cali, we usually had a preset track that ran around an area in a loop. It was always through public streets and wasn't always clear of non-racers. It was dangerous, but it was also exciting.

That's not what they are doing here. No, this is closer to drag racing. One stretch of road and two cars.

I watch as the first two competitors line up. After a couple of minutes, a girl walks out between them as they rev their engines. The woman holds out a piece of fabric, waving it around before dropping it.

As soon as she does, they take off. My heart races as I watch them.

If we were going based on the car alone, I would give it to the yellow Camaro. It's a new car with a decent engine, but it is often up to the driver, not the car. I can have the fastest, best car in the world, but if I can't drive for shit, I'll lose every time.

That's why the older Impala pulls ahead. It didn't have any bells and whistles on it like the Camaro, but the driver is a vet to racing. He handles the car like it's an extended appendage of his body.

Watching the way he handles the car makes the blood in my veins hum.

I want to be where he's at.

Before I can blink, the race is over. The Impala makes it into the next round as the man in the Camaro kicks the tire of his car, cussing about the loss.

Men can be such big babies sometimes. Their poor, fragile ego can't handle such blows as a loss.

I smile watching it. He would be doubly as pissed had it been me who won.

Fuck, I want to race.

"You seem to really enjoy this," Jordan whispers in my ear.

I nod. "It's exhilarating."

"You are something special, Roxanne."

"I know." I wink at him.

He smirks. "I have a feeling you really do know."

"So how does this work?" I ask. "Where I'm from, there was a specific route you had to go through. First one back was the winner."

He dips his head. "Street racing. We do that here sometimes, but it's easier to stay under the radar by doing drag races. This is round one. There are eight that entered tonight. These eight will race. Then the winners will face off until there are only two left. Then they will race and the winner gets the pot."

"Eight? So the pot is forty thousand dollars?" It's really not that much, but that's a lot to bet on a twenty-second drag.

"Not exactly. The organizers take a cut, of course. For a race this size, they would only take a quarter of it, so the pot is probably thirty thousand. Either way, a nice slice of money."

"I see. There's betting too, I bet."

He chuckles. "You're something else. Yes, there is betting. They take a cut of that too. There is also an entry fee. I paid ours back at the meet. It's a business like any other. They organize and take the risks, we come and enjoy.

It's all part of the circle of life."

I snort. "If you say so." The next race is starting up, so I ask him, "Can I walk closer? I mean, you can stay and talk to your friends. I just want to get a closer look."

"You sure? I can come with you." He says the words, but I can tell he wants to stay with his friends.

He was expecting a pretty face to hang off his arm. He wasn't expecting me to actually know my shit or want to pay attention.

"Yeah. I can sit by myself, Jordan. I'll be back in a little bit? I think I'll walk a little farther down so I can see better."

"Okay, but not too far. If shit goes down, you'll want to get back to the car quickly."

"Got it." I salute him.

As he turns to go back to his friends, I make my way away from him. I push my way into the front of the crowd, smiling when I see the cars lined up.

I watch every race, not once getting bored sitting there. Even between races, I studied the way the competitors set up for the next race.

There were no groups of people doing this for them. Each competitor set up their own area.

Jugs of water poured on the ground as the competitors do burnouts. Pep talks at the line. Clearing the way for the car to be pushed up to the line.

It's like a well-oiled machine. Each person knows their job.

When the final race starts, I angle forward.

I've watched the Chevelle race twice before now, but I haven't had a chance to spy the driver. Something tells me he is gorgeous. Maybe it's the way his tanned arm hangs out the driver's side window as he waits for his people to set up the race. Or the way he manipulates the car to his whim.

Something about him makes me want to get to know him more.

I watch their pre-race ritual, then hold my breath for it to start. Once the girl lowers her arm, they are off.

My heart races in my chest as I watch the cars barrel down the road. They are almost to the end when I hear it.

"*Cops!*"

All of a sudden, everyone is running every which way. I look around for

Jordan but don't see him anywhere. I run back to where I know he parked, but his car is gone. Several others are peeling out as well.

I feel a small well of panic rise up inside, but I push it down. I got this. Cops used to show up all the time back in Riviera.

Yeah, but Ross always made sure to get you out.

I ignore the nagging voice inside my head and make my way back to where most of the cars were. I'll try and hitch a ride.

A body slams into me. I grunt at the pain, looking up to see the man that Jordan vouched for me with.

"Ouch. Watch it," I grumble.

He pauses, looking down at me. Then he smiles, grabbing my hand.

"Let's go, sweetheart."

Before I can ask, he pulls me along with him until we are back where the racers had stopped. Most of them are gone, but a couple remain.

One of which is the hottie who won.

When he glares at me, the girl in front of him turns.

Hannah.

My cousin's eyes widen at the sight of me.

"Roxy, what are you doing here?"

I don't think she means at the races in general. I think she means literally what am I doing here standing in front of her.

The man next to me squeezes my hand. "We don't have time for this. Let's go."

"No," the hot stranger says. "She stays. Everyone else in their cars."

When the man next to me hesitates, the man barks out, "Now."

He glares at me before turning to climb into his car. Hannah gives me an apologetic look but climbs into another car with the man from the house the night I arrived.

The man next to me looks down at me. "Sorry, love. I don't have a choice. Run through those woods and you'll come out the other side on the highway."

He points to the woods on the side before letting go of my hand, running toward the passenger side of the Chevelle.

I hear the sirens approaching as they drive away. I don't hesitate. I run into the woods he indicated.

I run for at least twenty minutes before I start to slow down. I can feel my legs being scratched as I run through brush, but I don't care. My anger is getting me through.

I didn't need that guy's help in the first place. Had he not grabbed me and pulled me along, I probably could have gotten a ride with someone else. Hell, if Jordan had waited, I wouldn't be in this mess.

Let's not mention the asshole who seems to rule them all. What does he have against me? He could have easily given me a ride, but he's an asshole.

It doesn't matter. I don't need them. I don't need Hannah either.

She's supposed to be my blood, but she dropped me as easily as my mother did. Fuck her.

The nostalgia of our childhood can go fuck itself. If I had a car, I would leave tonight.

When I finally make it out the other side of the woods, there is a long stretch of road. The man said it was a highway, but there are no cars in sight. I don't even really know where we are. In the back of some undeveloped subdivision from what I could tell driving in, but there were so many turns and all the streets are curved, so who knows.

I set out walking instead. Several miles down the road, I see the lights behind me. Headlights slowing next to me. I tense at who it might be. I'm not stupid enough to think I'm safe. Even in some little town like this.

When the red and blue lights start to flash, I let out a sigh.

"Stop right there, young lady."

The older man's voice calls from behind me. I turn, crossing my arms over my chest.

"Can I help you?"

"What are you doing out here all alone?" He approaches me slowly, a hand resting on the pistol at his hip.

"Taking a walk."

"Well, I don't quite believe that. You look like one of them racing junkies. There was a race out here tonight. I bet that's where you were."

I don't respond. Ross taught me to keep my mouth shut. Anything you say might be used against you. Even if it seems innocent enough.

"Well, come on, girl. I'm going to have to take you in."

"Are you charging me with anything?"

"I don't know yet. Get in the car before I cuff you."

"You haven't read me my rights. That means I'm not under arrest, so I will walk. Thank you."

He cusses, walking over to me. Then he pulls out his cuffs, grabbing my arm.

"You are under arrest for illegal street racing. Anything you say can and will be used..."

As he continues reading me my rights, I zone out. I could recite them by heart at this point. It's not my first arrest. It won't even stick. He has no evidence that I was racing. I mean, I don't even have a car.

My only concern is how long I'll be tied up in jail.

Before, Ross would have me out within an hour. Here, I have no connections. I'll have to wait for my court-appointed attorney and hope to God they know what they are doing.

I've been here for hours. They have attempted to question me, but I only muttered one word. Lawyer.

Now I sit here. Waiting.

I can see the sun rising outside the window, giving me hope that my lawyer will be here soon. Whoever it is.

"Wheeler, you're free to go." I startle at the officer who stands before my cell. He opens the door, leading me out to the front desk.

They hand over my items before the receptionist gives me a warm smile. "They decided not to charge you."

I give her a nod in thanks. I guess I didn't need that lawyer after all.

I don't waste any time hightailing it out of there.

Then I walk all the way home.

By the time I come through the front door, it's late morning.

Hannah is sitting at the kitchen counter, waiting for me.

"What happened?" she asks, taking in my appearance.

I'm sure I look like a hot mess. My legs are scratched up, my tank top is wrinkled, and I smell like I spent the evening in a holding cell.

"Nothing. I'm going to shower and sleep."

"Wait," she calls as I turn to leave. "What did you tell the cops?"

I roll my eyes. "I'm no snitch. I said one word. 'Lawyer.' They were smart enough to know they didn't have anything to hold me with."

"I'm sorry, Rox," she murmurs.

I shake my head. "Don't be. I'm on my own and I'm fine with that. Blood doesn't mean shit."

"You're wrong. Blood does mean shit. That's why you're here. You're my blood and I will always do what I can to help you, but you're not family. I'm sorry, Rox. I wish you were because then you'd be protected, but I can't change that. Not unless he lets you in."

I nod. "The Shadow Crew is your family." Her eyes widen at my admission. She didn't know I knew. Good. "I get it. I had that before. A group I could count on until I didn't. You think they have your back? Until they decide they know what's best for you and they send you away. It taught me something valuable. You can only depend on yourself. Don't worry about it, Hannah. I understand and I don't hold it against you. I'll try to be out of here as soon as I can so you can get back to your family."

She doesn't say anything as I turn to leave.

Once in the shower, I think back to what I said.

I didn't realize how much I meant it.

Ross and the guys were supposed to be my family. They were supposed to have my back no matter what. They don't send away the other girls. So why did they send me away? Why did he refuse to let me in?

It really doesn't matter anymore. At first he made it sound like he would let me come back when it's safe, but then he told me I wasn't welcome back. I've only been here a couple of days and I already feel like they are in the past. That life is in the past.

Even if I go back and they welcome me with open arms, I would never trust them not to oust me again. Especially since they refuse to trust me with their crew business.

All it does is make me feel abandoned. The people I thought were my family abandoned me. Just like my mom did.

Just like Hannah will.

That's all my life will be. A series of disappointments.

CHAPTER FOUR
ROMAN

Hannah: She's home and said she didn't talk. I believe her.
Me: Good.
Hannah: She knows that we're a crew.
Me: Anything else?
Hannah: No.
Me: Good, keep it that way.

I set my phone down on the bench and turn back to my car. Walking forward, I run my hand along the side of my baby and can't help but admire her.

Roxy admired her too.

I shake my head, trying to ward off my wayward thoughts.

When I bought my Chevelle, she was a mess and I promised her that I would turn her into a work of art once again. And I did with a lot of blood, sweat, and swearing. I lean in and pop the hood and go about checking all the fluid levels. Anything to occupy my mind.

Anything to get her off my mind.

"Fuck me," I mutter under my breath as I see a woman lean over the hood of my car. "Who's that?"

"That would be Hannah's cousin, Roxy," Blaze says with a smile in his voice.

"Of course it is," I grunt.

I watch her perky ass as she leans over further, and I can't help but wonder what it would be like to take her from behind. But as soon as the thought crosses my mind, I push it to the side. There will be no getting naked or hearing her moan my name.

"Let's get this show on the road," I tell Blaze as I watch Roxy walk away from my car. I watch as she approaches Jordan, a local dumbass who thinks he's all that when really he's not. A streak of something hits me. Almost like I'm mad at her for talking to him. Or maybe disappointed.

I pushed her out of my mind until the races started and I felt her eyes on me as I approached the line. I saw her out of the corner of my eye, leaning forward, completely captivated by everything. Stepping on the gas, I rev the engine as I stared at her and couldn't help but smirk when her eyes fluttered and she bit her lip.

This turns her on. That was the only thought in my head.

As the race began, I blocked her from my mind once again, but every time I pulled up, I felt her eyes on me. And when the sirens started blaring and everyone panicked to flee, I couldn't help but watch her as she ran up with Marco at her side.

Holding her hand.

That new burning feeling inside caused me to react without conscious thought. I barked my orders.

Then I watched her run off through the rearview mirror as I sped away.

"Was that really necessary?" Marco asks as I speed up.

"You know it was," I say harshly, making him sigh.

When we heard that she was picked up, I couldn't help but wonder, what would she tell the cops? Would she say anything? Even if she did, there was nothing for her to see to report. Over the years, we've mastered operating behind closed doors. But when Hannah looked at all of us with worry in her eyes, I couldn't help but feel bad.

Hannah was family, and she cared about this girl. No matter how conflicted I was by my own reactions to her, I should have considered Hannah in it. This is her cousin after all.

As I work on my car, I can't help but come to terms with a few things.

She's gorgeous.

I want her.

But I won't have her.

Ross said she wouldn't cause any trouble, but a woman like Roxy? Trouble is her middle name.

And whatever trouble she's bringing to our doorstep, my crew and I want nothing to do with it.

"Wow, are you spit shining the interior parts today?"

Axel's voice brings me out of my thoughts. I realize then, I've been leaning here with a rag in my hand poised on top of the oil cap, but I haven't moved.

Standing straight, I turn to him. "Lost in thoughts. What are you doing here, man?"

Usually we all meet at the clubhouse. We all have our own places and sometimes we visit them, but no one ever comes out to mine. This is my oasis. The place I can go to let go of all the stress on my mind.

"I wanted to check in. Marco has been absent more lately, so I figured you might need someone to work through some shit with."

I shoot him a glare. I don't talk about shit with anyone. He knows that. He's right about Marco though. Marco is my second in command. He should've been the one out here checking on me. It makes me wonder once again what is going on with him.

"What do you think Marco is up to?" I ask, leaning against my car.

He shrugs. "I can find out if you want."

He could too. Axel is our computer guy. He doesn't enjoy racing like we do. He prefers the code and numbers on his computer. Hell, I think if he had his way, he would lock himself up in his apartment and become a hermit.

We don't allow that though. He's family, which means he participates in everything.

"Not yet. Let's give him some more time to work through it. I don't want to invade his privacy. Especially when it ends up being some stupid shit like he finally grew a heart and fell for some pussy."

"Is that your theory?"

"Marco is a Casanova. Of course, I think one day he is going to find a pussy that doesn't open at will for him. Then he's going to fall head over heels and be fucked up because he doesn't know how to do monogamy."

Axel chuckles. "What about you, man? You think you could do monogamy?"

An image of Roxy filters into my head.

"Fuck that, man. You know I don't chase pussy like him, but I still won't be tied down to one either. Can't trust bitches like that anyway. They sink their claws in before tearing you apart."

He snorts. "Hannah is in the inner circle."

"She's the exception. I mean, look at her and Blaze though. That's going to blow up one day and you know it."

"You're not wrong. So what about Roxanne?"

I stiffen. "What about her?"

Axel has a knowing look in his eye. "I saw the way you watched her. You saying you don't want a piece of that?"

"I promised Ross I'd keep an eye out for her. That's what I was doing."

"Oh, and letting her get arrested is taking care of her?"

I shrug. "I called and had her released. She needs to know the consequences of her actions."

"So that wasn't some test you devised to see if she could handle this life? To see if she would rat?"

"Of course not. There is no room for anyone else within our group."

He shakes his head. "Whatever you say, man. When you finally realize that spot at your side is starting to feel cold, I promise I won't say I told you so."

"Fuck off. When are you going to settle down?"

His eyes flare. "Never. I can barely stand you fuckers. There is no way I would be able to stand a female in my life permanently. Especially living with me." He shudders.

"You need to get over your issues, bro. I'm starting to think you need therapy."

"Fuck off." He turns to leave. Before reaching his car, he looks back at me. “Maybe a few tests to the new girl wouldn’t be so bad. You might not want her at your side, but if Hannah wants to keep her around, maybe she could be a lower level. Just a thought.”

Then he slides into his car, backing out without another word.

Yet his words are still ringing in my ears long after the dust settles from his retreat.

CHAPTER FIVE

Roxy

"You've been doing so great that Julio and I decided to give you some weekend shifts. Are you interested?"

It's been two weeks since I went to the races with Jordan. I haven't heard from him since either. I think he got the idea that the next time I see him I would castrate him for abandoning me.

It had nothing to do with the picture of a knife with the words I'll have your balls that I sent him the next day.

Not at all.

So instead of socializing, I threw myself into my new job. I offered to pick up extra shifts and gave it my all. After all, this is the only thing that is going to get me out of here.

I've only gotten two checks so far, but I already have two hundred dollars saved up. That along with the little bit leftover from what Ross gave me to get here and I'm happy with my progress. I left some money on the counter for Hannah to cover some sort of rent. I assume she got it because it was gone the next day, but I haven't seen her.

"Yes. Of course," I tell Janet.

"You sure? You're young. I know you kids like to go out on the weekends."

I roll my eyes. "I'm not that young. This job is more important than a social life at the moment. I'll be fine."

"If you say so. You'll work tomorrow then."

I smile brightly, moving back to my tables. A while later, Janet pops back.

"I sat you a table of five."

"Thanks."

I make my way out of the back, stopping short when I see the table she sat me.

If it isn't the assholes.

I still don't even know their names, but I dislike them already. The only one at the table I do know is my cousin.

"Good evening. Welcome to Julio's. I'd be happy to take your drink orders while you look over the menu."

"Jack and ginger ale," the main asshole with the sexy car answers.

Why is it that men that attractive with the nice cars are always the biggest douchebags? I bet he has a tiny ass dick too.

"Can I see your ID please?" I drawl in a bored tone.

I know the man is over twenty-one, but I'm technically supposed to ask if you look under forty. The tic in his jaw makes me want to smile in victory.

"Really?" he bites out.

"It's policy. I don't know you, so I need to make sure you're of age."

He grunts, pulling out his wallet, flipping to his license.

I scan it quickly.

Roman Carter. Date of Birth, October thirteenth, nineteen ninety.

"Thank you. For the rest of you?"

I repeat the process as each orders an alcoholic beverage. The only one I don't ask is Hannah since I know her.

I now know the asshole's friends are named Marco, Axel, and Blaze.

Blaze is the one from the house that first night. Marco is the one who asked Jordan if he was vouching for me and Axel, well, I hadn't met Axel before tonight.

Once I get their drink orders, I run to put them in before checking on other tables.

I finally make my way back to their table with their drinks.

"Do you know what you would like to eat?"

Marco smiles up at me, giving me a wink. "What would you suggest?"

He's a flirt. I could tell that from our first interaction.

"I like their chicken dinner tacos with a fried flour tortilla with a double side of their cilantro lime rice instead of beans."

"Wow. That's very decisive of you. I thought women didn't know how to make decisions," he teases.

Even though I'm still mad at him, I crack a smile at his easy-going demeanor. "What can I say? I know what I like."

"Enough flirting. Julio doesn't pay you to flirt. I want the beef enchiladas with spanish rice," Roman snaps.

I bristle at his tone. I wasn't flirting with Marco, but even if I was, I highly doubt Julio would care. He even tells me my smile will get me more tips.

Ignoring him, I turn to Blaze next. "What about for you?"

"Whatever the special is."

"You don't want to know what it is?"

He smirks. "Surprise me."

I shake my head. "If you don't like it, I'm not letting you send it back."

His smile widens. "I'm a garbage disposal, baby. I will eat anything." He pats his stomach.

I chuckle at his antics. He's the jokester of the group for sure.

Axel speaks up next. "Steak burrito with extra guac."

He meets my eyes briefly, before grabbing a chip to dip into the salsa.

"Hannah?" I ask.

She looks up, an apology in her eyes. "I'll have the nachos."

Marco is last. "I'll take your suggestion. The tacos sound delicious."

"Great. I'll get that in for you. Let me know if you need anything."

They are an odd group. Each one seems to fit a piece of a puzzle, filling in with their personality what the others are missing.

Why are you even sparing them another thought? I chastise myself.

Thankfully, the rest of their dinner goes by without issue. I even made sure Roman's meal was perfect. I had a feeling even a small mistake would make him complain. I feel like he's looking for a reason to lash out at me.

When I bring the check, Roman smiles at me, but not a nice smile. No, his smile reeks of wickedness.

When I asked if they were splitting the payment, he said no, so I hand him the check. "Here's your check."

He doesn't take it at first, then he smiles. "I think you want to buy us dinner. Isn't that right, Hannah?"

Hannah looks up at me, her eyes sad. "Right."

I feel fire fill my veins. She knew about this and yet she's sitting here with them. I can't blame her for taking their side though. I can blame him though. For treating her like shit. At least Ross and his friends treated me with respect. If I didn't want to do something, I didn't have to. Seems the same isn't true here.

"I'm not buying you dinner, so either cough it up or I'll go get Julio and he can deal with it."

"Running off to your boss? Is that what you do? Tattle?" Roman goads.

"No, but it's his business. I refuse to pay for your meals. If you couldn't afford it, you shouldn't have come in."

"Oh sweetheart." Roman says the words, but the term is an insult. "We could afford to buy this place. That has nothing to do with it."

"What is it then?"

"You live with Hannah. If you want to continue to live with her, you will show loyalty to the Shadows. That means you are buying us dinner. Unless you want your shit out on the lawn tonight."

I roll my eyes, meeting Hannah's.

Hannah speaks. "I won't throw you out, but he will. I've already made my opinions on this clear. You will always have a place in my home."

"Shut up, Hannah," Roman snaps at her, making her cringe.

I shake my head at him. She stood up for me at least. A little too late, but I'll take it. At least she tried. I have a feeling Hannah is in need of a backbone. I've been avoiding her because of everything, but I can't help but feel sad for her. I feel like maybe she latched on to these guys because they gave her something she was missing.

Isn't that what I did with Ross?

Taking a deep breath, I make a decision. I'm going to try to help Hannah be stronger. Stand up for herself more. Maybe in the process, I'll build my own confidence back up.

"Fine. I'll buy your stupid dinner. Get out of here before I regret it."

Roman tilts his head, looking confused. "You're giving in so easy? Disappointing. I thought you would put up more of a fight."

I laugh. "I'm not doing this for you. I'm doing it for her." I point at Hannah. "I don't care if you kick me out, but you're putting my cousin in a tough position. You're supposed to be her family, but you're dismissing her feelings on whatever this is. Be an asshole to me if you want, but leave her out of it. She's loyal to you. You win, so let it go."

"Rox," Hannah warns.

"No, Hannah. If he wants to treat me like shit, fine, but he needs to treat you better. If he doesn't, then you need to get out because you deserve respect and he's not respecting you right now."

Roman's eyes harden. "Let's go."

He doesn't say another word as he leaves. When I walk into the back, I pull my wallet out of my jacket pocket, pulling two hundred dollars from the money I saved for the one hundred twenty dollar bill. It still leaves me with a little over one hundred dollars left.

Asshole.

I meant what I said. Hannah might not be loyal to me, but she's still my cousin. She still offered me a place to stay and at dinner tonight, she spoke up. She didn't agree with his actions.

It's a baby step, but I'll take it. Maybe we can be more than roommates after all. Maybe she can even be a friend. An ally while I'm here.

Maybe I can even enjoy life here.

I just need to stay as far away from Roman Carter as possible.

"Fuck," I mutter to myself.

I left work later than usual, making me miss the last bus out for the night. I rub my hand down my face.

I could run back to the restaurant and hope someone is still there, but I doubt that. Julio left early tonight and Hector walked Janet and me out. It's a five-minute walk to the bus station, so I'm sure they're long gone.

I consider calling Hannah, but until I talk to her more, I don't want to get involved with her group's dynamics.

Shaking my head, I start to walk. Nothing like walking five miles after an eight-hour shift. I guess I should be grateful it's only five miles. It could be worse.

Setting out, I start walking down the road. I make it off the main stretch onto a side road when I notice a car down the block. It's parked on the side of the road with a man leaning against it. He's talking on a phone, but he seems familiar.

My body tenses as I realize how dark this road is. The main road is littered with streetlights, but this one has fewer and farther in between. Not only that, but I haven't seen a single car pass down this side road.

What was I thinking? I'm not backing down now though.

I continue to walk, slipping my keys out of the pocket of my jacket, I fist them.

Rule number one, never place them between your fingers. You're more likely to hurt yourself than your opponent. Fist them, sharp end coming out the outside of your hand and go for the eyes, throat, solar plexus, and groin.

When I get closer to the man, I freeze.

Blaze.

What is he doing out here?

I shake off my unease and continue walking. When I'm almost even with him, he turns, looking startled to see me standing there.

"I gotta go."

He hangs up the phone quickly, taking me in.

I don't pause. Instead, I avert my eyes and keep walking.

"Where are you going?" he asks, falling into step beside me.

"Home. Please leave me alone."

"You're walking all the way home? That's a long walk." He reaches out, grabbing my arm. "Let me give you a ride."

I pull out of his grip. "I'll be fine."

He glares. "Get in the fucking car, Roxanne. Hannah would have my balls if anything happened to her precious cousin."

"If I wanted a ride, I would have called Hannah."

He shakes his head. "Stop being stubborn. Your message at dinner was heard loud and clear. Let me respect your cousin by making sure you arrive home safely. I'll be on my best behavior. Scout's honor."

He makes a gesture with his hands.

"Um, were you even a Boy Scout?"

He scoffs. "Of course I was. What better way to learn to always be prepared?"

I shake my head, smiling at his answer.

"Fine, but any funny business and I'll gouge your eyes out."

He blinks at me for a moment before bursting out laughing. "Fuck, you're a spitfire. I swear you're here to shake shit up. Get in."

He walks me back to his car, opening the passenger door. "Madam, your car awaits."

"You're stupid," I tell him, but laugh anyway.

Once in the car, he turns the radio on. When I hear the reggaeton beat, I scrunch up my nose.

"You listen to this?"

He puffs out his chest. "Yeah. What, do you not like it?"

I shake my head. "I didn't say that. I like a variety of music. I just didn't peg you for the type to listen to it. Actually, I'm slightly impressed that you're actually cultured."

He chuckles. "There's a lot you don't know about me, brat. Hush now, this is my favorite part."

I can't help the laughter that flows as he throws his hands around, rapping what I think is supposed to be Spanish, but sounds like garble from his mouth.

When we finally pull into my neighborhood, I have to hold my sides from laughing so hard. Even when I was laughing, he only sang louder and tried to hit the beat harder. Almost like he liked hearing me laugh.

When he passed my house, I sober a little. "I think you passed my house."

He shakes his head, pulling into a house several down from mine. "This is my house. I think you can walk the several hundred yards since you were willing to walk five miles."

"You live here?" My eyes widen.

"Yep. At least for the last couple of years."

"Interesting. Do all of you live here?"

"Nah. Axel lives on his own in an apartment in town. Marco lives with his mom but sometimes stays at his sister's place too. Roman…" he trails off, looking over at me.

"No need to divulge secrets. I'm not that interested." I give him an out.

He laughs. "Roman spends most of his time at the clubhouse, but he has his own house as well. Out in the woods."

I nod. "Well, thank you for the ride home. When you aren't around your master, you're not actually that bad to be around."

He barks out another laugh. "Roman's not my master."

"Could've fooled me. Bye now."

I don't give him a chance to respond as I jump from the car, making my way down the street.

"You're a brat," he calls out behind me.

I can't help the smile covering my face as I ignore him. When I step up on the porch, I peek in his direction. He's still standing next to his car, watching me. He waves me inside, so I give him a small wave.

It's almost sweet that he wanted to drive me home and make sure I made it inside safely.

When I close the door behind me, I turn, kicking off my shoes.

"What are you smiling about?"

I gasp as I look up to find Hannah leaning against the wall at the end of the hall.

"Jesus, Hannah. Way to give a girl a heart attack."

She laughs. "Sorry. So? Why the smile?"

I consider my words. She and Blaze seemed close. Should I tell her that he gave me a ride home?

I decide to be honest. "Blaze gave me a ride home. You know your boyfriend is an idiot."

"I already told you he's not my boyfriend, but I agree he's an idiot."

The smile on her face eases the weight on my chest. I didn't want to upset her, but I hate lying when I don't have to. After she stuck up for me tonight with Roman, I want to be a better cousin to her.

We might not ever be best friends, but we can make the time here more pleasant. Maybe even keep in touch when I leave.

"Listen, about tonight," she starts.

I walk past her into the kitchen to grab a water. "Don't worry about it. I appreciate you standing up for me, but I don't want you jeopardizing anything for me. I can handle myself."

"I'm not jeopardizing anything. Roman's being even more of an ass than usual and I'm not sure why. I don't know what his issue with you is, but I made it clear to him tonight. He needs to leave me out of it. I won't stand for him treating you like shit. You're my guest. Also, I want to pay you for dinner. That wasn't right of him."

I shake my head. "Seriously, don't worry about it. I can afford to treat you to dinner. Besides, if he found out, he would make shit harder. Let him think he won this round."

She bites her lip. "Fine, but if he gives you any issues, let me know. I told him to back the fuck off."

I chuckle. "I'm sure he took that real well."

She shrugs. "He'll get over it. Want to watch a movie with me? I feel like we haven't actually had the chance to catch up."

I'm tired as fuck, but the hopeful look on her face has me softening. "Sure. Lead the way."

She smiles, grabbing two beers from the fridge before heading into the living room.

She hands me a beer.

"What have you been up to?" she asks as she turns on the TV, turning it down so that it's only background noise.

"Well, you know what I've been doing here. Back home, it was just life." I shrug.

"I know, but like, what did you do? Did you have a job? A boyfriend?" She wiggles her eyebrows at that.

I feel a blush creep up. "I had several jobs here and there. Nothing permanent. I graduated from college last May. As for boyfriends, I had friends that were boys, but nothing serious."

She nods. "I feel you there. Blaze never lets any guy get close enough to be serious with me. He thinks he has to go all big brother on me. Even when they are in the crew, he doesn't trust them with me."

Her eyes widen a bit, looking over at me like she shouldn't have said anything. I wave her off.

"I won't ask questions, nor will I repeat anything you tell me, so you can stop looking guilty for revealing some secret. Also, Blaze doesn't really look at you like a brother. Are you sure he's not interested in you? Maybe that's why he doesn't want any guys to come close."

She rolls her eyes. "I used to think that too. We've known each other since I was eighteen. At first, I thought he wanted to get in my pants, but back then, I was not about that. Then when Roman decided to bring me into the fold, he became distant. Now, he treats me like I'm one of the guys, which is good I guess."

She looks troubled at that. I have a feeling she likes Blaze more than she lets on.

"Except you don't always want to be treated like one of the guys. Sometimes you want to feel feminine. Like you're desirable."

My thoughts drift back to Ross. I knew how it felt to want to be desired by someone who wouldn't look twice at you.

"Sounds like you've been there before. Sucks, right?"

She holds up her beer to me. I clink mine with hers.

"Preach it." I take a sip before focusing back on her. "My first night here he was shirtless and you weren't wearing any pants. Actually, I think you were wearing his shirt."

She laughs. "That's pretty typical for us. He comes over and hangs out when he's bored. Sometimes he'll stay the night. He knows I like sleeping in men's shirts, so he usually gives me his. It's all platonic. He never even touches me."

The slight blush in her cheeks tells me she wishes he would.

"Why don't you just tell him you like him?"

She looks horrified. "That would ruin everything. We are such a tight-knit group. If he rejected me, I would be embarrassed to be around him. Then things would get awkward within the core group. Roman would be pissed and probably kick me out. I mean, he's known Blaze longer. Plus, I'm a girl. I don't even really know how I ended up there in the first place."

I laugh. "Slow down, girl. Take a breath. You're a badass chick. That's how you ended up there. Roman pulled his head out of his ass for once and saw that you were a loyal ass chick down to ride. That's why. I still think you should explore things with Blaze if you like him, but I get if you don't. I won't tell him. Fuck, I probably won't even talk to him again. He only gave me a ride tonight because he was worried that if something happened to me, you would be pissed off."

"Oh you'll talk to him again. Blaze hangs out here all the time. He has been giving you space because Roman wasn't sure if you could be trusted, but after tonight, all bets are off. Blaze will be coming over to hang out like he used to."

She looks down, biting her lip.

"What's wrong?"

She looks back up, her eyes anxious. "You're gorgeous, Rox. Like you could turn a gay man straight gorgeous. Can you maybe not sleep with Blaze? He's going to try to, but that might kill me."

I hold my hand out, gripping hers. "I don't give a fuck what he does, I would never touch him. He's not my type anyway, but even if he was, you're my cousin. I would never betray that. He's safe from me. Fuck, if you want me to, I'll stalk him and warn off all the other bitches too. You want me to fuck him up? I can really fuck his game up. Give me a couple of popular chicks and a sordid story about the gift that keeps on giving."

She looks at me, confused. "What?"

I burst out laughing. "Herpes, Han. I'll make the whole town believe he has herpes."

Her own laughter follows as we collapse against each other. When our laughter finally subsides, Hannah lays her head on my shoulder. I lean my own against hers.

"I know you didn't want to come. I know some shit went on back home, but honestly, Rox, I'm so glad you're here. I've missed having a girl around I can trust."

I swallow hard, the prickle behind my eyes a telltale sign that I feel the same.

"Me too, Hans. Me too."

CHAPTER SIX
ROMAN

"Hey, you got a minute?" Blaze asks, leaning against the car I'm working on.

"What's up?"

"Can we go to your office for a minute?" he asks, pointing over his shoulder.

I nod and we fall into step with each other. As soon as we both step inside, he shuts the door.

"Everything okay?" I frown as I sit down.

"Yeah, I just wanted to talk to you about Hannah."

"Is something wrong?"

Blaze leans forward, resting his arms on his knees. "I was actually going to ask you that."

"What do you mean?"

"Look, I get that you don't like that a Soulless is in our area. None of us do. But that shit you pulled the other night? It wasn't okay. You brought Hannah into it, and that's not right. She's been nothing but loyal to you since she joined and you made her feel like shit."

"I wasn't trying to hurt Hannah."

"But you did. You're putting her between a rock and a hard place. She's loyal to you, to us. But at the same time, Roxy is her blood. As long as we've known her, it's just been her and her dad. This is her opportunity to get to know a cousin she hasn't seen in years and you're making it difficult for her."

"This has nothing to do with Hannah," I grit out as I pinch my nose.

"But it does. Your actions toward her cousin affect her. Can't you just play nice?" he asks, earning a glare. "Honestly, I think if you got to know her, you would like her."

"Hannah put you up to this?"

"No," he says, looking away. "I drove Roxy home last night. Sure, she was guarded as hell, but she was nice."

"You drove her home?" I ask, surprised.

And here I thought he was holding out for Hannah. Why does that grate on my nerves?

"Yeah, I was pulled over and on the phone. Next thing I know is I see her walking down the street after closing."

"She was walking home at midnight?" I ask, glaring down at my desk, trying to hide my reaction from Blaze.

"She doesn't have a car. I'm guessing she missed the bus and decided to walk home."

"Why didn't she call Hannah?" I ask, making Blaze give me a look that says 'do you really need to ask.'

"Anyway, I drove her home. She was nice. That's all that happened. But it's a good thing she walked up on me instead of someone else. Who knows what could have happened. Hell, she could have walked up on a serial killer and Hannah's last memory of her cousin would have been you being an absolute dick to her," he says, making me flinch.

"I won't stop testing her, but I'll think about Hannah a little more before I do."

"That's all I'm asking for," he says as he stands. "Now I'm going to dip out. I have to stop by and grab some stuff for my mom."

I watch him shut the door behind him as he walks out and can't help but groan. I meant what I said. I won't stop testing her. There's a reason she was never brought into the fold with Soulless and I want to know why. If she is as amazing as the rumors say behind the wheel of a car, then the Soulless would have been idiots not to mark her as one of theirs. There is more to her story. Axel asked me to consider making her a lower level, but in order to do that,

I need to figure out why she never was one in California.

Still, from here on out, I'll be better at my plan of attacks. I'll consider the others more before I make a decision.

The woman makes me impulsive. She's dangerous.

As the barista hands me my card back, my phone vibrates in my pocket. Pulling it out, I look at the text on the screen as I move out of the line only to bump into someone.

"Watch it," I growl as I pull my now coffee-soaked shirt away from my body as my skin burns.

"Look here, asshole, you're the one who ran into me. If you would have been watching where you were walking instead of looking at your phone, you would have seen me. And as far as I'm concerned, you owe me a new one," Roxy sneers.

My jaw tics as I take in her standing right in front of the counter, just having picked up her coffee. Not only did she get coffee on me, but herself as well. I can see her nipples peeking through her gray shirt. My eyes roll down her body and take in her tiny black shorts and black combat boots.

Why does she have to be gorgeous?

"Hey, my eyes are up here," she says, snapping her fingers in my face.

Reaching forward, I grab her hand.

"Don't," I hiss, trying to see the red, angry skin on her hand and wrist.

Roxy's eyes flash as she pulls out of my grip and mutters under her breath, "Asshole."

"Ma'am," the barista says hesitantly, getting our attention. "I made you a new drink."

"Thank you," Roxy says, smiling at the girl.

And fuck if it isn't a beautiful smile. I wonder what it would be like for her to aim it at me? Shaking away the thoughts, I say, "No wonder the Soulless didn't want you, you're clumsy as fuck."

Roxy's jaw tics as she brings her attention back to me. "Think whatever you want, but let's just do each other a favor. You stay out of my way and I'll stay out of yours," she says as she picks up her coffee.

"With pleasure," I growl as she rolls her eyes.

I watch Roxy walk away and can't help but bite my lip, looking at the way her hips sway as she walks.

"Sir, your coffee," the barista says, a lot less nicer than she did to Roxy.

I raise a brow and can't help but wonder what the fuck is up with women today?

My phone ringing catches my attention.

"What's up, Hannah?" I ask as I grab my coffee and carefully walk out.

"Where are you?"

"Grabbing coffee. Why? What's up?"

"I was wondering if we could meet up for a minute," she says vaguely.

"Sure. Everything okay?"

"It is. Meet me at the park in five?"

"Sounds good," I say before hanging up.

It's a nice enough day. I walk through town toward the park. Once there, I take a seat on the bench as I enjoy my coffee. Tilting my head back, I close my eyes and enjoy the sun on my face and the moment of peace.

I feel her before I see her.

"What's up?" I ask as I bring my cup to my mouth, taking a drink.

I watch Hannah shift out of the corner of my eye.

"Spit it out, Han."

"I want you to give Roxy a chance," she blurts out, making me groan. "Hear me out, please."

"Let's hear it," I say as I lean back and kick my legs out in front of me.

"I think if you got to know Roxy, you would like her. She might be loud and speak her mind, but she's loyal to a fault."

"If she was so loyal, why didn't Soulless bring her into the fold?" I ask, raising a brow.

"The only person who can answer that is the leader of Soulless, but I genuinely think she would be a good addition to the crew. I want to bring her into the fold. I want you to fast-track her in."

"You know there is no fast-tracking when it comes to earning someone's trust," I point out.

I think back to my conversation with Ross and think about what he said. He never said that they ended on bad terms. If anything, he sounded like he cared for her. The question is why?

I roll the empty coffee cup between my hands as we sit in silence, and I think about what Hannah's asking. Standing, I walk to the trash can and toss the cup. As I walk back to Hannah, I put my hands in my pockets.

"I'm not making any promises, but I'll think about it."

It's a lie. I won't just think about it. I've already been thinking about it, thanks to Axel. Still, watching the hope in Hannah's eyes makes it worth it.

"Really?" she says with a smile.

"But only if she can pass the tests I throw her way. I'm not going to take it easy on her and you're not allowed to interfere."

"I won't," she promises. "When will you talk to her?"

"Don't worry about that. I'll see you later."

"Thank you!" Hannah yells from behind me. I raise my hand, letting her know that I heard her.

Looks like I have to give the new girl a chance now. The problem is, I don't want her to be lower level. I don't know how to come to terms with that.

CHAPTER SEVEN

Roxy

"Where are you going?" I ask Hannah, curious.

We've spent most nights together the last three weeks. Blaze joins us sometimes, but not always. I haven't really seen the others, but that's okay with me.

"Crew business. I'll be back in a couple of days."

A horn honks from outside. I walk her to the door, stepping out on the porch with her. Roman sits in the car, staring at me.

Ever since our run-in at the coffee shop, I've seen him a couple more times. He's come in to eat by himself and I've seen him around town, but other than that, we seem to be staying out of each other's way. Thank God.

As usual, I don't give him the time of day, pulling Hannah into a hug.

"Be safe out there. I'll see you when you get back."

She pulls back, grabbing her backpack from the floor inside the door, then turns to leave.

I stand on the porch, watching as she gets in the passenger side.

I smile when she waves, offering her a small wave back. I turn back to the house as they start to back out.

I wonder if there will be any races with the ringleader out of town. Only one way to find out. I haven't been since the first. I've been itching for a fix.

With him gone, I think I'll take my chances. Fuck, I wish I had a car.

Before I can close the front door completely, a car door slamming catches my attention.

I pull the door back open, watching as Roman jogs up the path. He doesn't say anything. He just grabs my arm, pulling me back outside.

"What the fuck? Don't touch me," I grunt, pulling back.

Roman refuses to let go and I hit him, stopping him dead in his tracks.

He spins, getting into my face. "Do not ever hit me again," he hisses.

"Let me go," I demand.

Roman ignores me and starts pulling me again.

Once I'm outside, he pulls the door closed behind me before locking it then dragging me down the driveway.

Hannah gives me a confused look as he pulls me to the passenger side, opening the door.

"Rox here is going to come along. Let her in the back."

I want to fight him, but the shocked look on Hannah's face stops me.

"Next time, don't manhandle me. I would've walked to the car on my own," I say as Hannah gets out.

I slide in the back, pulling the seat back so Hannah can get back in the front. Thankfully, I slipped on a pair of flip-flops to step outside with Hannah. Other than that, I don't have anything on me.

There's no talking once Roman gets in the car. He turns the music up and drives.

The ride goes by in the blink of an eye. With the music flowing through the speakers, I focus on the car itself.

I've been panting after this car since I saw it. Sitting in it now makes me feel like a kid on Christmas. My panties are goners.

Finally, we pull up to a beautiful house, pulling me from the inappropriate thoughts I have about what I would like to do inside this car. The house is surrounded by mostly trees with a river on one side. It's secluded even though it's only thirty minutes away from the town. It's a little slice of heaven.

"Out."

I roll my eyes at Roman. Hannah gives me a small smile when she reaches in to grab my hand.

"Let's go inside," she tells me.

"No. You go. I want to talk to her first." Roman stands in front of me, folding his arms over his chest.

"Oh. Are you okay with that, Rox?" Hannah asks, showing me she'd stay if I wanted.

Roman scoffs, but I ignore him. "It's fine, Han. I'll be in soon."

She nods before giving Roman a look.

As soon as the door to the house closes behind her, Roman speaks.

"I'm trusting you more than I should by letting you be here. I need to know that you can keep your mouth shut and follow directions."

I roll my eyes. "First off, I didn't ask to be here. You legit dragged me to your car. Second, I know how to mind my own business. Third, I will follow directions that I want to. I don't blindly follow anyone."

His face becomes harder. "Get on your knees."

I chuckle. "Fuck you."

"I'm serious. Show me you can follow a simple direction, otherwise you won't come."

"I'm not going to suck your cock or whatever else you have in mind. I don't need to prove myself to anyone."

He shakes his head. "Hannah wants you in. Did you know that? She came to me asking me to make an exception to my rules to bring you in. 'Fast track' she said. There is no fast track to trust and loyalty."

"I don't need your trust, nor did I ever offer my loyalty. My loyalty is to my cousin."

"If you plan to stick around, you will want both from us. Now, on your knees. I won't ask again."

"I don't plan on sticking around. Do your worst."

He huffs out a breath before advancing on me. My body wants to step back, but I stand my ground. I don't want to give him the satisfaction of thinking he has intimidated me.

Once he reaches me, he grabs me and slings me over his shoulder, making me scream.

"Put me down, asshole." I elbow him in the back of the head.

He grunts but keeps walking. I can't see where we are going, but the sound of water rushing makes my heart stutter.

"Let me go or I'll make you regret it."

"Fine," he says and then I'm flying through the air.

My body crashes into the water, giving me seconds to hold my breath.

"Jesus, what the fuck?" I scream out as soon as my head breaks the surface.

"What? Can't handle a little water?"

Roman stands on the bank, glaring down at me.

I can already feel my body start to shake in the cold water.

"You're such a fucking asshole. One of these days, I might just kill you."

His body goes tense, his jaw tightening. He strides into the water toward me. I don't back up. I hold my ground. What's the worst he can really do to me? Hannah's just inside. There's no way she would let him murder me right here. Besides, I know how to fight.

"Want to say that again, little girl?"

I press closer to him, my whole body against his. Nose to nose, I stare into his eyes.

"One of these days, I might just kill you," I hiss.

His hand shoots out, grabbing me by the throat, but I don't react. Even when he applies pressure, I keep his eye.

"You're brave. I give you that, but you are also borderline stupid. Your words have consequences. You might want to consider that before you keep on this track."

My voice comes out breathy, but strong as he continues his pressure. "I'm not weak. I say what's on my mind. I'm not afraid to stand up for myself and I'm not going to give up without a fight."

He pulls me closer by my neck. Then he shocks the hell out of me by pressing a hard kiss to my lips. It's a quick kiss, but it's enough to render me speechless. Heat floods me despite the cold water flowing around me.

He drags his lips across my cheek until they are at my ear.

"Talk like that will get *you* killed."

Then he lets me go.

I stumble back into the water but thankfully stay on my feet as I watch him climb the bank of the river.

I huff out a curse as I follow.

What the fuck was that? Why did he kiss me? Why did my body like it?

My thoughts run rampant as I claw my way up the bank.

When I stand, I try to wring out my shirt the best I can, shivering as the wind blows.

I watch as Roman stalks toward the house. Reluctantly, I follow him, hoping to be able to clean myself up a little.

Stopping and grabbing my flip-flops from the ground where they landed as he manhandled me, I slip them back on my feet.

At the door, I consider kicking them back off, but fuck him.

I walk into the house, noting that it's not much warmer in here. Hasn't anyone heard of heat?

Roman has disappeared, so I follow the sounds of voices to the living room.

"What the fuck happened to you?"

I narrow my eyes at Blaze. "Nothing. Where's the bathroom?"

He points down the hall, turning back to Hannah and Axel as they all share a look.

I fume all the way down the hall until I find the bathroom.

Once inside, I take in my appearance. Thankfully, I didn't have anything important on me. Roman never gave me a chance to grab my wallet or phone.

Still, it's going to be a bitch to walk around in wet jeans. The shirt will dry soon enough.

Reaching under my shirt, I undo my bra before wringing it out in the sink. I grab a towel hanging haphazardly on the bar, cringing at the thought of who might have used it, but beggars can't be choosers.

I scrunch my hair into the towel and begin to dry it. Once it's as dry as I can get it, I put my bra back on and make it out to the living room.

Roman stands there in dry jeans as he flicks through a magazine. I don't bother taking a seat. As much as I want to ruin his furniture, I still have no idea whose house this is. I would feel bad if I found out it was someone like Axel's.

Axel lives in an apartment in town, remember. Roman lives in the woods. This has to be his house.

Before I can sit down, deciding this has to be his house, a noise outside captures my attention.

The front door swings open and I smile.

"Love, what are you doing here?" Marco's smile is big as he makes his way over, tucking me under his arm.

We haven't seen much of each other either, but when we do cross paths, he is always nice to me. I even met his mother when he brought her in for dinner.

"I have no clue," I answer honestly.

"Why are you wet?" he asks, pulling away.

I shrug. "Accident."

"Enough. Let's go," Rome growls.

Marco glances over at him, but Roman is already on the move.

"Come on, this will be fun."

I scoff at him, but let him lead me toward the door.

We follow the others outside to find an older Toyota Corolla in the drive. Nothing like what they normally drive.

"Everyone in." Roman heads toward the driver's side as I follow Marco to the back.

I shiver when a particularly cool breeze blows.

"Fuck. You're freezing. Didn't you bring a change of clothes?" he asks, his hands running up and down my arms.

"I didn't really get a heads up. I'll be fine," I mumble.

Next thing I know, something hits me in the back of the head. I pull back and find a hoodie on the ground at my feet. I pick it up, looking over to Roman.

"Put it on. Let's go."

I roll my eyes at him, holding it to Marco.

"Hold this a second."

He nods as I pull my shirt off my body. Marco whistles as I trade him the shirt for the hoodie.

I feel the group's eyes on me, but I'm not modest. My body isn't perfect, but it's just a body.

Ignoring them, I pull the hoodie over my head, noting the warmth still on it from Roman's body. I also cannot deny that I love the smell of sandalwood on it. It's intoxicating.

"If you're done with your strip show, we have places to be. Don't make me regret bringing you," Roman says, making me roll my eyes.

I don't respond, climbing into the back. It's a tight squeeze. Axel is sitting up front while Blaze is behind him with Hannah sitting in the middle. I push in next to her, angling my body so Marco can fit next to me. Once the door is shut, I try to not crowd Marco, but it's no use.

He laughs at my attempt, grabbing my thigh to pull me halfway into his lap.

"Comfy?" he teases.

"You're going to be soaked. My jeans are still wet."

He shrugs. "It's okay."

I look toward the front as Roman turns the car on. His eyes are on me in the rearview.

"Don't look suspicious. One of you is going to have to crouch."

I let out a deep sigh, turning my back toward the door, settling more firmly on Marco's lap. He groans as I burrow down into him until my head is even with his shoulder. I pull the hood up, curling into his chest, my legs spread out toward Hannah.

"There. No one can see me," I murmur.

Roman doesn't respond, but I feel the car move. Marco's arms wrap around me. I can feel his body heat radiating through the hoodie. After several minutes of silence, I give in. I close my eyes, letting my body fully relax. I don't know how long this drive will be, but at least I'm going to try and enjoy it.

Six hours.

That's how long I've been curled up in this position on Marco's lap. My body is itchy from my impromptu dip in the river.

After thirty minutes, Roman finally gave into Hannah's whining that it was too quiet. He put some music on low so she could hum along. Three hours in, my legs were cramped and my body begged to be moved, but I didn't say a word. I think Marco could tell. Either that or he was as uncomfortable as I was. His hands started massaging where he could, attempting to help me out.

When we pulled up to the lone cabin located deep in the woods, I didn't even take the scene in. I jumped out, stretching my legs.

"Alright, settle in for the night. We will meet in the morning to discuss the plan," Roman says before turning to walk into the cabin.

I pause next to Hannah as she grabs her bag from the trunk, watching as the boys do the same.

I'm the only one who has nothing else to wear. All I have is dirty jeans, a wrinkled T-shirt, and a borrowed hoodie.

Of course.

"The guys all have their own rooms and I bunk with Blaze, but I'm sure Roman got you a room too, so just go find somewhere to chill out. You can hang out with me if you want, but I figured you might want a shower first," Hannah says.

I nod my thanks, letting everyone go into the house ahead of me.

Why did he even bring me? I think to myself.

Not wanting to appear weak, I make my way into the house. You can tell it's a vacation house of some sort. The decorations are obviously meant to reflect the woods surrounding us. To the left is an open layout living room kitchen combo while another sitting room is to the right with a door off it. Straight ahead is a hall leading toward another door and a staircase leading upstairs. Walking through the house, I note that the room off the sitting room is a large bedroom with a bathroom, but the bag on the bed shows it's taken. Finding no other rooms downstairs, I make my way up finding two other rooms and a bathroom. My heart starts to sink when I realize there is only one door left. So four bedrooms and six people. Asshole. That means I'll have to bunk with Hannah, but I don't really care.

That's not until I reach the end of the hall, peeking in the last room. Hannah is laid on the bed, her head resting on Blaze's chest as they talk low.

Fuck.

I don't want to interrupt whatever that is. Even if it's nothing, Hannah deserves to have some alone time with her crush.

Backing away, I let out a huff of breath. After using the bathroom quickly, deciding against a shower without clean clothes, I make my way back downstairs. I hear typing and glance around the corner to see Roman in the sitting room on a laptop. I duck back, not wanting to deal with him. I can hear voices in the kitchen as well but ignore them. Instead, I head out to the back porch.

Once I step outside, I close the door quietly behind me. I smile at the view. It's gorgeous, nothing but trees as far as I can see. The back of the yard is sloped down, a trail leading into the trees. It's beautiful.

I almost want to take a walk, but when the wind blows, making me shiver, I think better of it. Besides, I'm sure Roman would abandon me here if he thought I ran off.

Instead, I walk over to the porch swing, lying down on it while staring at the sky. I try not to let it bother me, but sometimes, when it's quiet and I'm feeling overwhelmed, my emotions get the best of me.

I don't even really care that Roman is being a dick to me. That he made me come and didn't even consider the accommodations to include me. I'll sleep out here if I have to.

Still, that small part of me that still feels the cut of my own mother's abandonment pulls at me until my eyes are burning with unshed tears. I give myself a moment to feel it, then I take a couple of deep breaths, pushing it back down. Closing my eyes, I focus on the sounds of nature.

An hour or so goes by as the sun fades, leaving me in the dark. It's chilly, but it's peaceful too.

I must doze off because the next thing I know, something lands on top of me.

I jerk up, startled.

"Shit, sorry," Marco says, jumping up. "I didn't see you there."

I move over, making room for him. After spending six hours on his lap, this seems like nothing.

"It's all good," I rasp as I rub my eyes.

"What are you doing out here?" His voice is friendly as he takes a seat, pulling out a joint.

"Enjoying the quiet."

He lights the joint up, puffing on it before holding it out to me.

I give him a small smile of thanks before taking it.

"Really? Seemed like you were sleeping."

I shrug, passing the joint back after my own hit.

I hold it a moment before blowing it out. "I might have dozed off."

He smiles. "It's cold out here. Go sleep in your room."

"There're only four rooms and Hannah was otherwise occupied. It's all good, I can sleep anywhere."

His eyes narrow. "There aren't five rooms? I mean, Hannah always shares with Blaze, but with you being here, you should have a room."

I shrug. "I don't think I was meant to come on this trip. He didn't even give me a chance to pack anything."

Marco winces. "Fucking asshole. I'm sorry, Rox. You can borrow some of my stuff."

I shake my head. "It's okay. I think this is another one of his bullshit tests. He wants to see if I'll break, but he doesn't realize I'm not as fragile as he thinks."

Marco laughs, handing me back the joint. "He doesn't know how to handle you. Most people around here respect him enough to stay away. You seem to keep popping up unexpectedly. I'm surprised he brought you at all."

I feel the calming effects of the weed filling me.

"I just want to race. I don't care what else you are up to. Fuck, I don't even want to be a part of your family."

"Family is everything. You don't want that love and support?"

I shake my head. "I had that, and they sent me away. They treated me like a kid even though I was their best driver. I'm over that shit now. I've learned you can only count on yourself. Trusting others will only lead to disappointment or betrayal," I say, making Marco flinch.

"Damn. They did a number on you."

My heart clenches. Not just them.

"Well, at least take a shower. There's a washer and dryer, so you can clean your clothes at least."

I nod. "I guess I could do that. Maybe I'll take some toothpaste if you have some?"

He grumbles, "The asshole didn't even make sure you had a toothbrush? I'm going to ream his ass."

I chuckle. "Stay out of it. You're sweet, Marco, but I can fight my own battles."

"Yeah, but it's fun to rile him up."

"Leave it," I warn him, standing. "I'll go get a shower then."

"I'll grab you some toothpaste when I'm done."

Nodding to him, I make my way back into the house. Once upstairs, I look in the cabinets in the bathroom, smiling when I see the little travel-size shampoos and conditioner.

Something is going right for once. Stripping out of my clothes, I lay the hoodie across the counter while leaving my jeans, bra, and underwear on the floor.

I speed through a shower, feeling better now that I feel clean. I had my moment to give in to my emotions, but now I feel stronger. I am stronger.

Once dry, I put the hoodie back on. It's long enough to cover me for the most part. I consider putting my underwear back on, but they really need to be washed. Poking my head out of the door, I look both ways. The coast being clear, I make my way down the stairs to find the laundry room. I pause when I hear raised voices.

"You didn't even give her a chance to pack fucking toothpaste. That's a dick fucking move."

I recognize Marco's voice immediately.

"Watch it," Roman hisses.

Someone takes a deep breath, blowing it out.

"I get you don't trust her, but don't treat her like shit because of your issues. I'm letting her have my room. I'll take the couch."

"No, you won't. You'll go to your room and get a good night's rest because we need you at the top of your game tomorrow. I'll sort the room situation."

"She better be in a bed. I hope you know what you're doing."

I creep back upstairs, not wanting to be caught eavesdropping. Shutting myself back in the bathroom, I listen as steps come up the stairs and enter the room next door. I poke my head out and start to make my way back down the hall, but Marco pops out, scaring me.

"Here's the toothpaste." He gives me a warm smile.

"Thank you."

I pop back into the bathroom, using my finger to attempt to brush my teeth. Once done, I wash my hands before grabbing my clothes again and the toothpaste.

I pause in the doorway. Marco is lying on his bed without a shirt on. His pants have ridden lower on his hips, leaving every ridge of his chest on display leading down into that delicious "V."

"Enjoying the show?" he says, but doesn't move to look at me.

"Sorry," I blush. "I was returning this."

I toss the toothpaste at him, cringing when it hits him.

He chuckles. "You can have my room if you want it. I can sleep on the couch."

I shake my head. "Really, I'm fine. I'm going to go find that washer and dryer you mentioned."

He smiles. "Downstairs next to the bathroom under the stairs."

"Thank you."

Leaving the room, I make my way down the stairs. As I hit the bottom, I look left as I turn right, trying to keep myself from running into Roman.

Too bad fate had other plans.

He's not in the sitting room at all and as I round the bottom of the stairs, I face-plant right into him.

"Fuck," I curse, dropping my clothes to hold my aching nose.

"Watch where you're walking," Roman grunts, but his hands come to my shoulders to steady me.

His eyes take in my body, noting my bare legs underneath his hoodie. His eyes flare with heat before he covers it back with his blank mask.

I bite back the apology on my tongue. He doesn't deserve it.

"I'll just get out of your way."

When I go to bend to grab my clothes, he holds me in place.

"Let me."

He bends quickly, picking them up, folding them under his arm. I don't miss how his eyes take a quick glance up as he is bent as if he is trying to see up the hoodie.

"I'll take those," I say as I clear my throat.

"Come with me." He grabs my wrist, pulling me behind him back into the sitting room. Then he pulls me into the room off of it, dropping my hand.

"You'll sleep in here tonight. There's a T-shirt for you to sleep in. I'll go throw your clothes in the wash."

"I can do it and I don't need your shirt, I can wear your hoodie."

He shakes his head. "I want to wash that too, so change."

He turns, shutting the door behind him.

I think about disobeying him for a moment, but it's not worth it. So instead, I change into the T-shirt, which shows a lot more of my skin than I'd like.

Opening the door, I find Roman standing on the other side.

"Here." I hand it out, not opening the door much wider.

"I'll get these in the wash. Where's your T-shirt?"

"In the car, I think."

"I'll grab it. Good night."

As he takes a step away, I open the door, reaching out for his arm. "Wait."

He turns toward me, eyes darting down to my thighs before meeting my face again.

"What?"

"Um, my bra. Can you make sure the strap doesn't get hooked around the middle piece. Oh, and it can't go into the dryer."

"Jesus, you're demanding. Anything else, your highness?" he sneers at me.

"I wouldn't say no to a glass of water. You know, seeing as I'm practically naked, thanks to your stunt."

"Whatever. Go back into the room before you distract the guys."

"Yes, sir." I fake a salute.

His eyes flare again, but he turns, hiding his reaction as he walks away.

Shutting myself back in the room, I make my way over to the bed, getting under the covers. Then I stare at the ceiling.

CHAPTER EIGHT

ROMAN

I drop her clothes piece by piece into the washing machine.

"Fuck," I hiss quietly, holding her panties in my hand. I drop them like they are on fire into the washer and slam the lid shut. After starting the machine, I lean against it and hang my head. After a moment, I open the lid again, making sure her stupid bra isn't caught like she asked.

What is it that drives me crazy?

Pushing off the washer, I head out of the laundry room and move toward the bathroom. I close the door softly and turn on the shower. Stripping off my clothes, I step into the water and brace my hands on the wall, hanging my head between my arms. My mind flashes back to earlier and the way Roxy felt in my arms. The way she looked soaking wet. Her eyes were on fire, but there was no denying how turned on she was. The way her chest heaved and her nipples were poking out, begging for attention. When I pulled her body into mine and claimed that smart mouth.

Pushing off the wall, I groan as I reach down and squeeze my cock. I stroke myself as I think about how she took off her T-shirt without a care and wore my sweatshirt. Tightening my grip, a flash of her bare legs peeking out from under the hoodie comes to mind. Then when she was only in my T-shirt. The idea of her in nothing but my shirt sends me over the edge, making me come on my fist.

"What the fuck is she doing to me?" I whisper to myself.

I haven't come that fast since I was a kid who learned how his dick worked. Reaching forward, I turn the water to cold. As I wash my body, I can't help but think about how much I hated looking at her in Marco's arms. All curled up into him as he gave her comfort. The way I couldn't help but want her to be in my arms instead.

I shut off the water and step out. As I dry off, I look into the mirror and silently remind myself that I don't have time for a relationship, let alone one with someone like Roxy. The crew comes first and they need my full attention.

Wrapping the towel around my waist, I walk out of the bathroom and grab my bag off the couch. I walk into the laundry room and drop the towel as I put on a pair of gym shorts. The washer dings, letting me know it's done and I change the load over, hanging her bra on the door, before walking back to the living room.

Sitting down, I can't help but think about catching a little bit of sleep, but I know that I have work that needs to be done. Reaching forward, I grab my laptop off the coffee table and get to work.

Still, my mind drifts to her as I try to focus. It's not until hours later that I realize I haven't gotten much done. I'm almost ready to call it a night when the door opens.

My eyes settle on her immediately, my cock coming to attention as she stands in the doorway, her hair a mess as my shirt falls to her upper thighs.

It's not until I take in her face that my body tenses.

I DON'T KNOW when I fell asleep, but I wake startled by a noise outside. I gasp as my eyes try to take in the room. No one is in here with me, but I could have sworn I heard something. I glance at the nightstand to look at the digital clock.

Three in the morning.

My heart catches when I see the glass of water. He actually brought me water. I try to push down the warm feelings from the gesture.

Another noise draws my eyes to the window. For half a second, I could swear I see a face staring back at me. I jump, turning the light on, but it's gone.

Stumbling to the door as my heart races, I open it.

Roman's eyes lock on me the moment the door opens as he sits on the couch. He takes in my body first, but when his eyes meet mine, they harden.

"What's wrong?" he asks, abandoning his laptop on the couch to make his way to me.

I shake my head, feeling foggy.

"I think I saw someone outside my window. Or maybe I didn't. I'm not so sure now."

"What?" He grabs me by the shoulders, leading me to the couch. Then he sits me down, grabbing a blanket to throw over my lap. "Stay here."

Then he pulls a gun from his waistband and leaves the room before I can respond.

Several minutes pass by and I almost fall back asleep on the couch. Then he's standing over me.

"There was no one there."

I nod. "It was probably a nightmare."

"You freaked out over a nightmare? How do you not know the difference?"

"Sometimes they seem so real. Like I'm actually experiencing them. They used to happen a lot more when I was a kid, but I usually take some melatonin before bed which helps keep me under. I haven't had one where I was awake and still dreaming in a long time."

I know I'm being more honest because I'm still between an awake and asleep state, but I can't help it.

"Well, you can go back to bed."

I shake my head. "Can I sit out here with you for a little bit? Being in there might plunge me back into it and I really don't want to end up screaming."

He pauses. "What if I sit in there with you? You won't get any restful sleep out here."

"That might help," I admit softly.

He nods, grabbing his laptop before leading me back into the bedroom.

Once I'm settled back under the covers, he turns off the light before climbing on top of the blankets next to me. I turn to face him.

"Thanks for the water."

"What water?"

"The glass on the nightstand."

"I don't know what you're talking about. Must have been Hannah. She checked on you a while ago."

I try to push away the disappointment at his statement. I thought it was him.

I wanted it to be.

Fuck, I need to get my shit together. No attachments.

I don't know why I keep getting caught up in him like this. I think I see a small kindness and lose my head.

"Oh. I'll thank her then."

After that, neither of us speak again. He types on his laptop while I close my eyes, attempting to fall back asleep.

SOMETHING SHIFTS AT my back, stirring me from sleep.

I groan, but then an arm snakes around my middle, pulling me back into a warmth. For a moment, I try to grasp on to the feeling.

"What..." I mumble, not sure if this is a dream or not.

"Shh. Go back to sleep," a warm voice rumbles from behind me as a hand brushes through my hair.

Unable to grasp on to the moment of awareness, I fall back into a slumber feeling safe and warm.

CHAPTER NINE

Roxy

The first thing I notice when I awake the next morning is the sunlight filtering through the window.

I burrow deeper under the covers, not wanting to wake up. I've never been a morning person, but the lingering feeling of my last dream makes me want to sleep forever.

It was the kind of dream I usually only get from reading a good book. Where my mind falls into the romance of it all.

My eyes pop open as I realize who exactly featured in my dream.

Roman.

Ugh. Why did it have to be that asshole?

I turn over, letting out a sigh of relief that he's not in bed with me.

I could have sworn I woke up with him cuddling with me, but that was obviously part of the dream. I doubt he would ever willingly cuddle with anyone, let alone me.

Even his offer to sit in here with me last night was probably selfish. He probably didn't want to hear Marco bitch at him for making me sleep on the couch.

Pulling the covers off, I stand and start to stretch, my hands above my head.

A cough from behind me startles me.

I turn abruptly, finding Roman standing in the doorway to the bathroom with steam billowing out around him. He has a towel wrapped around his hips, leaving his chest bare for me to stare at.

I swallow hard as my eyes rake his body. Once to his face, I see his eyes also taking me in.

Then I blush hard because I'm not wearing panties and stretching definitely gave him a good view of my bare ass.

"Hi," I manage to squeak out.

He shakes his head, a smirk on his lips. "We leave in twenty. Take a quick shower. I already put your clothes in the bathroom."

"Oh. Okay. Thanks." I nod, making my way toward him.

He barely gives me any room to pass him, my body rubbing against his. My breath hitches, but I don't pause. I shut the door behind me, resting against it a moment.

I startle when he knocks suddenly.

"Yes," I call out.

"Nineteen minutes now. Hurry up."

Of course. He's such an asshole.

Walking over to the shower, I turn it on. Then I turn to the sink to find my clothes folded in a pile with my bra and panties on top. On top of them is a brand new toothbrush still in the package and a travel-size toothpaste.

My heart warms.

Roman is a mind fuck.

One second he's a dick, then the next he does something sweet. I have no doubts that he is ruthless as fuck, but why is he doing these small things?

It's all probably a fucking game to him. Make the new girl lose her mind.

Still, I use the toothbrush before taking a quick shower using the male body wash I find inside.

As I dress, my heart stutters again. Under my jeans is the hoodie he let me wear yesterday. I bite my lip.

Instead of putting it on, I finish getting dressed. Then I grab the hoodie, leaving the room, determined to find him.

"Oh good. You're awake. The boys are loading the car, then we can get going," Hannah says.

"Oh. Yeah. Hey thanks for the glass of water."

She gives me a funny look. "You're welcome?"

Before I can question her odd reaction, Roman pokes his head in the front door.

"Let's go."

"Hey," I call to him before he shuts the door.

"What?" he snaps.

I throw the hoodie at him. "I don't need this."

He tosses it back. "It's yours now. It smells like shit anyway."

Hannah laughs as he turns, leaving us.

"He's such an asshole." I take a deep inhale, smelling the laundry soap. "It smells like fresh linen."

She shrugs. "Let's go. You think he's an asshole now? Make him wait and he gets worse."

"Marco, do a sweep," Roman demands as we reach the car.

After several minutes, Marco comes out, shutting and locking the door behind him.

"All good, boss."

Roman nods. "Good."

Then we are in the car again, positioned the same as yesterday.

"For future reference," Marco whispers in my ear. "Never leave anything behind. Even a toothbrush."

My face blushes. I forgot that I left the toothbrush in the bathroom.

"Thanks," I whisper.

He squeezes my hip lightly before focusing out the window.

I glance out the windshield, but movement in the rearview mirror catches my eyes.

Roman looks at me, his eyes narrowing. He doesn't say anything. I have a feeling he's not happy that Marco seems to like me.

Only an hour later, Roman pulls into a parking lot.

"Let's run in and get some food."

My heart starts to race. I have no money on me. The last time I ended up out with them, Roman made me pay. It was a test, but I don't feel like figuring out how to get us free food.

As everyone gets out, I lean against the car. Roman looks back at me as the rest of the group make their way into the restaurant.

"Move it, kid."

I bristle at the new nickname. First, little girl. Now, kid. He's not even that much older than me.

"I'd rather stay here."

When the rest of the group stops, he waves them on, coming to stand next to me.

"What's wrong now? This place isn't up to your standards?"

I roll my eyes. "I'm not hungry. I'd rather stretch out my legs while I can."

"Are you uncomfortable on Marco's lap? Looked like you were enjoying it well enough."

I scoff. "I have no choice, but no. Riding for six hours on another person's lap isn't comfortable. At least I'm not wet this time."

His lip curls up. "That was your own fault."

"Whatever you say. I'll watch the car. You go eat."

He shakes his head, unlocking the car before handing me the keys. "Don't run off with it. You won't like the consequences."

Then he stalks off into the restaurant. I slide into the driver's seat but set the keys in my lap. I don't want to waste the gas by turning it on or kill the battery by only having the radio on. Instead, I lean back in the seat, locking the doors.

Several minutes pass before a knock at the window startles me.

"Open," Roman demands.

When I do, he looks toward the passenger seat.

Climbing over the center console, I settle into the seat.

He climbs in, closing the door behind him. Then he reaches into the bag I didn't realize he had and pulls out a wrapped sandwich.

"Eat."

"I'm not a dog. You can't order me to do what you want."

I watch his jaw clench. "Can you stop being difficult for five fucking seconds and just eat the goddamn food?"

"Why do you care? What am I going to have to do to pay you back for this food? I know your generosity isn't free."

"You're paranoid. Just eat the food and shut up."

Then he reaches over, plucking the keys from my hand, and starts the car.

When he pulls out his own sandwich after turning on some music, I relent. I really am hungry. I haven't eaten since breakfast yesterday.

We eat in silence. Even when we are both done, all Roman does is take my trash and place it in the bag before placing the bag on the floorboard.

When the others make it back to the car, laughing and joking, I start to get out.

"Stay," Roman grumbles, getting out.

I sigh, but stay in the car. Following Hannah's advice, I decide to follow along for now. I'd hate to get stranded out here with no way to get home.

After a couple of minutes, the rest of the group piles into the back, Hannah lying across their laps.

When Roman gets back in, he turns down the music before driving. Another hour passes before he starts to slow down in a small town.

"You see that shop right there?" He doesn't look, but jerks his head as we pass.

I look out the window.

Frank's Auto and Body Repair.

"Yeah."

"Good."

Then he drives down the road until we are at the edge of town. Then he pulls into a little motel. After disappearing inside, he comes out, indicating we all follow him into the room he rented.

Once inside, he closes the door and curtains.

"Alright, we need eyes inside that shop. Kid, you're up."

"What? I thought I was going in?" Hannah says nervously.

"Nope. It's time for the kid to earn her keep. She wants to keep poking in our shit, well she can prove she has what it takes. She needs to prove her loyalty. What do you say?"

Roman meets my eyes, a challenge in them.

I don't owe him anything, nor do I need to prove myself, but a small part of me wants to prove him wrong. He thinks I'll back down. I won't accept his challenge. I'll show him.

"I'm down. What do you need me to do?"

He whips out his wallet, handing me over a credit card. I look down and see the name Mary Watson on it.

"You take the car in for an oil change. Keep an eye out for anything suspicious. Report back."

I scoff. "What are you looking for so I know what I'm looking for?"

He's silent a beat. "Suspicious activity. That's all you get to know."

I shake my head. "How much is on this credit card?"

He shrugs. "Boosted it off some rich-looking lady yesterday. You'll be lucky if it's still active."

Fuck.

So there's the danger. I could be getting caught.

"Fine. Keys."

"Wait." Marco steps up. "What about back-up? When it was Hannah, you were—"

"Enough. My decision is final," Roman cuts him off.

I don't have to guess how he was going to finish that. Hannah wasn't being sent in alone, but I am.

Another test.

One I didn't even ask for. I didn't want to be a part of his crew. I didn't mean to keep turning up when he doesn't want me to. Still, the overachiever in me wants to do this.

He wants loyalty? He can't have it. I gave it freely once and they fucked me over. I will keep my mouth shut though. I will do this job for him and hopefully figure out what the fuck he's looking for. I don't need his trust, nor do I want it. At this point, I just want to go home.

Hannah. I'm doing this for Hannah. If I don't, she will have to.

"Don't worry about it, Marco. I got this," I say as I strip off the hoodie, leaving me in my tight T-shirt and jeans.

I wink at him as I grab the keys from Roman and walk out the door.

I don't give myself a chance to feel the nerves. He wants me to get an oil change? I'm not some wilting female who knows nothing about a car. These guys will see right through that facade. I need as much time as possible and an oil change will only take fifteen minutes, tops. I have my own plan.

Taking the piece of shit car over to the shop, I smile when I step out. I already have the attention of one of the guys in the back.

I wink at him before heading inside. Once inside, an older gentleman is at the counter.

"Hello, my name is Mark. How can I help you?"

"Yes, I need the brakes changed on my car."

"Sure thing. Let's go take a look."

"I got this one, Mark." A man closer to my age steps out of the office.

Mark smirks at him. "Sure thing, boss."

So he's the boss here. He has piercing green eyes with shaggy curly blond hair. Attractive would be an understatement, yet the neck tattoo and his demeanor scream dangerous.

I lead him out to the car, leaning against it as I hand him the keys.

"My name's Zade. So brakes, huh?"

"Let's cut the shit, shall we? I can change the brakes myself. Hell, I could give it a full tune-up if I wanted, but I'm on a time crunch and not from here, so I need someone else to do it. So are you going to overcharge me? Fuck it up? Maybe try to sell me a bunch of extra shit I don't really need?"

He chuckles. "Well, with an evaluation like that, I don't think I will. Seems like you might call me on my bullshit."

I smile at him. "One hundred percent."

"Good."

He looks under the hood, takes a reading of the odometer, then glances under the car.

"Okay, let's go inside and work up a price."

Walking back inside, I take in the waiting room again. There's nothing out of the ordinary here. Chairs and magazines to keep the customers entertained.

Then, to my surprise, Zade leads me into the office.

"Please have a seat."

"Tell me, do all your customers get this VIP treatment?"

He smirks. "Only the pretty ones."

I roll my eyes. "I'm more than a pretty face."

"I'm starting to realize that. You can change your own brakes. Not many women can do that."

"Sure they can. They don't want to learn is all. Why would they, when they have men so readily willing to do it for them? I prefer the independence."

"I bet you do." He types on his computer. "I have the brakes in stock. I'll be real with you. Usually I would charge four hundred fifty, but because you amuse me, I'll do it for three-fifty."

I bark out a laugh. "How considerate, seeing as parts are only one hundred dollars, give or take."

His smile widens. "Okay. Fair enough. Two fifty."

"Done." I smile back.

"Great. Wait here and I'll go grab the paperwork from the printer."

He steps out of the room, leaving the door cracked.

I don't hesitate. I swing around the desk, looking at the paperwork. Nothing suspicious laying out. Then I open the top drawer as quietly as I can. I don't find anything there either. I'm about to open the next drawer when I hear him coming back. I stand from the seat, leaning against the desk to look at the photo on the wall.

It's a framed photo of several men with their arms thrown around each other. I recognize more than one of them. Some of them I saw at the races when I first got here, but one of them I know I've met before. Not here, but back in California.

I see the mark, making me swallow hard.

Fucking Roman.

He sent me in to spy on the fucking Devil's Den.

I mean, Roman thinks I'm some clueless ditz. When I was around Soulless, I never knew what they were doing, but I could tell the Devil's Den weren't to be fucked with. They were loud and proud about who they were. It's how I figured out Soulless was more than some little club. No, it was a crew of criminals.

These crews don't ever mingle from what I can tell. Anytime they would come to Cali, shit always went down, and it was never good. I need to keep my involvement with them to myself and get out of town as quickly as possible.

Fuck.

"Whatcha doing, beautiful?"

I glance over my shoulder, frowning at Zade.

"I have a name," I tell him.

"I know, but you never told me it, so I improvised. Forgive me."

I chuckle. "Mary."

I use the name on the credit card, knowing if I use my real name, he may be able to connect the dots.

I glance back to the photo. "Nice photo."

He comes up next to me, close enough I can feel his breath on my neck. "My brothers. I could introduce you if you wanted to hang out later."

My body shivers at his insinuation. The Devils are known for their heathen ways. Orgies are not uncommon for them. I'm sure he'd have no problem sharing me with all five of the other men in the photo.

"Maybe another time. I'm on a timeline, remember?"

"That's right. Where did you say you're from?" he asks, tilting his head to the side.

"I didn't." I look away.

"Feisty. I like that."

I walk back around the desk and sit again. He pushes the paperwork over to me.

"I need you to sign this. Normal shit."

"Perfect. Can I hang out in the garage while they work? I want to make sure numbnuts doesn't fuck it up." He shakes his head, laughing. "For you, I'll make an exception. Give 'em hell."

CHAPTER TEN
ROMAN

The click of the door closing echoes throughout the room. We all watch through the window as Roxy climbs into the car. As soon as she pulls out of the parking lot, everyone starts talking at once. Standing in front of the window with my arms cross, I close my eyes and push the worry to the side.

Should I have sent her off by herself?

Shaking my head, I stand up straight and turn toward everyone right as a pillow comes sailing at me, hitting me in the chest.

"What the fuck, Roman!" Hannah cries out.

Blaze pulls her into him, wrapping his arms around her and leans down, whispering in her ear.

"What's the plan?" Axel asks.

"We let her go. See if she comes up with anything."

"That's it?" Marco scoffs. I look over at him, leaning against the wall, arms crossed.

"That's it." I nod, shooting a look toward Hannah. "If anyone can pull this off, it's Roxy. No offense, Hannah."

"None taken," she mumbles.

"She's got this," Blaze says, trying to comfort Hannah.

"Why did you send her in alone?" Marco asks.

"Because she has no ties to us. If she gets caught, it won't come back on us."

"That's such bullshit," Hannah says, turning into Blaze's arms, burying her face into his chest.

Blaze shoots me a pissed-off look.

"You're the one who told me to fast track her," I point out.

"Look, arguing isn't going to get us anywhere," Axel cuts in, stopping the fighting. "All we can do is wait. Like Roman said, an oil change won't take too long. She will be back soon enough and we will all be on our merry way."

"I don't like it, but it was a good call," Marco says, pushing off the wall. "As long as they don't know her ties to us or Soulless, she should be fine."

"We will be on our way home in the next hour," I say confidently before turning back to the window.

As I stare out the window, I can't help but wonder once again, did I make the right call?

Someone turns on the TV and I hear the bed squeak with the weight of someone getting comfortable. I hear Axel, Hannah, and Blaze start talking among themselves.

Marco steps up alongside me, shoving his hands in his pockets.

"Are you sure about this?" he asks after a few beats of silence.

"I have to be."

"That doesn't answer my question."

"Well, it's the only answer I have."

"You know best, right?" I don't like the sarcastic tone of his voice.

"Do we have a problem?" I turn, giving him my full attention.

"I don't know. You tell me. You used to ask my opinion before making a move and now you don't tell me anything."

"That's not true."

"When it comes to Roxy, it is. I can't tell if you're blinded by your attraction to her or if it's because of her association to the Soulless. Either way, you're not acting like your usual self."

"Same could be said about you. Anything you want to tell me?"

"I'm right as rain," he says as his eye twitches. "All I'm saying though is you better get your shit figured out," he says before walking away.

As the clock ticks, the tension in the room grows. The longer she's gone, the more I feel the need to take action. What if they caught onto her? What if she's hurt? I barely resist the urge to start pacing as I reconsider my actions for the first time in a long time.

This was a mistake.

When the car finally turns into the parking lot, you can feel the tension dissipate. My heart is still pounding in my chest, but relief fills my body, calming me.

She made it back.

I refuse to acknowledge my feelings about that fact.

It's because she's going to be a soldier. Even my mind hears the lie in that statement.

Whatever I'm feeling gets pushed aside. We have a job to do.

Hopefully she didn't fuck everything up.

An hour and a half later, I'm out of the garage and back to the motel. I even gave Zade a fake number when he asked. Seems he has taken a liking to me.

As soon as I knock on the door, Roman opens it, pulling me in before pinning me to the door.

"What the fuck took so long? An oil change is only fifteen minutes," he says harshly, but there is a flicker of something behind his eyes.

Is that… concern?

I roll my eyes. "I know, which is why I got the brakes changed and spent an hour in the shop along with at least fifteen minutes in the office."

"What?" he growls.

"Can you back up? You're annoying me."

I push against his chest, but he doesn't move. I let out a sigh.

"You said you wanted info. I'm not an idiot. I walked in there and asked for a brake job. I guess I'm just pretty enough to catch the attention of Zade."

Before I continue, Roman curses, punching the wall next to the door, leaving a hole.

"You fucking talked to Zade?" he says through clenched teeth.

"Yes. Had a whole conversation with him actually. He even asked for my phone number."

"You didn't." His words are a warning.

"Of course not. I didn't even give him my real name. I'm sure when he calls the random number with a Miami area code and asks for Mary, he will find I gave him the wrong number. I'm hoping by the time he figures it out, we're long gone."

"She's right. We need to go," Marco says from behind.

"Fine. You debrief us on the way. Marco go check and make sure they didn't put a tracker or some shit on the car."

"They didn't, but feel free to check," I snap back at him.

The rest of the group gets up, collecting their items before heading to the car. Once Marco clears it, we get back in.

"I can sit back there. Give Hannah a chance for comfort," I say as I glance back from the passenger seat.

"No," Roman bites out.

I roll my eyes. It's his way or no way, that's for sure.

Once we cross the edge of town, Roman breaks the silence.

"What happened?"

"Nothing. I tried looking in his desk but didn't find anything. He has a picture hanging behind it with six guys all with the same tattoo."

I glance over at Roman, watching his fists clench on the steering wheel. "Are you fucking careless? You tried looking in his desk? Do you know what he would have done to you had he caught you?"

I shake my head. "I can handle myself. Anyway, the office was a waste, but the shop wasn't. I'm assuming what you're looking for is the boxes of parts with the serial numbers scratched off? Looked pretty illegal to me." I shrug.

"What?" Axel asks from the back seat.

I turn, looking at him. "I told Zade if he was going to work on my car, I wanted to watch. He let me after I negotiated a cheaper price. Mary will thank me for that. Anyway, while the guy was changing the pads, I started wandering around the shop. No one questioned me."

"You have a motherfucking death wish," Blaze mutters under his breath.

"I don't get what the big deal is. Did I get what you needed?"

"Yes, but at what cost? Do you know how reckless that was?" Marco says softly.

"What do you mean?" I frown.

He breathes out a heavy sigh. "Nothing."

Hannah glares at him. "You know what. Fuck you guys. I know she's not in, but she did just risk her fucking life for you, so you can tell her more than that. They sent you into enemy territory to see what they have going on. These assholes keep showing up to our races to start shit, then the cops end up showing up. There has also been a lot of theft of car parts in our area recently. We think they are in on it. Affecting our money flow."

"*Enough*," Roman demands.

I turn and glare at him, but he's not paying attention to me. He's breathing heavily as his fists continue to clench and unclench on the steering wheel.

"I see. Well, no harm. He had no idea who I was. I didn't get caught."

"You're clueless. This town is less than two hours from ours. They come to our races every weekend. You think he won't recognize you? He won't connect the dots?"

I shrug. "And if he does? I'm not your problem. I'm not in the club, right? Isn't that why you sent me in? So that you didn't have to risk your own people? I mean, Hannah was going to get an escort, but you sent me in alone. I'm expendable. I don't have the stupid little tattoo to protect me. I get it."

"What do you know about our tattoos?" Roman asks, shooting me a look out of the corner of his eye.

I wince. I forgot I'm not supposed to know about them.

"It seems like a symbol of being part of a club. I get it. No hard feelings. You don't owe me anything. Besides, if this place is only two hours from us, why the fuck did we drive six hours yesterday?"

"We needed to make sure we wouldn't be tracked. Instead of heading straight there, we went around the town and stayed north of it, coming in from a different direction," Marco says from the back.

"I see. So if you're now worried about me being recognized, why were you going to send two of them in? Wouldn't they be recognized immediately?"

"Zade wasn't supposed to be there. We had bad intel."

"So it's a good thing I went in. Everyone is safe. Mission accomplished."

I force a bright smile on my face.

"We will finish this conversation when we get back," Roman grits through his teeth.

"Whatever you say, boss man," I say sarcastically as I scoot down in the seat to get comfortable. I lean my head against the window and close my eyes.

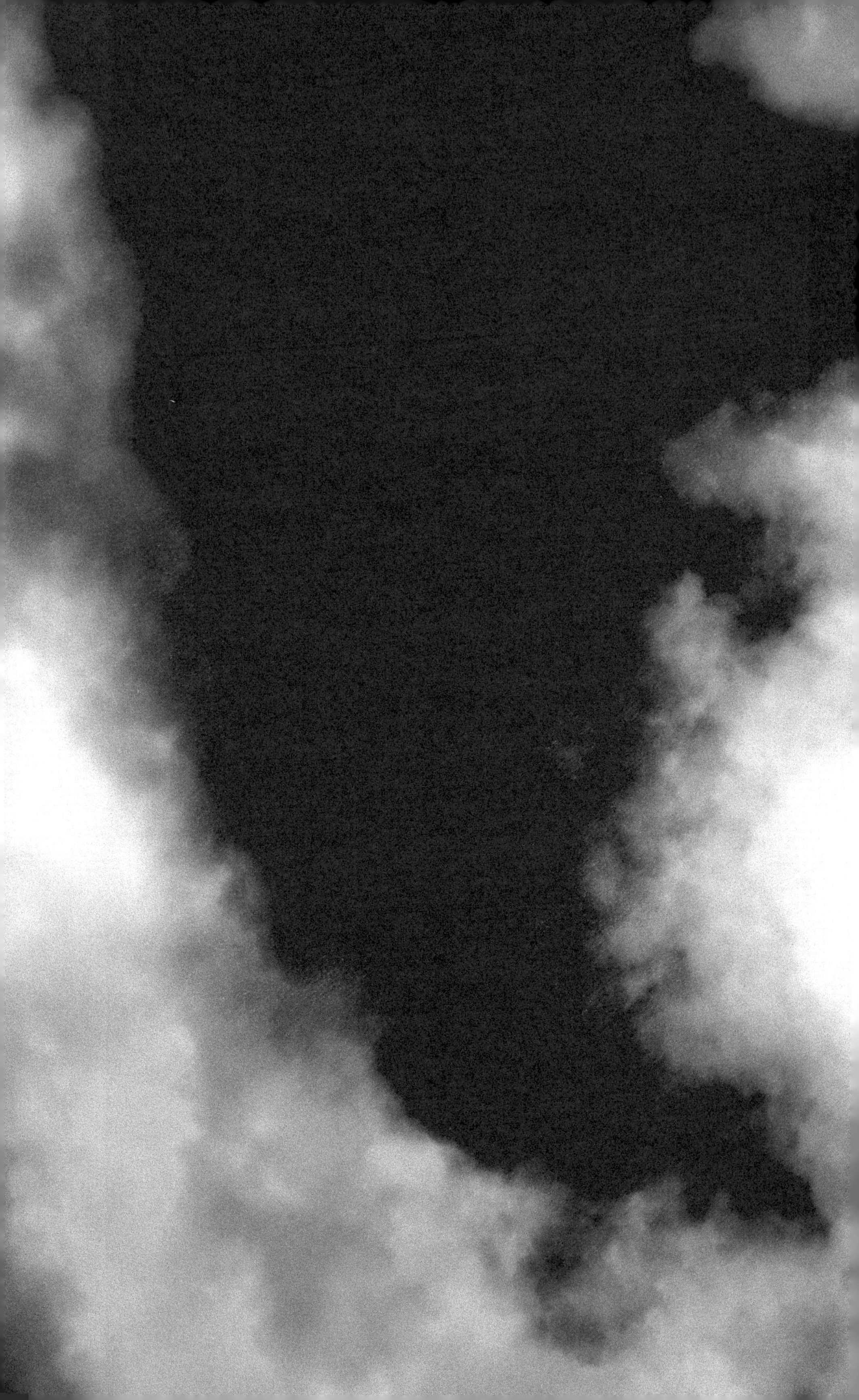

CHAPTER ELEVEN
ROMAN

As I pull into the driveway leading to my house, I glance over at Roxy. Again. Ever since she curled up and passed out, I can't stop looking at her. It reminds me of this morning and how I woke up before the sun rose to find her pressed against me with my arms wrapped around her. How perfectly her body fit against mine. Running a hand down my face, I slow down. I see Roxy stir out of the corner of my eye.

"We're here," I murmur, waking her up.

"You don't say," she deadpans as she sits up, brushing her hair out of her face.

Ignoring her, I put the car in park and shut it off before getting out. Slowly everyone gets out.

"About fucking time," Blaze mumbles as he stretches.

"I had your elbow digging into my ribs the entire time," Axel says as he shoots a disgusted look at Blaze.

"Yeah, well I had to lie across all of you," Hannah says.

"Can we talk about how bony your ass is?" Marco says, wincing.

"Be nice!" Hannah snaps, slapping him in the chest.

"Don't worry, Han, I think your ass is perfect just the way it is," Blaze tells her, making her blush.

"Smooth talker," Roxy says under her breath as she comes to stand next to me.

"Is it cool if we all head out?" Axel asks me.

"Yeah, I'll see you tomorrow," I say as I slap him on the back.

"Later," he calls over his shoulder as he walks to his car.

Marco nods his goodbye as he heads toward his bike.

"I'll take the girls home," Blaze says as he wraps his arm around Hannah, tucking her into his side.

For two people who claim nothing is happening between them, they sure as hell act like a couple. It causes me to worry. I would be happy about it if they both weren't so skittish. I'm afraid if they ever tried to take it further, one would get hurt, changing the dynamic in our group.

The group dynamic has already changed with Roxy, that nagging voice in my mind reminds me.

"Later," I tell him.

As they walk by, Roxy moves to follow and I grab her arm.

"Not you," I murmur.

Blaze and Hannah pause, looking at us. "I'll bring her home later," I tell Hannah.

"You good?" she asks Roxy.

"I'll be fine," Roxy says confidently.

Moving my hand from her arm, I slide it down and grab her hand. I pull her toward the house.

"It's so pretty," Roxy whispers, making me look over my shoulder as I place the key into the lock.

"What?" I ask as I unlock the door.

"I might not like you, but I sure as hell like this porch," she says, making me laugh.

"Glad you approve," I say as I open the door. We walk in and I shut the door behind me. "Kitchen's through there." I point to a doorway.

Roxy offers a small smile as she walks by me toward the kitchen. I lean against the door a moment, asking myself why I asked her to stay. I didn't do it consciously. It was an impulse my mouth refused to deny.

Taking a deep breath, I round the corner to find her at the fridge with the door open as she bends down, ass out. I can't help but lean against the doorframe and watch her.

Damn, her ass is delectable. I could just sink my teeth into it.

"You want one?" she asks as she holds up a beer, shaking me from my thoughts.

I offer a nod, not trusting myself to speak.

Roxy shuts the fridge with two bottles in hand. She quickly opens them both as she walks toward me. I hold out a hand, taking one from her. Without breaking eye contact, I take a drink.

"Thanks, Roxy. You're the best, Roxy," she mocks before taking a drink.

"Want to tell me what all happened today?"

"I already told you." Roxy rolls her eyes as she brushes past me.

"Where do you think you're going?"

"Outside. If I have to deal with you, I should at least get to decide what I want to look at."

I fall into step behind her and can't help but watch her ass sway. Roxy opens the front door and looks over her shoulder. "Like what you see?" she quips.

I resist the urge to chuckle. Of course she caught me staring. A woman like her knows she is fine.

"So tell me what happened?" I ask as she hops up onto the railing, leaning against a pillar.

"I told you already. Nothing happened. We made idle chit-chat. I watched him change the brakes and wandered around the shop. That's it." She shrugs as she raises the bottle to her mouth.

"What did you chit-chat about?" I ask as I step up next to her and lean against the railing.

"He told me he thought I was pretty and how he wanted to eat me out on the hood of his car while I screamed his name." She shrugs again. "Is that what you wanted to know? He told me he could tie a cherry stem with his tongue and honestly, I almost took him up on the offer. I don't think I've ever been with a guy who could do that. His oral skills must be impressive."

I slam my bottle down on the railing, spilling beer out as I grab her legs, forcing them apart as I step between them. The rage I feel inside wants to go back to that shop and kill that motherfucker for coming onto her, but I can't. Not when I have her here in front of me. So instead, I take my frustrations out on her.

"Hey!" Roxy yells, grabbing on to me with one hand as she tries to hold on to her beer bottle with the other.

Her legs wrap around me as if on instinct. She is balanced precariously on the railing, but with my grip on her, she won't fall. I won't let her.

I slam my mouth down onto hers and kiss her with everything I have. Every ounce of hate, frustration, and attraction. Roxy gasps, giving me entry into her mouth. I groan as her tongue meets mine.

"Did he touch you?" I ask harshly between kisses.

"Who?" she gasps as I trail kisses down her neck.

I nip her right below the ear, making her arch into me. "Zade. Did he touch you?"

"Of course not, you fucking idiot," she snaps, rubbing her jean-covered pussy against me.

I quickly reach for the button of her jeans and undo it, sliding her zipper down.

"Lift," I say as I slap her on the ass.

Roxy complies without a word, and I slide her jeans off. She moves to jump down, but I hold her in place.

"Here's what's going to happen. I'm going to bury my face in your pussy while you balance on the railing. Then you're going to wrap those long fucking legs around my waist as I fuck you against the siding. Understood?"

"As long as I get to ride you while you sit in that chair, I'm game." She nods, looking over my shoulder, I see one of the front porch rocking chairs.

"Fuck me," I mumble under my breath.

"Oh, I plan to," she says as she sets her bottle down.

"Did I say you could put that down?"

Roxy ignores me and rips off her shirt, tossing it on the ground. She then removes her bra, dropping it.

My mouth waters as I look at her tear drop breasts and can't help but lean forward, pulling a nipple into my mouth. Roxy hisses as she arches into me, as I graze my teeth along her nipple. Letting it go, I blow on it, making it pebble.

"I want to fuck these."

"Maybe later. You said you wanted to eat me, so get to it," she says as she pushes my shoulders, making me fall to my knees.

I want to spank her ass for that sassy attitude, but the way my dick hardens at it? Yeah, that's a problem.

I pull her forward, making her reach back and grab on to the railing.

"Hold on and don't move."

Her legs settle over my shoulders as I begin to pepper kisses to her inner thighs. The closer I get, the more restless she becomes.

"Stop teasing me, Rome," she moans out.

Rome. Fuck if her calling me by my nickname isn't sexy as fuck.

Leaning in, I swipe my tongue the length of her gorgeous pussy, smirking when she voices her approval. Not wasting any more time, I dive in with only one goal.

Making this woman scream my name as she comes on my tongue.

Focusing my tongue on swirling across her clit, I slowly drag my fingers down the back of her thighs and onto her ass. When I trail them between her cheeks, her body jerks, but the gush from her tells me she likes it.

My dirty girl, I think.

Then I pause. My girl?

"Don't you dare stop," she growls at me, reminding me of my task.

Shaking my thoughts away, I go back to work, eating her like she is my last meal. I slowly introduce my fingers, sliding first one, then two fingers into her folds before thrusting inside her. When she starts grinding against my face, I match her pace, listening to each little sound spilling from her sweet lips.

It doesn't take long before she's clamping down on my fingers, her thighs tightening around my head as she comes.

Fuck, she's beautiful. I think as I glance up to watch her face contort into pleasure. I keep lapping at her until she pushes against me, her breath hiccuping.

"Sensitive. It's too sensitive."

Slowly lowering her legs from my shoulders, I chuckle. "We aren't done yet, Rox. I still owe you at least two more."

Her hazy eyes meet mine. "Two?"

"Another when I fuck you on this rail and a third on the chair. I'm a man of my word."

I watch as her body trembles at my words. I think she's going to deny me.

Yet she surprises me again. "What are you waiting for, boss man?"

The way my body jerks into action is new. The impulse to give in to her every demand is unbearable. As I stalk toward her, I can only think one thing.

Fuck, I'm in trouble.

Roxy

Roman is the epitome of danger. Not only does he do dangerous things for work and drives a sexy as fuck car that screams danger, but the way he just played my body like a fiddle? Fuck, he's dangerous.

When he first kissed me, I almost pulled back, but then I decided not to. What does it matter if I fuck him now? I'll be gone sooner rather than later. At least I can get a couple of orgasms while I'm here, right?

Wrong. I was so wrong. I have never come as hard as I just did on his mouth. Not only that, but the way he is stalking toward me promises more of the same.

I'm truly fucked.

My heart races as he settles between my legs. Here I am, sitting naked as the day I was born on the railing of his porch while he stands fully dressed, his mouth still glistening with my arousal.

Reaching down, he pulls his shirt up, wiping his mouth on it before he tosses it to the ground. Then he leans in, pressing a hard kiss to my lips.

My body rocks back, causing me to move my hands from the railing to grip his shoulders for stability.

"I got you, baby," he murmurs as he kisses down my neck.

Then he removes one hand from my hip to unbutton his jeans. He continues to kiss and nip my neck as he works, the sound of his zipper sending a jolt of electricity to my body.

When he finally pulls back from my neck, he presses another kiss to my lips.

"Hold on to me."

I do as he asks, watching as he moves his hands from my body to push his clothes down before he fumbles with a foil packet. After a moment, he finally gets it open, sliding the condom onto his length slowly.

Even that action has my body heating. For some reason, watching him stroke his length is hot as fuck. I could watch him do it all day.

Or you could help him, that dirty part of my mind tells me.

Pulling at his shoulders, he looks up at me with a smirk.

"Patience." His voice is husky.

I huff out my irritation, but before I can make a comment, he's there. He's pushing at my entrance while his mouth greedily nips at my own.

I open my mouth to him as my legs pull him closer, making the tip slide in.

I let out a squeak at the feel.

I'm no virgin, but I also haven't been promiscuous either. I've only had three partners, and it never felt like this with them.

Just the feel of the head inside me is enough to bring me a slight pinch of pain and a whole lot of pressure.

Roman groans, pressing his lips to my temple.

"Fuck, you are so fucking tight. You feel like a fucking dream."

He slowly thrusts in a little more, taking his time while I adjust to his girth.

Roman is big. I mean way bigger than the guys I was with before. When he is finally fully seated, my core clenches around him, causing him to still.

"God, it's like you were made for me. A perfect fit. I can feel every twitch."

I don't even know if he is actually talking to me. I hear his words, but I cannot respond. I'm too entranced with the way he jerks inside me every time my body clenches around him.

After a moment, he slowly begins to move. I roll my hips along with him, loving the way my clit brushes against him with each pass.

My body is coiled tightly, even after already releasing all the tension once before. The way my body is tingling, I know it won't take much more to send me over the edge. I'm already teetering there, begging for the release I know he will give me.

Mindless words slip from my mouth as I give into the havoc he's wreaking on my body.

"Please," I beg him, but I'm not sure what I am asking for.

Roman's hand on my hip pulls me closer to his body as he continues to thrust. Then his other hand buries itself in my hair, gripping onto my neck. The next moment, his lips are on my neck. After a few open-mouthed kisses, I feel the sting of his teeth sinking in.

That's what sends me over.

I bear down on him as I moan out his name. I can feel my nails digging into him as my eyes slam shut. I am panting as I feel my body jerk in his hold. The waves of pleasure keeps rolling through me as he slows his thrusts, holding me against his chest.

After a few moments, he stops, planting kisses against my head as I lean it on his shoulder.

"Fuck, I almost couldn't hold out. You're a fucking siren."

Then he's moving. I whimper as jolts of pleasure and pain flow through my overworked clit as he moves us, keeping his dick firmly inside me.

When he sits in the rocking chair I mentioned earlier, I don't move. I rest against him as his hands brush up and down my back.

"You okay?" he whispers.

"Yeah. Need a minute."

"Take all the time you need."

He continues to touch me in a gentle way, but it's too much for me. I can take angry Roman wanting to fuck me out of his system, but this gentler one is cracking the walls I've built around my heart.

So when I catch my breath, I go on the offensive. So far, he's been the one controlling this. He withheld his own release. Not anymore.

Leaning back, I grab his face, pressing my lips to his as I clench around him. His cock jerks inside of me in response.

"Now it's my turn," I whisper as I start to roll my hips against him.

His hands grip my hips, but he lets me set the pace. As my body takes from him what it needs, my mouth works against his, mimicking the pace of our bodies. When his fingers dig into me, I know I have him close.

I work my body harder against his, noting the building pressure inside me myself, but trying my best to hold out. I need to get him off. I can't let him get another one on me.

His body begins to thrust up into me as we move together. Then he pulls back from my mouth, cursing out as his body jerks inside me.

At the feel of it, my own finally gives in to the pleasure it's been seeking.

I collapse on top of him, both of us panting from our exertion.

After a moment, I finally breathe out.

"I still fucking hate you, Roman."

He snickers through his heavy breathing before kissing my temple. "If this is how you hate, then hate away, baby."

Shaking my head, I pull away from him, groaning as he slides out of me when I stand.

"I'm going to clean up then I want to go home."

The lust in his eyes fade as his mask falls back over his face.

"Of course."

I hurriedly grab my clothes, making my way into the house. My mind is still whirling as I remember the way he lit my body on fire. After a quick peek back, I curse to myself.

I'm in so much fucking trouble.

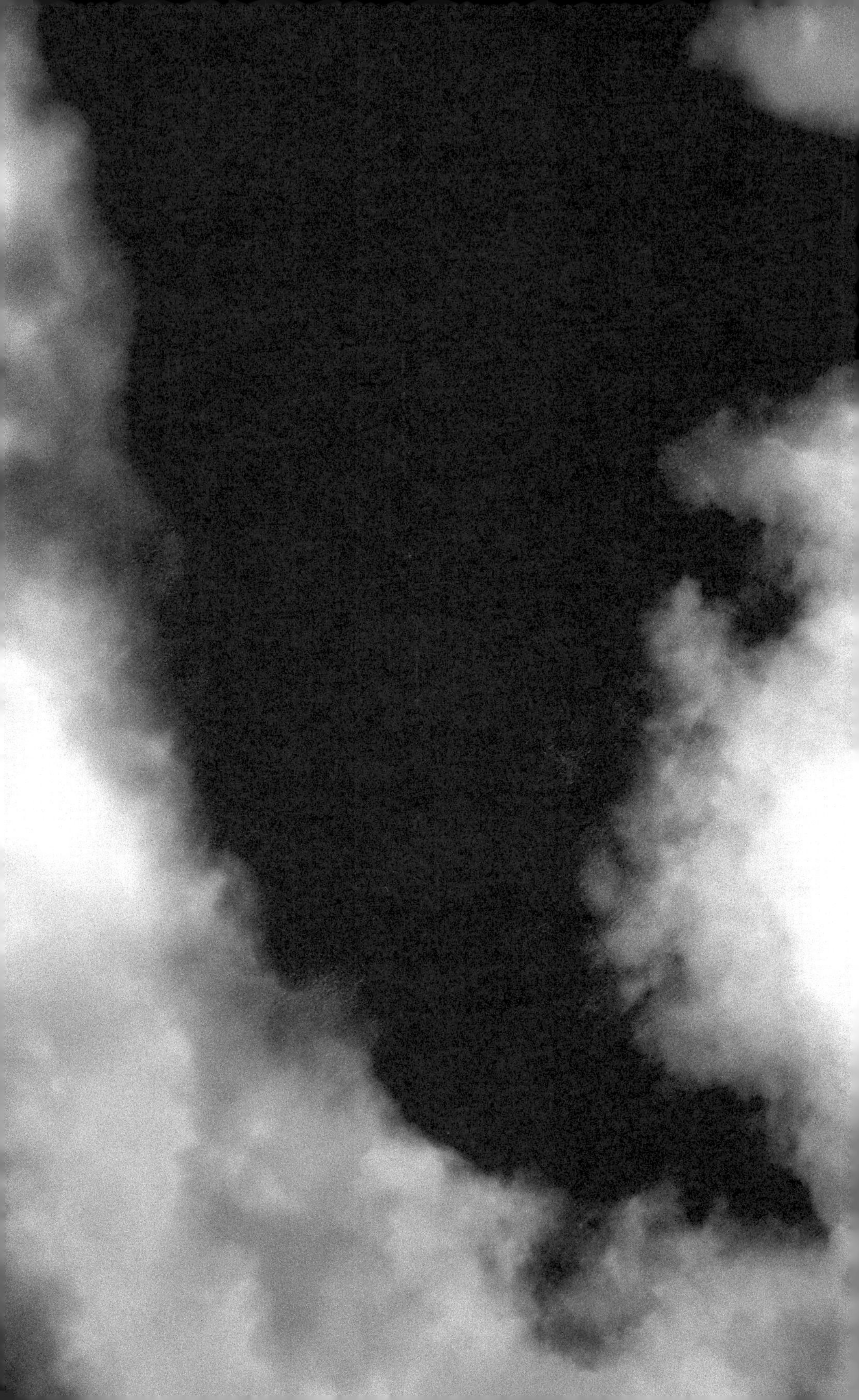

CHAPTER TWELVE

Roxy

"Pack a bag. We got places to be, biatch," Hannah calls to me as soon as I walk through the door.

I breathe out a sigh. "I'm tired as fuck, Hannah. I need a nap."

She laughs. "A nap? It's ten at night. That would be sleeping."

"I have to work again tomorrow night. Go do whatever without me."

I flop down on the couch, bringing my foot up to rub the soles of my feet.

I've been picking up double shifts and avoiding the fuck out of the Shadow business. I know Hannah wants me in, but after I had sex with Roman, I think that would be a terrible idea. I need to keep my distance. I'm leaving as soon as I get a car and nothing is going to stop me. Especially not some good dick.

"No can do. Boss man wants you there, so you have to come."

My heart races at the admission. Does he really want me there? Does he want to fuck again or did he feel that jolt of connection I felt?

Knock it off, I think to myself. I don't need the distraction.

I narrow my eyes at her. "Your 'boss man' doesn't dictate my life. He's not my boss."

"Not yet. Come on, it'll be fun."

"Like the last trip we took was fun? I mean, I suppose I should be grateful he's allowing me enough time to actually pack, but honestly, I'm not down for doing your 'crew business' when I'm not even in your crew."

Her eyes soften. "This isn't crew business. We are having a lock-in at the clubhouse. It's only going to be us and the guys. It's a bonding thing we do periodically."

"So why the hell would you care if I come?"

"You're my cousin and one of my best friends now that we've reconnected. Don't make me be the only girl there."

"You just said Roman demanded my presence."

She shrugs. "I may have hinted that he should invite you. You know how it is with men. If you want something, you have to make them think it was their idea in the first place."

Why do I feel disappointed at the admission?

I shake my head. "You're manipulative as fuck. You know that, right?"

She sighs. "You try being the only girl in a group of four men with wildly different personalities. Some may think it's some kind of fantasy coming true, what with a harem of guys, but it's exhausting. You learn to tread very carefully to keep the peace. Trust me."

"I'm still not going."

"You have ten minutes to get dressed before Blaze gets here. I suggest you use your time wisely."

Rolling my eyes, I get up and head to my room, calling out to her, "Not happening, Han. Give it up."

Determined to get some fucking sleep, I go to my room and change into a large T-shirt, leaving me in only my panties underneath. After turning off the lights, I curl up in my bed, more than ready to pass out.

I am almost asleep when a knock at my door sounds.

"I'm not coming, Hannah. Go without me," I call out.

The next thing I know, the door is kicked in. My heart races as I sit up.

Blaze stands before me, a smile on his face.

"Hannah, grab her a bag. I'll get her in the car."

"What?" I screech as he makes his way toward me.

He doesn't respond. Instead, he grabs my arms, pulling me out of bed. I try to struggle, but it doesn't faze him.

He picks me up fireman style, slinging me over his shoulder. I pound on his back as he makes his way down the hall, well aware my ass is now exposed.

"Put me down, asshole! I don't even have pants on."

He chuckles. "Your fault. You were given a warning."

When his palm lands on my ass, I grimace. I am going to kill him. Reaching down, I dig my nails in his back, determined to draw blood.

He grunts, then moans, "I love when a girl is rough. Keep it up."

I stop immediately. This asshole is sadistic. Or maybe a masochist? Either way, I'm not playing into his fantasies.

When he gets to the car, he tosses me in the back seat, shutting the door behind me. I try to pull the handle, but the fucker put the child lock on.

I go to scramble into the front seat, but Hannah slides in, throwing a bag at me.

"I put some shorts in there for you. You may want to put them on." She eyes my legs before casting a quick glance to Blaze.

Thankfully, he is starting the car and not paying me any mind.

I know how she feels about him, but I didn't ask for him to kidnap me from my bed. Still, my loyalty to her has me slipping on the booty shorts she grabbed for me.

"I don't get why you guys want me here so bad," I mumble.

Blaze smirks, glancing at me in the rearview mirror. "I love that you don't see what the rest of us do. You're so oblivious."

I glance to Hannah, but her jaw is tense. She doesn't like this line of discussion.

To try and ease her, I reply, "I'm not sleeping with any of you. You know that, right?" I say it even though I've already slept with one of them.

The rest don't need to know that though.

One and done. I got him out of my system.

Liar. That internal voice is a bitch.

He shakes his head. "I wouldn't touch you, Rox. You're gorgeous, I'll give you that, but you're Hannah's cousin and you already have two men panting after you. I don't need that drama. Trust me, you're firmly friend-zoned with me. I know, I know. It'll be hard for you to move on, but it's for the best."

Hannah relaxes, a small smile on her face. I can't even be mad at his words when it did what I wanted.

"I'll be sure to buy some chocolate and rent sad movies to move on," I say sarcastically while aiming a smile toward Hannah so she knows I'm playing.

"Good. Now that we have that settled, how are you at playing video games?"

I narrow my eyes. "Why?"

"I need to know who to bet on. Usually, it would be Marco all the way, but you're a wild card. If I can get a leg up, I want to."

I feel the smile flit across my face. "Let's just say, I'm no stranger to pulling all-nighters playing video games."

"Perfect. Don't tell the others. Let them be surprised."

"Are we duping your friends, Blaze?" I fake outrage.

He winks at me in the mirror. "You're my friend now too, brat. We can be on the same side on this."

Hannah laughs. "Roman is going to lose his mind. Let's do it. I'm terrible at games, so they'll assume you are too. Such a male way of thinking."

"Hey, I asked her. I didn't assume." Blaze pretends to be offended.

Hannah reaches over, patting his cheek. "I know. Which is why you're my favorite," she says, making him smile.

She can't see it, but he likes her too. I can tell by the way he keeps shooting glances at her the rest of the trip or the way he does something stupid to see her smile. They are so in tune with each other that it's crazy.

I'm almost jealous. I wish I had someone who knew me as much as these two knew each other. Someone who cared like they do.

Like the way Blaze turns down the air without a word, because Hannah shivers. Or the way Hannah turns the station when a song that makes Blaze tense comes on.

It's an intimate knowledge that comes from years of knowing one another, but it's more than that. It's the way they each pay close attention to one another because they legitimately care about the other person.

By the time we arrive, I've made a decision. They might not be willing to put their necks out there to reveal their true feelings, but I can help push them in the right direction a little bit.

"Come on. This is going to be easy money." Blaze claps his hands as he slides out.

I wait for him to slide his seat forward so I can get out.

"Money? You better be splitting it with me."

He gives me a cocky grin, pulling me under his arm. "Of course. Fifty-fifty. I'm a fair man."

As we get closer to Hannah, he pulls her under his other arm. "In that case, I have two hundred you can bet for me."

His smile widens. "I think we are going to get along just fine."

When we get inside, the others are already in the kitchen around several boxes of pizza.

"Right on time," Blaze murmurs before letting Hannah and me go to head farther into the kitchen. "The party has arrived," he says, making everyone turn and freeze. I don't miss the eyes taking in my appearance.

Roman's jaw tenses. "What the fuck are you wearing?"

I quirk my eyebrow. "My sleep clothes. It seems I had no choice in this little party tonight. So much so that Blaze pulled me from my bed to get me here." I walk closer to Roman, patting his chest. "Don't worry, I pulled the shorts on in the car so I wouldn't be indecent."

Marco snickers as Roman glares at Blaze. "You pulled her out of bed naked?"

Blaze holds his hands up. "Not naked. She was wearing the shirt and panties. I didn't even look. I swear."

I wink over at Marco as he smiles at me before addressing Roman again, "Eh, if he did, it doesn't matter. It's my body. Now, are you going to move so I can grab a plate?"

I nudge him over with my hip. His hand flies down, gripping my hip to keep me against him as he leans down to whisper in my ear.

"Go put more clothes on."

I shrug. "I don't think Hannah grabbed me anything but shorts and another shirt."

I can hear his teeth grinding. "I'll give you sweats."

I peek up at him, trying to control my smile. This man thrives on the control he has.

I'm about to knock him down a peg or two.

Leaning across his body to grab a paper plate, I brush my front against his, watching his eyes darken.

My body hums in response. It obviously remembers our time on the porch, even if I've been trying to forget.

I grab a piece of pizza before finally responding, "I'm comfortable in what I'm wearing. I'm not ashamed of my body and I don't care if your friends or you look at it. Why would I cover up? Unless I'm making you uncomfortable. Is that it?"

He growls. I mean an actual growl and it does things to my body. The sound moves through me as a tingle starts from my head moving through every nerve ending until it reaches my toes. It's erotic in a way I never considered.

Fuck, I need to get laid. Again.

Not waiting for his response, I grip his hand, pulling it from my hip before taking my plate into the living room. Marco follows closely behind me, taking the end seat on the couch. I sit next to him, giving him a small smile.

"You're something else. That was hot as fuck, by the way," Marco whispers.

"What was?"

"You. Standing up to Roman. No fear in your eyes. Fuck, I'm hard just thinking about it."

I give him an incredulous look. "That's gross, Marco. I don't need to hear about your dick."

He looks sheepish. "Sorry. I'm just saying. You're not like anyone I've ever met before."

I chuckle. "That's because I'm one of a kind."

Then I press my shoulder into his to let him know I'm not upset by his comment. I like Marco. He's sweet. He hasn't been an asshole to me like Roman or picked on me like Blaze. Axel, well, he doesn't say much, so it's hard to gauge how he feels about me.

Marco, though, makes sure I know he likes me. I am starting to get the feeling he is becoming infatuated with me beyond friendship, but I'll keep my distance and discourage that line of thinking. As nice as he is, he's not my type. I apparently only get horny for unavailable alpha assholes who want to tell me how to live my life.

First, Ross. Now Roman. It's like my body wants to punish me by desiring the only guys who my mind knows it shouldn't have.

The others join us, cutting off all further discussion of me as they start to talk about other shit that happened during the week.

None of it was crew business per se, but more like a family catching up as if they haven't all been in a room together in a while. It almost feels like a family dinner.

The way they are all so comfortable around each other is natural. Axel took the armchair next to Marco like he has done it a million times before. Marco had taken his spot on the couch while Roman took the one on the other side of me, leaving me in the middle of them. Blaze took the only other chair next to Roman. I must have taken Hannah's spot, because she easily slid into Blaze's lap.

Once we finish eating, Blaze shoots me a wink.

I shake my head at him. He might have been an ass at first, but he's starting to grow on me. Much like fungus, but not as unpleasant.

"Who wants to play some video games?" Blaze teases.

Marco laughs. "I'm always down."

"Hannah, you want to try?" Axel goads, making me smile.

I haven't heard him so carefree before. It's like being here with his family has made him more relaxed. Even with me here, he's not so stiff.

"Shut up, Axel." Her tone of voice sounds angry, but it's softened by the smile on her face.

I look around at each of them, feeling a warmth inside I haven't felt, well, ever. Even with Ross and his friends, I never quite felt like I belonged. They kept me at arm's length, but right here, right now, I feel like part of them. Not some outsider intruding.

When Roman nudges me from my right, I glance over at him. "What do you say, kid? You think you can play?"

I shrug, nonchalantly. "I can try. Depends on the game."

"It's okay, Rox. You do your best. It'll still be fun," Marco says from my other side.

I glance over, giving him a small smile. "You'll tell me which buttons do what?"

I hear Roman grumble as he gets up from the couch, moving to the video system under the television.

Marco lays his hand on my knee. "Of course. I'll help you out in the first round, then we can play a round for real."

I glance over to Blaze, trying to tamper down my smile. This is too easy.

Blaze leans into Hannah's neck, trying to withhold his laughter. Hannah's cheek blushes as she sits perched on his lap.

When Roman comes back after handing out the other controllers, he hands me mine.

Before he can sit, Marco pulls me into his side, making Roman shoot him a glare.

These two have issues and I do not want to be in the middle of it.

Still, I need to play this up for Blaze's sake.

"Okay, so the 'X' jumps, the 'O' kneels or slides if you're moving, the square will reload your ammo, and the triangle will switch your weapon out. To fire, you press this button here. It's called 'R2.' Then you use this thing here to move while the other toggle will move your view. That's the basics. You got it?"

He's so close, I can smell his cologne. If I turned my head to the left, his lips would brush against mine.

Still, even with that, my body is hyper focused on the brooding male on the other side of me. The way his thigh is pressed against mine like he has no care for my personal space.

Where Marco is considerate of me and is only touching my arm as he shows me the controls.

They are night and day, yet only one of them makes me burn inside.

"Thank you. I have it." I pull away from him, smiling to myself when he arranges himself so he is not pressed against me.

It's so considerate. I move my right leg so it's not touching Roman, but he only moves with me, pressing closer to me.

"Stop fidgeting."

I glare at his barking tone.

"Asshole," I breathe under my breath, but the twitch on the side of his lips tells me he heard me.

Fuck him. I don't care if he did.

"Are we ready to play?" Axel's impatient tone cuts through my thoughts.

I give him a coy smile. "I think so. Hopefully, I don't disappoint you."

Blaze chuckles, calling out, "I'll put five hundred on the newbie."

Axel laughs. "I'll take that bet. I got five on boss man. He's looking like he's ready to dominate tonight."

Marco shakes his head. "You know I always win. I don't know why either of you are bothering to bet against me."

They both shrug, but it's Axel that speaks up, surprising me. "You have a distraction tonight. Seems it may work in my favor," he says, winking at me.

He fucking winks at me, and I'm stunned. Axel, who has barely ever spoken more than a couple of words to me at a time. The same man who wears a blank mask like it's a second skin.

"Close your mouth, brat. You'll catch a fly," Blaze calls from across the room.

"Fuck you. I'm confused as to who this is in the room with us. Were you abducted by aliens, Axel? I didn't know your face could make expressions."

He shrugs, but smiles. "You weren't in before."

"I'm not in now," I tell him.

"No, but close enough. Now let's kick some ass."

I let them kill me a couple of times, shooting a look at Blaze as I scrunch up my nose as if I'm upset at my performance. Blaze looks a little worried now, but I shook him a wink and he relaxes.

That's right. Trust me.

"Come on, Rox. I'll help protect you."

I pout. "It's okay, Marco. Maybe you should go without me. I'll camp over here."

"Noob," Axel whispers under his breath.

As soon as Marco starts paying more attention to his own screen, I make my attack.

"What the fuck?" Axel calls out.

We aren't playing teams. No, we are playing free for all. That means I can kill each and every one of them.

One down.

"What happened, Axel?" Hannah asks.

"Someone snuck up behind me and fucking knifed me. Wait, Roxanne? Was that you?"

His voice turns incredulous as the screen tells him who committed the murder.

"What? How do you knife?" I play along.

Axel mutters, "Lucky fucking kill."

I continue on, sneaking around shooting each one. Blaze doesn't comment when I kill him, but as I kill each of the others, they start to catch on.

"Did you fucking hustle us?" Roman grunts from next to me.

"Did I? I mean, I never said I didn't know how to play. Did you guys assume because I was female that I wouldn't be able to do well?"

Marco bursts out laughing. "Point made. All hail the Queen."

When the round finally ends, Blaze jumps up, holding out his hand to Axel.

"That's cheating. You knew, didn't you?"

Blaze pastes an innocent look on his face. "Me? No, but I had a feeling she was badass. I mean, she has proven us wrong more than once."

"Asshole. Fine, here is your money."

When he hands over the money, Blaze counts out half, handing it to me. "I gave you the extra ten since he only had twenties. Fuck, it was worth the entertainment. Watching the disbelief on their faces? Yeah, that was great."

"You're such an asshole, Blaze." Axel shakes his head, laughing.

Blaze shrugs. "Takes one to know one, I guess."

As we start the next round, I look around the room, smiling at the scene. I never thought I would get comfortable like this again.

I'm still planning to leave, but right now, I'll live in the moment.

I'll enjoy this.

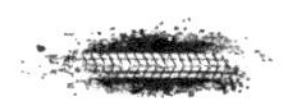

"You can have my bed, I'll sleep out here." Marco yawns as he stands to stretch.

The night went on to the early morning hours.

The rest of the group tapered off throughout the night. First it was Hannah, pulling Blaze with her. They can claim they are only friends all they want, but as soon as she started toward the bed, Blaze was right behind her.

Then Axel bowed out an hour later, grumbling about a woman kicking his ass.

Once it was just Marco and Roman with me, they decided to put a movie in. That turned into three movies, neither willing to get up and go to bed.

I have a feeling it has to do with me. Especially with the way they each drew closer to me as the evening progressed. Marco still attempted to keep his distance, but Roman had no problems throwing his arm around the back of the couch as he began to play with my hair.

It wasn't until I started yawning every couple of minutes that he got up and announced we should all go to bed.

I know I need to get at least a couple hours of sleep. I still have to work tonight and since it's Friday, I know it will be packed. Still, I'm not liking the idea of sleeping in Marco's bed.

"It's okay. I can sleep on the couch."

"That's not very gentlemanly if I let you do that."

I shake my head. "I don't need you to be a gentleman. Just go to bed, Marco. I won't compromise on this."

Roman is hovering in the kitchen, listening to our conversation.

"It's not like it's actually my room, Rox. It's a spare room that I use when I'm here. You'll be more comfortable in there."

I shake my head, unwilling to compromise for him. After tonight, I know he likes me as more than a friend. I need to keep him firmly in the friend zone though. I don't need to encourage anyone to pursue anything with me when I still plan to leave eventually. I don't need an attachment to keep me here. I already fucked up once with Roman. I won't do it again.

"Go to bed, Marco," Roman bites out when Marco opens his mouth, presumably to argue again.

He shoots a glare at Roman, but then leans down to kiss my cheek. "Fine, but if you change my mind, you know where to find me."

"I won't, but okay."

He shoots me one last glance before he heads down the hall. When his door clicks closed, Roman makes his way over to me.

"You can take my room. I won't sleep anyway," Roman's deep voice rumbles.

My body is begging to say yes, but that's a terrible idea.

Distance. I need to keep my distance.

I narrow my eyes at him instead. "What makes you think I want your room any more than I want his?"

He gives me a playful smirk. "You telling me your heart doesn't race when I'm close?"

He leans in, brushing a kiss against my cheek as his hand grabs my wrist, pressing into it gently.

I already know what he's doing. My pulse *is* racing. He can feel it thrum through the pulse point on my wrist.

"Who says it doesn't do that when Marco is close?" I whisper, unable to raise my voice anymore.

He tenses. "Does it?"

I clear my throat, pulling away from him. "It doesn't matter. I'm sleeping on the couch."

He grunts but doesn't pull me back to him. Instead, he heads down the hall. I move to the couch and start to settle in when I hear footsteps. I heave out a sigh, ready for another fight, but then something hits me in the face.

"Hey." I sit up, looking over the back of the couch, pulling the pillow that hit me away from my face.

Roman glares at me, pulling a blanket over the back to cover me.

"What is this?" I ask, hesitantly.

"You want to sleep on the couch? Fine. Be stubborn, but the least you can do is accept some form of comfort."

I bite my lip, watching as his eyes track the movement.

"Thank you," I manage to whisper.

He nods once, moving back to the hall.

Once I hear his door shut, I pull the pillow under my head before arranging the blanket over me in a more comfortable way.

As I drift off to sleep, I smile. The pillow smells like Roman and as much as I don't want to admit it, he is becoming my favorite smell.

I DON'T KNOW how long I doze off for, but a muttered curse wakes me.

I sit up, looking over the couch toward the kitchen.

Axel looks over at me, looking apologetic.

"Sorry," he whispers.

I shrug. "What time is it? I didn't bring my phone."

"Eleven." He turns back to the coffeepot, continuing to fill it up.

It was just beginning to get light when I passed out, so I'd guess I got about five hours sleep.

Standing, I stretch, hearing my bones crack.

"Can you make me a cup too?" I ask him.

He smiles so I head down the hall and use the restroom. Once I get back, he pushes a cup over to me along with the sugar and cream.

I smile, fixing my coffee.

When he heads toward the French doors leading outside, I follow him silently. He pauses at the couch, grabbing the blanket that I was using before proceeding.

Once outside, he leads me to the porch swing overlooking the river.

He sets his coffee on the railing to the porch before wrapping the blanket around my shoulders.

"Sit," he says, grabbing my coffee from me so I can do as he asks without spilling it.

Once I'm settled, he hands me back my mug before grabbing his and sitting next to me.

Then we sit in silence. It's nice. Comfortable even. Nothing but the sound of the river and nature as we are enjoying each other's company.

After a while, he finally speaks. "You're good for us. Blaze treats you like a sister. Marco wants to date you, which is new for him. He doesn't date. Roman..." he trails off for a moment before clearing his throat. "You're here which says a lot about Roman."

I look over at him as he continues to look out over the land. "What about you?"

He glances over, giving me a small smile. "I wasn't sure at first. I'm the analytical one. The overthinker. At first, I thought you would cause issues. You still might, depending on how you handle the situation with Marco."

I nod, understanding what he's saying. He sees it too.

"I'm not planning to do anything with him. It's not like that for me."

He looks at me for a long second before continuing, "He thinks he wants more with you, but it's because you're different. You're not the one for him.

You belong to someone else. He will see that sooner or later."

He takes a sip of his coffee as if he didn't just say I belong to someone.

"Um, there's a flaw in your thinking."

He quirks a brow at me. "Enlighten me then."

"I don't belong to anyone."

He smirks. "Not yet, but you will. You don't see it because you're in it, but as much as you want to run from this place, you're already rooted here. Hannah would be devastated if you leave. Not to mention the rest of us, but Hannah more so. She used to talk about you a lot. She always used to say she was going to reach out to you. She missed you, but she never did."

"What do you mean?"

"She was scared you would reject her. She said after you turned thirteen, you became distant. You stopped calling. She always wanted the girl she thought of as more of a sister back, but she was scared you didn't want her anymore. She has some abandonment issues."

I scoff. "Her? She had her dad at least. Uncle Mike was always good to me. Unlike his piece of shit sister. My mom pretty much left for good when I turned thirteen. She paid rent and kept collecting welfare on me, but she was never actually there. I stopped calling because I didn't have a phone. Not because I wanted to. Then too much time had passed. I had a new life. New friends."

"I'm not saying you're wrong, but Hannah is allowed to feel that way too. She would never admit it because she had her dad, but her mother did a number on her. I think that's why she moved away from him after high school. She wanted to find a place to belong."

I swallow hard. I never thought about it that way. That even having her dad, she might have felt insecure about relationships.

"Is that why she refuses to acknowledge her feelings for Blaze?" I whisper.

I mean, she has acknowledged them with me, but he doesn't know that. If he is as observant as I think, he has caught on.

He presses his lips together. "They are both insecure. She's worried this is all temporary. It's why she doesn't rock the boat with us. She goes along with it because she wants to do whatever she can to please us. Except when it came to you. I think that's when I realized you were more than a random chick. Anyone who can make Hannah raise hell must be something special.

As for Blaze, he thinks she's fragile. He doesn't want her to take off if they don't work out. At least, that's what I think from watching them together. Blaze has never said anything and well, Hannah won't."

I nod. "I can see that. It's sad."

"It is, but eventually they will act on it or they will settle down with someone new. If I had to place my bet, I'd bet on them pulling their heads out of their ass. Blaze chases every guy that Hannah dates away while the girls Blaze messes around with are never in his bed more than once. It's a fucked-up situation."

"I'd say." After a pause, I ask, "So you think I'm good for you guys?"

I can't help the hope that floods my chest.

"I think you're what we need to shake things up. We have been content in our core group for so long, but we aren't getting any younger. Roman hasn't let anyone else in since Hannah, and that was eight years ago. He's letting you in whether you want it or not. It's up to you if you want to accept it."

"And if I don't?"

He shrugs. "Then I suggest you leave town sooner rather than later. We are all already attached to you in some form or another. Leaving now would hurt, but it would hurt more if you waited."

I swallow hard. "You would be hurt?"

"Not like the others, but yeah. You're a cool chick. You can beat my ass at shooting games and you call Roman out on his shit. I wouldn't mind being your friend."

"Friends. I can do that." I smile up at him.

"So you'll stay?"

I consider his words. "I can't make any promises, but I'll seriously think about my next steps."

He stands before leaning in, pressing a kiss to the top of my head in an unexpected tender gesture. "That's all I can ask for. I'll go make some breakfast. Come in soon, okay?"

Then he leaves me with my swirling thoughts.

Could I stay? Were they really letting me in? Roman acts like he hates me half the time, but maybe if the others want me here, he will keep me.

Did I want to be kept?

CHAPTER THIRTEEN

ROMAN

I have never questioned my loyalty to Marco and what I would and wouldn't do for him. I want nothing more than for him to be happy. But watching him walk toward Roxy, I can't help but be envious. I see the way his eyes light up when she's near and I hate it.

I want her attention. I want to hear her snap at me one second then moaning my name the next. I want her next to me, under me, and over me.

Pushing off the fence, I rub my face, trying to shake off my possessive feelings toward her. I see the way she tries to avoid us, and I don't know how much more I can take. Worst of I don't know how my best friend will take it when he finds out that I've had her and that I want her again.

I'm thirty years old and I've never thought about being in a relationship much, but Roxy, she makes me want to try whether she realizes it or not. When she's cold, I want her to wear my hoodie. I want to make her coffee every morning and watch as she shakes off her dreams from the night before.

The thing about Roxy though, is she's as skittish as a bunny and I'm going to have to coax her into this.

"Hey Roman!" someone yells.

I turn and see one of the regular guys leaning against the hood of his car drinking an energy drink.

"What's up, Dick?" I nod.

"The name's Rich," he says, shaking his head. "You racing tonight?"

"When don't I?" I ask, raising a brow.

"True." He nods. "I need you to win me some money then."

"I'll try," I deadpan before turning and walking away.

"Did that guy really just tell you he needs you to win?" Blaze asks as he walks up next to me with Hannah under his arm.

"He did."

"Idiot." Blaze laughs.

"Be nice," Hannah scolds, slapping his chest.

"I'll see you at the line," Blaze tells me before veering off with Hannah to do what they need to do.

Over the last few years, we've all figured out what we need to do to make these races go off without a hitch and I love it.

As I approach my car, I can't help but feel adrenaline teasing me, knowing it's almost time. There's nothing better than being inside a high-performance car and pushing her to her limits. I run my hand along the fender, admiring her. As I open the door, I look over the roof and spot Roxy in the crowd and can't help but wonder, what would she look like behind the wheel of my baby?

One of these days, I'm going to find out.

Roxy

THE IDEA OF staying has been weighing on my mind more and more recently. Between the movie nights with Hannah and Blaze and the random lunch dates with Axel, I'm starting to really settle in. The thought of leaving doesn't feel like it used to. Instead, I'm kind of dreading it.

Then there's Marco and Roman. Thankfully, I've avoided being alone with them so far. The only time I really hang out with them is in a group. I know Axel knows my intent, which is why I appreciate when he always inserts himself into whatever plan Marco makes to get me alone.

Marco notices it too, but he hasn't called him out on it. At least not in front of me.

That's why I'm surprised to find myself alone with him after Roman demands my presence at tonight's races. He even went so far as to call Julio and make sure I had the night off.

When I see him, I plan to bitch him out for it, but so far he hasn't shown his face.

"You're with me tonight," Marco says as soon as I climb out of Blaze's car.

"Yeah? Why is that?" I ask.

"I figured you would want to get to know a little more about the business."

They've been doing this more lately too. Slowly showing me parts of the crew without actually telling me the important shit.

I get it. I'm not in yet, but it's obvious some of them want me in.

Roman's the only hold-up. If I'm being completely honest with myself, it hurts that he is holding out on me like Ross did, but another part of me expected it. That's the part still planning to leave.

It's the same part denying the electrical field that surrounds me and Roman anytime we are in a room together.

We've already caved to our desires once, will we do it again?

I know Marco can sense it too because he always amps up his attention when Roman's around. Almost like he wants me to pay attention to him instead. He is always touching me when Roman is in the room. It's never inappropriate, but I know he is trying to stake some sort of claim.

I hate their pissing contest. It makes me uncomfortable being between the two of them.

Can I even call it that? Roman sometimes acts like he wants me, but then he acts like he can't stand me. His mood swings give me whiplash.

Yet even with that, I eat up the moments he does give me. The subtle brushes of his hands against my body. The small gestures telling me he is paying attention, like the way he can make my coffee the way I like it. Or the way the more crisp bacon ends up on my plate at breakfast.

"I guess so. Does it even matter? Roman is never going to let me in for real."

Marco grits his teeth. "He's being difficult, but he will come around. Give him time."

I roll my eyes. "Roman is alpha male to his core. If he doesn't want to do something, he won't. It's obvious he doesn't want me in."

He shakes his head. "You know nothing about him then. If he didn't want you around, you wouldn't be here. End of story."

I don't bother responding. I've had different versions of this conversation with Axel and Blaze as well. It's pointless.

He leads me around the crowds, slinging an arm over me as he talks to each one.

I don't miss the exchanging of cash as they talk about the lineup tonight. I yearn to go look at the cars, but every time I try to venture away, Marco pulls me back to his side.

After an hour and a half, I'm bored out of my mind.

"Can I go hang out with Hannah now?" I whisper to Marco as we leave another group.

He chuckles. "Have you been paying attention at all, or are you that done with all of this?"

"I'm bored and you wouldn't even let me drool over the cars. I'd rather be at work at this point."

He shakes his head. "Come on. It's about time to head out anyway."

When he leads me over to the same area he stood at my first race, I smile.

"Jordan kind of explained it to me, but why do you check cars?"

He looks back at me. "Everyone pays to go. Whether it be to race or watch. You don't pay, you don't go. We haven't always done it this way, but a couple of years ago, some people crashed and started a huge fight that ended up with a lot of arrests and media coverage. These races work because, for the most part, it's kept on the down-low. Even when the cops come, it's usually because we call them ourselves to break up the crowd. We don't want anyone to get seriously hurt or for it to become a place to hash out beef. So by greeting everyone going, we can keep an eye on things."

I cock my head to the side. "That's actually impressive."

"Thank you." He beams. "It was my idea, which is how I ended up with this job. My idea, my responsibility."

I nod, understanding.

Roman rolls past us, his eyes taking me in. I give him a small wave, but he doesn't reciprocate. The only indication that he even notices is the small smirk on his face.

Then the first car pulls up. Marco leans down, eyeing the passengers. Then he waves them off.

One after one, they follow each other.

I stand at Marco's side, smiling at some faces I recognize.

They blend together for me, but Marco addresses each and every one.

Then a familiar Mustang pulls up.

I snort, making Marco smile at me over his shoulder.

"Hey, man. Who's the girl?" Marco asks.

I lean down, eyeing her. She looks nervous.

"Did you bring a narc with you, Jordan?" I ask.

"What?" Jordan's eyes widen when he takes me in.

I didn't notice him earlier. I don't think we approached him.

"Jordan, my man. You know you have to stop doing this. Either you pay prior to line up or you don't go."

"Come on, man. I got here late tonight."

I shake my head. I doubt that's the truth.

Looking back to the girl, I find her eyes on me, but she averts them quickly.

"Marco," I drawl.

He holds a finger up to Jordan, straightening to give me his full attention.

"What's up, babe?"

"The girl is skittish," I tell him.

He looks back to her then to me.

"You're out tonight. Sorry, should've shown up on time."

"What the fuck, man? Just because this bitch says so? She's mad she didn't get to ride on my dick." His eyes narrow at me.

Marco tenses, but I only laugh.

"In order to ride, you have to have something worth riding. There's a reason you never called after that night. Weak men are cowards. Move along and take your meek girlfriend with you."

Marco looks like he wants to punch him, but Jordan revs his engine, taking off, not following the others who have slowed down to keep the line in sight.

Then the next car pulls up and we are back in business. When the last one finally rolls through, I smile.

"Blaze, my man, you going to let me race your car tonight?" I ask him.

He looks at me, horrified. "Hell no. No one drives my baby, but me."

"It was worth a shot," I say as I slide in the back.

Marco slides in beside me, smiling at me.

"How'd you enjoy your crash course into Marco's job?" Blaze asks as Hannah turns to look at me.

"It's boring as fuck. The fact that he can people that much in one night is a fucking miracle."

Hannah laughs. "You people every night at work."

"It's different."

Marco asks, "Really? How?"

I shrug. "It's the setting. I'm getting a paycheck from it."

"I get paid for this too, honey. Don't think I do this for free."

I roll my eyes. "Whatever."

"Your resting bitch face is on point, Rox. I watched you tonight. I could tell you really didn't give a fuck about being nice," Hannah informs me.

"Was I supposed to?"

Blaze snorts. "You're perfect the way you are, brat. Don't ever change."

"Stop flirting with me, Blaze. You're like my brother. It's creepy as fuck."

He bursts out laughing. "This is why I love you."

When we finally pull up to the secondary site, we all get out together.

"So what next?" I ask them.

Blaze grabs Hannah's hand. "We have our jobs to do. See you in a bit?"

Marco nods. "You're still with me. Now we observe."

I let him lead me around, keeping an eye on the crowd. Thankfully, he keeps me closer to the edge of the races, so I can at least still watch, but the constant movement is starting to annoy me.

"Why don't you ever just stop?"

He pulls me toward him as some drunken idiot stumbles past me to puke next to a tree.

"That's why. We have to monitor the situation. Make sure it doesn't get out of hand."

"You don't even get to enjoy the best part of all of this. Does that mean you don't race?"

"Nope. We all have our parts to play. Roman races. Sometimes Blaze.

Axel is on radios while I'm on crowd control. It's like a well-oiled machine. When we do our parts, everything flows. One of us gets distracted, shit goes down."

"Like my first race? When the cops showed up?"

He smiles. "We knew they were coming. I might have delayed our exit."

"What do you mean?"

"I saw you watching the race up close. I knew that douche would run off, not caring if you got caught. That's why I ran into you. I was looking for you. I was so pissed when Roman made me leave you."

I shake my head. "Why would you care?"

"You were new. I wanted you to have a good impression of the races."

"I can handle myself."

He snorts. "I know that now. I didn't back then though."

"Well, in the spirit of being honest, do I really have to stay with you all night?"

He frowns. "Is it really that bad to be around me?"

I roll my eyes. "You know that's not what I mean. I want to watch the races. I already missed the first three."

He huffs out a sigh. "Fine. Roman races next. Blaze will be there helping him prepare. Stay with them and I'll come back and get you in a bit."

"No need to get all pissy about it."

He gives me a small smile. "I was enjoying our time together tonight is all. We don't really get time just the two of us."

I swallow hard. Fuck. This is why I was avoiding being alone with him.

I nod weakly. "I'll go find Blaze and Hannah."

I feel his eyes on me as I disappear into the crowd. When I get up to the start of the race line, I hesitate.

Blaze is nowhere to be seen and neither is Roman, but they haven't lined up to race yet.

I ignore the people around me as I wait, feeling nervous for some reason. Something in my gut is telling me something is wrong. I look around again, trying to keep an eye out for any of our group, but I don't see any of them.

Several minutes go by, then I hear it. The sirens.

"Fucking seriously?" I cuss to myself as I take off running with the crowd.

I don't even know where to go. I feel like running back to Blaze's car would be pointless. All the people rushing that way are jamming me up. I glance back over to the woods.

Fuck it, I spin, heading the opposite way down the edge of the road. I am scanning faces in case I see one of the guys or Hannah, but so far, no luck. I break away from the crowd about to head across the road when I hear the engine.

I freeze as a car comes to a halt in front of me.

"Get the fuck in," Roman hollers out the open passenger window.

I don't hesitate. I run to the door, flinging myself into the car, barely closing the door before he peels off.

I watch as Roman maneuvers around the people scrambling to their own vehicles. Once free of the crowd, he really opens the car up, speeding down the side roads. His headlights are off, but he manages to handle the car with ease. My own heart races imagining running into something in the darkness.

For a brief second, I have a flashback to my accident. I haven't been able to remember much about it, but I remember now. The car next to me pressed into me, making me veer left. That's when I saw it. A small pillar on the ground. Hitting that is what caused me to flip.

I can see myself fly through the air when Roman speaks, startling me back into the present.

"Stay with me, kid."

My eyes snap open. I look over to see his eyes focused on the road. How did he know I was lost in my head?

Finally, he turns down a trail, coming to a stop when the road can no longer be seen.

"We will wait it out here for a little bit," he informs me.

"Okay."

He gets out, moving to the front of the car. I hesitate a moment before following.

"Thank you for not leaving me behind again."

My heart is thrumming in my chest at what this could mean.

He shrugs. "I owed you one for not ratting us out the first time."

Of course he did. Fuck, I need to get my feelings under control. I feel like I'm back in California with Ross all over again.

He always flirted with me making me think he would one day want more. Even when he would run off with other women, I thought he was waiting for me to be old enough. I think that's what hurt most when he sent me here. Maybe I read him all wrong. Maybe I thought he was flirting, and he was just being nice.

There's no way I read this wrong with Roman. He is attracted to me. That much he proved when he fucked me on his porch, but obviously it isn't more. I don't want it to be anyway. At least, that's the lie I keep telling myself.

Truth is, I know my feelings for him are complicated.

"I see. Well thanks anyway," I mumble.

He lets out a heavy breath. "Don't sound so crushed."

I turn to glare at him. "I'm not."

He scoffs. "Sure. I saw you with Marco tonight."

"Yeah. He doesn't seem to hate me as you do."

"He doesn't hate you at all. Seems he's getting pretty close to you. Are you trying to snare him in your web?"

"I'm not trying to steal one of your guys away if that's what you're asking."

"I'm curious as to who would distract my best friend away from his duties. He was supposed to be keeping an eye on things tonight. We almost didn't make it out in time because of his distraction."

"Got it. Let's forget the fact that you ordered me to be here. Next time, I'll avoid him. Anything else, master?" I sass.

He smirks. "Do you want him, Roxanne?"

I scoff. "Not that I have to tell you a damn thing, but no, I don't. I don't want anyone. Relationships make you weak."

Then as an afterthought, I mumble, "Really any kind of attachment makes you weak."

"So if I was to..." He moves closer, pressing his body near mine. "Lean in right now..." One hand grips my hip while the other reaches up to cup my cheek. "And kiss you, would you say no?"

His face is close to mine. So close we are sharing the same breath. Still, I don't move. Instead, my body lights on fire. I have never felt the electricity flowing through my veins the way it does whenever he's near.

"I didn't push you away the first time, did I?"

He leans in, pressing a surprisingly gentle kiss to my lips.

"Would you tell Marco you don't want me?" he asks, making me tense.

Of course this is another game. All this man plays is games. At least when it comes to me.

"I would because, like I said, I don't want anyone." I try to step back, but his hands hold me in place.

"That's not exactly the truth though, is it?"

"What's that supposed to mean?"

"It means that if I trace my hand down your body, slipping it into your panties, I would find you drenched."

At his words, I feel the familiar tingle, but I ignore it.

"You think you know everything? Sure. My body physically reacts to you. Especially when you're close like this, but it means nothing. It means my body is physically attracted to yours. The problem? Mentally, I cannot stand you. You're egotistical, controlling, and an all-around asshole. At least Marco is sweet and honest. I don't think I've heard a single truth from your lips. All you do is play games. I'm done with it."

I push harder against his chest, his hands tightening in my hair and on my hip. I'm likely to have bruises tomorrow.

"You want a truth? Fine. You are driving me fucking crazy. The way you taste, the way you fuck. Walking around like you don't have a care in the world. Putting yourself in danger over and over again. Flirting with Marco. Glaring at me. It makes me want to strangle you."

My breath catches. "Do it then. End me. What's stopping you?"

His chuckle is dark. "I never said I wanted you to stop breathing, kid. Strangling doesn't always end in death, you know. Sometimes it can end in pleasure."

My breath hitches at his words. The thoughts of his hand around my neck while he thrusts into me….

My body shivers at my errant thoughts.

Before we can continue this line of conversation, his phone dings.

He drops his hands, stepping back.

I finally take in a deep breath. What am I thinking? I shouldn't be here with him. He is obviously deranged.

He types out a message before turning to me. "Get in. We have to go." Wordlessly, we both move and get into the car.

Whiplash. That's what I feel like I get every time we are in a room together.

The silence in the car is deafening as he drives at a much safer pace. It's not until we get back to the clubhouse that he speaks again.

"Next time, don't run off on your own. Stay with one of us at all times. It's the best way to keep you safe."

"I can take care of myself." I move to get out, but he reaches out, pulling me toward him by my hand.

Then, he cups my cheek, brushing his nose against mine. "I'm well aware that you can take care of yourself, Roxanne. You've more than proven that, but still. When you are on crew business, you stay with one of the crew. I know you'll fight me on this, but it's non-negotiable. It's how I take care of my own. Got it?"

"I'm not crew."

He growls, "You're not family. Not yet. But when you are with crew doing crew shit, you are an extension of us. With or without your mark."

"I don't want a mark. I don't want to be crew," I protest, even though the lies burn slipping out of my mouth.

The more time I spend with them, the more I find myself wanting to stay. Wanting to be in their little group.

"I'm well aware of your feelings on the subject. You've made them more than clear. Still, as long as you're with Hannah, you are under our protection, so please, for once, do as I ask. Can you do that?"

My heart is hammering in my chest as I stare into his eyes. Every nerve in my body is humming at the way he rolls his forehead against mine as he is cupping my cheek. His tone is demanding, but his actions feel more like pleading.

Roman doesn't beg though. I have to be misreading this.

"Stop involving me in crew business and I won't have a reason to be protected."

He shakes his head, letting out a breath. "I wish I could."

He says the words so quietly I almost don't think they are for me. Before I can ask him what he means, he presses a hard kiss against my lips. My body sways toward him, wanting to melt into him. My mind is screaming at me to pull away, but when he bites my bottom lip, I gasp, opening up to him. His tongue slides inside, starting a war of wills with my own.

I don't even question my next move, my mind clearly taking a backseat to my body.

When I slip across the center, climbing onto his lap, he doesn't slow. Instead, his hands find my hips, helping me settle onto him more firmly.

With the wheel at my back, I press closer to his chest, my hands rubbing over his shoulders as I press my center down onto him.

Fuck.

He's hard as fuck. My body is on fire at the thought of this man being as turned on as I am.

I rock my hips against him, his hardness pressing against my core through my jeans. I wish we both had much less clothes on. Even being in the car is amping up my body. It's my two favorite things. A sexy ass car and a fine ass man.

The longer we kiss, the more my body gyrates against his. I know I'm moaning, but I can't help it. My head is dizzy with the intoxicating smell of him mixed with the fresh leather smell of his car.

"Fuck, Rox. You are sexy as fuck. I've been dreaming about how amazing it felt to be deep inside of you," Roman groans as he finally pulls his lips from mine.

When he kisses along my jaw, my breath catches.

I've fucked in the past, but it was never like this. Not like it is with Roman. It was always a quickie that consisted of tearing clothes off and lasted less than five minutes.

Roman isn't in a rush. He takes his time, exploring my face and neck with his lips while his hands dig into my hips.

I can feel my breaths coming quicker as he pulls my hips harder against him.

"Each moan you let slip is making my dick even harder," Roman whispers against my ear.

That only elicits another moan from my body.

I can feel that familiar feeling build inside me. The one that tells me I'm going to burst any second.

I don't even have a second to consider the fact that I've never felt this with another person before it hits me.

My breath stops as my core clenches around empty air. My mind goes blank as my eyes fall closed, the only sound a ringing in my ears.

My head must have fallen forward because when I finally blink my eyes open, my forehead is rested against Roman's shoulder, his hands rubbing my back as he holds me to him.

I can feel my chest heaving as I pant against him.

"That was so fucking beautiful. Fuck. That's the single hottest thing I've ever seen in my life."

Roman whispers against my hair, pressing kisses to my head.

"What the fuck," I pant out.

"That was something else for sure," he answers me.

When I go to move my head from his shoulder, he groans as my lower half moves against his.

"Careful, kid. I'm on edge here," he warns.

I'm about to respond when I see headlights pulling up the drive.

"Fuck," I curse, scrambling off his lap.

"What are you doing?"

"I do not need them seeing what we just did," I tell him honestly.

He sighs, letting me go to rub his hand across his face. "You regret it."

It sounds like a statement, but the look on his face tells me he is asking a question.

I bite my lip. Did I regret it?

I'm still in the post blissful feeling of my orgasm mixed with a slight panic from being caught.

"I don't know," I whisper.

He nods, looking disappointed.

"Let's get out before they wonder why we are sitting in the car alone. Might want to fix your hair too. You look flushed."

I groan as he exits the car. I pull my hair out of the bun it was in, pulling it back up. I feel my cheeks and know they must be red. They are warm to the touch.

When I step from the car, Roman looks at me over the top.

"Here." He tosses me his keys. "Go inside and clean up."

I don't question him. I head up to the house, leaving him and the rest behind.

When I'm finally shut in the bathroom, I take a long look at myself in the mirror.

There are red marks all down my cheek onto my neck. Not enough to leave a bruise, but it's enough to know something happened.

Fuck.

I pull my hair down, running my hands through it. Hopefully it's enough to hide the marks.

When I look back at myself in the mirror again, I consider his words.

You regret it.

The longer I consider it, the more it frightens me because I don't think I do.

I think I liked it.

CHAPTER FOURTEEN

Roxy

I must be losing my mind. That's the only excuse that I have for being here for the third Friday in a row. Instead of working and collecting tips to get out of this place, I'm standing at the meet.

Last Friday, I was with Axel. He still shows up to the meet, but once we leave here, we go to a bunker he has set up out in the woods. Fucker has a bunch of cameras being fed into a portable computer system. His job is complicated and boring as fuck, but at least I got to watch the races from the screen.

This week, I'm stuck with Blaze and Hannah. While Marco collects money for admission, Blaze and Hannah collect the bets. From what I understand, they work as a team so Hannah isn't left alone. It's a protection measure.

On top of the betting, Blaze also accepts any requests for races. Sometimes they can be same night if they have an opening on the ticket, but most of the time it's for future races.

It's interesting to see how they work, but the intrigue wanes almost immediately. I could never do any of their jobs.

I'm anxious to see if I get to follow Roman around next week. Now his job is the one I want. I want to be the one racing. It's been far too long.

Slipping away from Blaze and Hannah I walk along the cars, checking them out. I keep my eye on them so I don't drift too far. Roman would have my ass if I did.

I stop at a blacked-out Nova and can't help but stop and admire her. As I'm leaning over the hood I feel him approach.

"What do you think?" Roman asks, leaning over me, pressing my back to his front.

"She's gorgeous."

"I'd have to agree," he says, wrapping his hands on my hips.

"Roman," I warn.

"Maybe I should blackout mine."

"Don't you dare." I say as I turn in his arms, forcing him to step back, giving me space.

"Shouldn't you be with one of the others?" he asks, rubbing his bottom lip.

"As much as I love all of them, their jobs are boring. Important, but I have zero desire to watch them work."

"What would you rather be doing?"

"You know what I'd rather be doing."

Roman's watch beeps.

"What's that all about?" I ask, unable to help myself.

A wicked smile overtakes Roman's face. "Come on," he says as he grabs my hand.

Roman and I speed walk toward his car and once we approach he opens the passenger door.

"Get in."

I wordlessly do as he says, settling in as he rounds the hood of the car. I can't help but take in how good he looks in his dark jeans and white T-shirt. The way his shirt molds his biceps.

He opens his door and slides in and shoots me a smirk.

"Like what you see?"

"You know you're attractive, you don't need me to tell you that." I roll my eyes, making him chuckle.

Roman starts the car and heads toward our destination. As we pass

Marco at his station, I don't miss the frown on his face as he notices me in the car with Roman. I ignore the pinch of guilt I feel.

Truth is, I am content sitting in this car with Roman. I haven't felt even a small iota for Marco that I feel for Roman.

I really need to have that talk with Marco.

At some point my knee starts bouncing with prerace jitters. I can't help but be envious that he gets to drive and I can't.

Roman's hand lands on my knee and squeezes. "Chill. You'll have fun tonight. I promise."

"If you say so." I sigh.

A few minutes later we pull up and Roman parks the car. He leans back his seat slightly, making himself comfortable.

"Don't you want to get out?" I ask, biting my lip.

"Why should we when we're up in a few and we have the best view."

"I don't know, don't you want me to get out so you can do your prerace ritual?"

"I think you can keep your fine ass right where it is."

We watch as the fine as Nova pulls up to the line along a newer Camaro.

"Who do you think will win?" Roman asks, nodding toward the line.

"The Nova, no questions asked."

"Think you could beat the Nova?"

"If I had the right car? Most definitely."

"Even without seeing how the driver handles her?" he asks, moving his hand higher up my leg.

"I'm good," I say, making him hum.

"Don't I know it," he says under his breath as he sits back up.

We watch the first race together, his fingers drawing patterns onto my skin. I'm so distracted by the feeling that I almost miss the Nova pulling ahead to claim the win.

When Roman removes his hand from my leg, I let out a breath I didn't realize I was holding.

He chuckles. "Looks like it's go-time."

Roman starts the car before pulling up to the line. I look out my window and watch a Challenger pull up to the line next to us.

I can see Blaze out the back window doing something. I look out at the crowd as Roman and Blaze go through their rituals. Once we are pulled up to the line, I smile.

"You got this," I tell him.

"Are you sure?" He smirks.

"If you don't win, you don't deserve this car."

A girl with tiny shorts and a black tank top walks up and stands in the gap between the cars. She raises a white flag with one hand and points to the other driver. Once he nods saying he's ready she points to Roman. I turn slightly in the seat and stare at Roman. He dips his chin as his hand flexes on the steering wheel. I watch the woman drop the flag out of the corner of my eye as Roman takes off.

The G forces push me back into the seat and I can't help, but moan at the feeling.

It's been too fucking long since I've gotten this kind of high. Roman handles his car with ease as we speed down the straightaway, blowing the other car out of the water.

"You like that?" he asks as he circles back to the head of the starting line.

"You know I do."

ROMAN

Having Roxy in the passenger seat of my car has awakened some primal part of me. All I want to do is haul her off like a caveman, claiming her as mine.

She would kill me, but it would be worth it.

Fuck, the way she moaned when we took off from the line? That fucked me up. If I had been against a real opponent that stood a chance, I might have lost my first race in years.

All because of her.

Still, there is one thing I am dying to see.

"You want to drive?" I ask as Blaze gives me a thumbs up, letting me know I'm good to go.

Roxy shifts in her seat again, rubbing her thighs together. She's been doing that since the first race.

"You know I do." She scoffs.

Reaching over, I grab her, pulling her into my lap.

"What the fuck!" she gasps, making me chuckle. I slide out from under her and settle into the passenger seat.

"Better pull up, they won't wait forever," I say, nodding toward the line.

"Really?" Roxy beams.

"Better get up there before I change my mind."

Roxy quickly adjusts the seat and pulls the car forward and to the line.

"You're going down," she mutters as she sees the Nova already lined up and waiting.

This is the last race of the night. Once we win this, it's all over.

This week's flag girl steps forward and asks the driver of the Nova if he's ready at his nod she looks over and does a double-take when she sees someone else in my driver's seat making me laugh.

She hesitantly points at Roxy who nods as she takes a deep breath.

Once the flag drops Roxy pushes down on the gas and I can't help but reach over and grab onto her thigh. As she shoots down the strip I can't help but slowly move my hand higher up her thigh. Somehow Roxy handles my baby like she's been driving her for years and it makes me hard as fuck.

When we reach the end, signaling our win, I dread going back to the crowd.

"Don't stop. Keep going," I say harshly as I squeeze her thigh, making her thighs clench together.

"Where am I going?" she rasps.

"Take a right out of here." I turn my hand, cupping her through her jeans and run my middle finger along her seam. "I can feel the heat radiating off of you," I murmur, making her hiss.

"Did driving turn you on?" I ask as she pulls out of the area we race. "Take the third left."

I remove my hand from between her legs making her whimper. Turning in my seat I lean forward and reach for the straps of her tank top. Slowly I lower both straps down her shoulders before doing the same to her bra straps.

"Roman."

"Shh. Keep driving."

Reaching under her arms I pull her tank top and bra down so they sit below her breasts.

As I play with her nipples Roxy counts quietly under her breath as she squirms.

"You see the tree line?"

"Mmhmm," she murmurs as I tweak a nipple.

"Park in there. There's a pull-off but be careful. Don't scratch my baby or I won't let you come."

Slowly Roxy pulls the car into the trees and throws the car in park. She launches herself at me, fusing her mouth with mine, grinding her pussy against me.

Opening the car door I grab Roxy by the hips. "Hold on," I demand.

I get us both out of the car without dropping her and kick the door shut. I press her back into the car, making her scramble to hold onto me.

"Don't you dare, I don't want to fuck up the hood."

"If we fuck it up, I'll fix it. Relax."

I step back and raise a brow silently asking for permission as my hands land on the button of her jeans. At her nod, I undo the button and slide the zipper down. All at once, I slide her panties and her pants down as she arches up and removes her tank top and bra. I trail my hands up her calves to her thighs and spread her legs.

Dropping to my knees I run my tongue along her seam. She tastes sweeter than I remember. I can't help but groan. Roxy sighs as I rest her legs over my shoulders and lick her. Weaving her hands into my hair she pulls me in close making me chuckle.

"You're so wet. Is this all for me?"

"Don't get cocky, it's from racing," she snaps.

"I'll show you cocky. But I'm telling you right now, if I eat this pretty pussy again that's it. You're mine. Do you understand?"

"Wh-what?" Her voice stutters.

"You heard me. Now shut up and take it," I growl before diving in.

Her back arches off the hood of my car as I attack her clit with my tongue, using my teeth to nibble here and there.

Fuck she's sexy. Seeing her on the hood of my car like this as she moans out my name? My cock is begging to be set free at how hard she's making me.

I don't let up. I don't take my time. My only mission is to make this woman come as hard as she can on the hood of my car.

I continue to taste and tease her with my tongue as I reach up with one hand to grip one of her tits. I knead and pinch it while my other hand moves to assist my mouth. Thrusting two fingers up inside her, I set an unrelenting pace.

Within a minute, she explodes on my tongue as she screams my name.

My dick twitches in my pants, desperate for his turn with her.

I don't hesitate. Flipping her over onto her stomach, I smirk when I spot the wet spot not shining on the hood of my car. Knowing it's from her release fills me with a sense of pride.

Roxy's hands flatted on the hood when I grip her hips to pull her back.

"Spread 'em, baby."

When she immediately moves to do my bidding, a sense of satisfaction rolls through my body. I love having her at my mercy.

Slapping her ass once, she jerks, but then she moans.

"Fuck, do it again." Her words are a surprise, but I give her what she wants.

I land another three smacks, relishing in the way she gasps then moans with each one.

Reaching my hand down, I smirk. "My dirty girl likes to be spanked huh? If you wanted to be spanked, all you had to do was ask."

I toy with her clit a moment, watching the look of pleasure fill her face.

"Fuck me, Roman. I need you inside me right the fuck now."

I chuckle, pulling a condom out of my pants.

I always keep one in my wallet, but before Roxy, I didn't use them that often. After the last time we fucked, I made sure to keep a couple on me at all times.

Quickly ridding my lower half of clothes, I slide the condom on, loving the view in front of me.

If I thought Roxy spread eagle on my hood was hot, it has nothing on her bent over, panting for my dick.

I rub my now sheathed dick through her folds before finally pushing in.

She moans as her sex starts to clench around me. She just came, but she's already so close to another one. The fact that I made her this way? Yeah, that's a powerful feeling.

Stopping when I'm fully inside her, I land one more slap on her ass. Feeling her clench around me is torturous, but I had to know how much she liked it.

"Stop playing with me, Rome. Please." She moans.

Not needing another word, I start to thrust inside her. I don't go easy. No, I give her my all.

Digging my fingers into her hips, I know I'll leave a bruise, but the pain only makes her clench harder against me.

Feeling the familiar tingle at my spine, I know I only have moments before I blow, but I need to take her with me.

With one hand, I reach down, twisting my hand in her hair as I pull her back to me. The other hand reaches for her clit, swirling hard against it until she screams out, her body shaking in my arms.

That's when I burst, my dick twitching inside her as it releases everything it has for her. I slow my thrusts until I stop completely. Releasing her hair, I wrap my arm around her upper body, holding her to me.

Leaning forward, I nip at her ear, making her giggle.

"You left handprints on my car," I tell her, staring at the proof that I just took her against my car.

"It was your fault," she huffs.

I squeeze her tighter to me. "It's hot as fuck. I think I should have them etched permanently into the hood. What do you think?"

She gasps, pulling away. I groan as my dick slides out of her heat.

When she turns, she smacks my chest. "Don't you dare defile this car. It's beautiful as is."

I smirk, pulling her back into me. "Should I be concerned about how much you like my car?"

She gives me a saucy grin. "No. It's the only reason you got laid tonight."

Before I can respond, she steps away, grabbing her clothes from the ground.

Once we are back in the car, me back in the driver's seat, I reach across to grab her hand.

She tries to pull back, but I tighten my grip.

"If it's the car that keeps you in my bed, then you can drive it any fucking time you want."

Pulling her hand to my mouth, I kiss it lightly.

She doesn't respond, but I can see the blush on her cheeks.

Roxy is mine.

I just have to convince her of it.

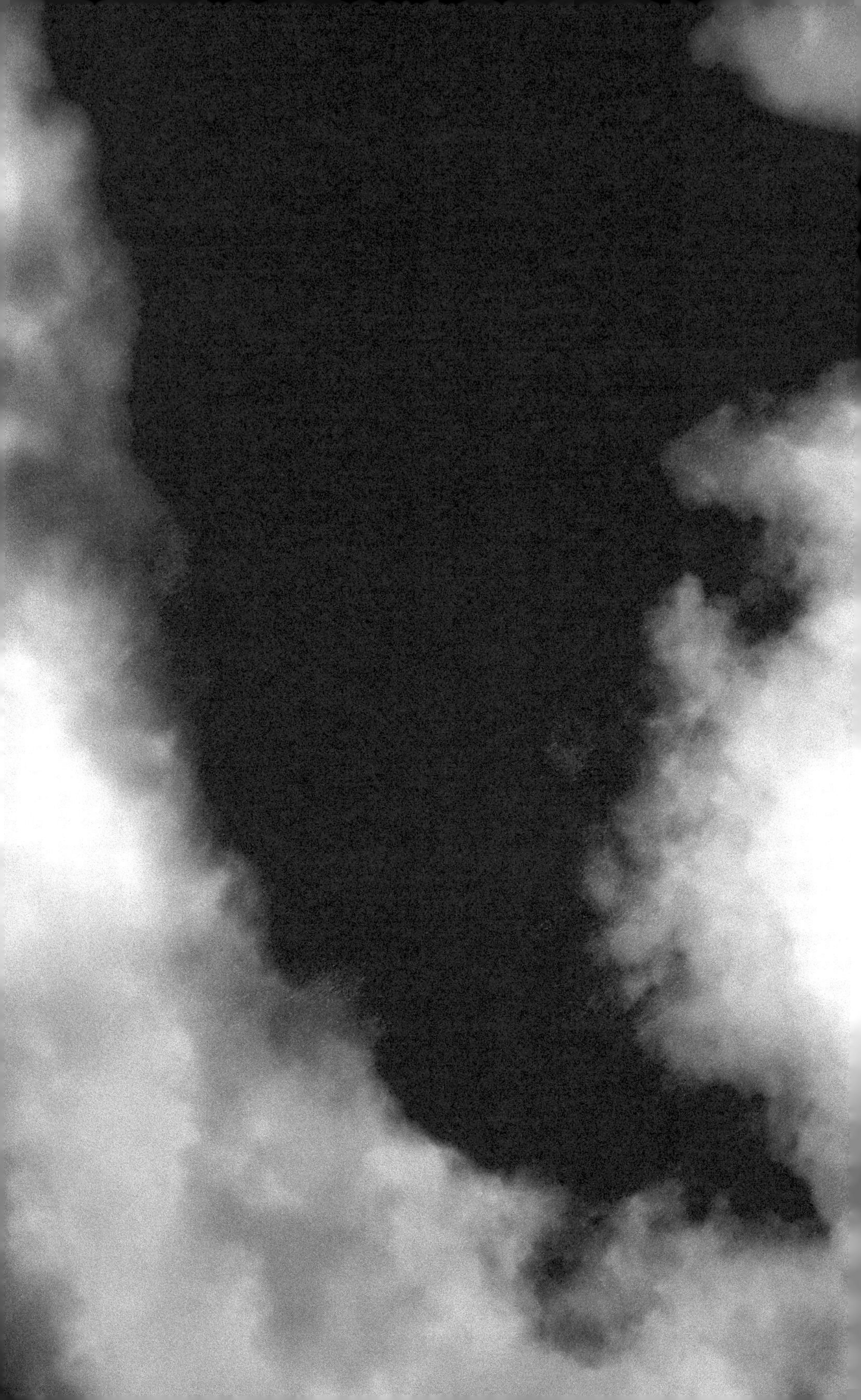

CHAPTER FIFTEEN

Roxy

"I sat you a table of five. They requested you."

I smile at Janet. "Thanks."

As soon as I enter the dining room, my smile falls. Why are they here?

Sitting at the table are Roman, Axel, Blaze, Marco, and Hannah.

It's not that I don't want them here. It's the opposite. The fact that seeing them made me want to smile is the problem.

I've become attached. Not only to each one individually as a friend, but to Roman as more.

The way he claimed that I was his has been freaking me out. I'm not equipped to handle this. Everything good in my life is always ripped away.

Walking up to the table, I grab my notepad. "Welcome to Julio's. What can I get you to drink?"

"Really? You're going to act like you don't know us?" Blaze teases.

I roll my eyes. "Fine. Why are you here annoying me?"

Marco speaks this time. "You've been avoiding us."

I shrug. "Not really. I've been busy. You know I have this thing called a job and a life. Whether you like it or not, I kind of have to keep living it."

They aren't wrong though. I have been avoiding them. After my last run-in with Roman, I've been scared shitless to be around him. I'm not sure I can hide the way my body reacts to him. It was bad enough after the first time we slept together but now it's worse. It's as if his cock broke the dam, leaving behind a craving for the man who has the power to both make me burn in anger and desire.

"Don't be smart with me," Roman demands. "We need to talk."

"And I need a million dollars. Why don't we want in one hand and shit in the other and see which one fills up faster, huh? Now, what do you want to drink? I have other tables."

"That's not how this works," Roman spits.

"Okay, water for all of you. Got it. I'll be right back with that."

I turn, ignoring Roman calling my name. Fuck him. Jesus, he is such an asshole.

An asshole who knows how to use his tongue.

"You okay? You look a little shook," Janet asks.

I smile. "Assholes. You know how it is. Actually, can you take five waters to them? I think I need to get some air before I lose my shit on them."

She giggles. "I got it. Go take your time."

Walking through the kitchen, I smile at Roberto, the cook. "I'm stepping out back for a minute."

He nods, going back to his cooking.

I take a step out the back door, letting it close behind me. When I knock, Roberto will let me back in.

I walk a little bit down and lean against the wall. Taking a deep breath, I try to center myself again.

It's not just the old hurt that's making me avoid the Shadows. It's how I've started feeling about Roman. I've always thought he was hot, but I actually like him. I like seeing who he really is. The way he cares for his family. His loyalty and passion.

The way he smiles at me. The teasing, flirting and lingering touches all leave me wanting more. The butterflies I thought were long dead awoke in my stomach. I feel like I'm thirteen and staring at a handsome man for the first time all over again.

Then I heard his words from before.

You're not family. Not yet.

I know he added the yet part as if I might be someday but fuck if it didn't hurt. I didn't even want to be a part of it but fuck if he didn't keep pushing me into it.

My chest aches. The feeling of unworthiness settling it. Never enough for anyone to stay.

"Mary," a familiar voice says behind me.

I tense. Fuck.

I paste a smile on my face, turning to Zade.

"Hey, fancy meeting you here."

His eyes flicker recognition along with humor.

"Same. Imagine my surprise when the phone number I called was to an old lady in Miami."

I shrug. "Can't fault a girl for being safe."

He smiles wider. "Yeah? How about the fact that the transaction on your credit card was flagged as fraud?"

I fake outrage. "Oh? Was it? My bad. Must have not recognized the name of the shop."

He shakes his head. "You can drop the act, Roxy. I know who you are."

I swallow hard. Fucking Roman. He is always getting me into these fucked up situations. For one brief moment, I actually miss Ross. At least I knew the score with him.

"Yeah? Seems my reputation precedes me then, huh?"

"I'd say so. I knew I had recognized you, but I didn't put it together until the charge was disputed. I was surprised to see the Queen of the Riviera race scene slumming it here in Chita. What brings you to my neck of the woods anyway?"

I shrug. "Needed a change."

"Did you finally get sick of those assholes treating you like a trophy? They never did swear you in, did they?"

His eyes are roaming my free skin, looking for a tattoo that's not there.

"What do you want, Zade?"

"Why were you at my shop?"

"I needed the brakes changed and didn't have the time or place to do it. Sorry about the credit card. I boosted it to get me the hell out of dodge." I shrug.

"So you fled Cali?"

I laugh. "Not at all. Soulless and I came to a mutually agreed upon decision that California was no longer the best place for me. I wanted to branch out and see other places. Here I am."

"So no ink claiming you. You could be a Devil's girl if you wanted," he says, taking a step forward.

I shake my head. "I told you back at the shop. I enjoy my independence. I don't want to tie myself to anyone."

He grins. "Good thing you haven't. It leaves me open to do whatever I want to you without fear of retaliation. You're not a Soulless girl. You're definitely not a Shadow girl even if you tend to hang around them. Seems like you're only good for one thing. Neither club willing to claim you. To protect you. Do they enjoy having you on your back?"

"I don't lie on my back for anyone. I think we are done here."

"Oh we are just getting started."

He steps toward me, but I back up, looking around for somewhere to run. I shouldn't have walked back here alone. I just needed a damn minute from Roman. He's always getting me into shit.

"You can run if you want, but you won't get far. My guys are posted at the end of the alley."

I see movement telling me he's right.

"What do you want to do to me then? Rape me?" I say the words with confidence, but inside my gut is churning.

I can defend myself, but not against more than one attacker. Especially since I see two more guys coming up behind Zade.

"I don't need to rape girls to get some. That's beneath me. I don't have such reservations about teaching lessons though. I think I need to send a message to the Shadows. It would be foolish of me to turn down such a unique opportunity."

"Roman will kill you," I tell him, trying to keep him talking while hoping someone comes to check on me.

He laughs. "That's the beauty of it. Did they not teach you what the mark means?"

"Doesn't matter. He won't stand for you to hurt me."

I know what I'm saying isn't true. Roman might have started acting less indifferent to me, but I doubt he would risk his crew for me.

"Oh my sweet girl. Without a mark, he would be risking his entire crew's lives if he were to retaliate. See this crew system we are a part of has rules. There aren't many, but one of which states that one crew cannot attack another for retribution for harm done to a non-marked member. You're a sitting duck, girl."

I take a deep breath in. "Fine. Let's get to it then, shall we. See if you can stand up to little old me."

I brace myself for the fight to come, but he doesn't fight fair. Cowards rarely do.

"That's cute, but I think you should save your energy. You're going to need it."

The two men jump forward to grab me. I try to twist out of their reach while throwing a punch, but it's only seconds before they have me pinned against the wall. I never stood a chance.

Zade walks closer, running his hand along my face. I spit at him, not caring if I anger him. If I'm going to die, I'm not going down without a fight.

"You bitch. You're going to pay for that."

"As you keep saying. Go ahead and show me how much of a coward you are. Or is that just it? Are you all talk?"

His first punch hits me in the gut. I grunt as I try to bend over, but the other two hold me up.

Then I look up and smile at him. "Is that all you've got?"

I shouldn't taunt him. I know I'm only going to make it worse on myself but fuck him. Fuck all of them. I'm not some weak girl that needs protecting. If I had a fucking mark, this would have been avoided. Zade even had said as much. So their reluctance to mark me is what led to my death. Good. Let them feel the guilt from that for the rest of their lives. They deserve it.

When the next punch hits my rib, I suck in a breath. I can't be for sure, but I think I heard a crack.

Zade continues to throw his fists at me, aiming for my middle mostly, but landing a few to my face. I don't know how long he takes, but when he's done, I'm barely conscious. His goons are the only thing holding me up anymore.

"Let her go," Zade commands.

I can't even brace myself for the fall as my face meets concrete.

Zade crouches down and brushes the hair out of my face.

"It's a shame, I hate hurting women but sometimes its unavoidable. Tell Roman, if he knows what's good for him, he will mind his own fucking business."

Zade stands and kicks me one last time before turning and leaving the alley.

Once I'm sure he's gone, I open my eyes to look around. I don't see anyone, but I'm only feet from the door.

I lean up, trying to pull myself, but collapse back to the ground.

Maybe a nap would be good. Get some energy back. Yeah, I'll close my eyes for a second.

A loud bang forces my eyes back open.

"What the fuck?" I recognize that voice, but my vision is blurry. "Get the car back here now!" I hear the shuffling of feet. "Stay with me, Roxy." Roman's voice roars above me, but it sounds odd.

Almost like he's yelling from down a hallway. Darkness starts to creep in.

Then nothing.

ROMAN

SWINGING THE KITCHEN door open the first thing I see is Roxy laying on the ground beaten. "What the fuck." I say to myself. "Get the car back here now!" I yell over my shoulder as I run toward Roxy. "Stay with me Roxy." I demand as I put my fingers on her neck, checking her pulse.

Her heart beats steadying under my fingers. I take a deep breath, relaxing slightly. Ever so gently I run my hands along her checking for any visible broken bones. Sliding one hand under her neck and the other under her legs I get ready to lift her.

"What if you hurt her more?" Hannah asks making me look up. I see her wrapped up in Blaze's arms as he keeps her away.

"We need to get her out of here," I tell her as I carefully scoop her up and pull her into my chest. "Call the doc."

Axel comes to a screeching in front of us and Blaze grabs the door, opening it for me. Carefully I slide in with Roxy in my lap.

"We'll meet you at the club house," Hannah says as Blaze shuts the door.

Axel takes off driving like the devil is on our asses.

"Where's Marco?" I ask as I run my hand through Roxy's hair.

"I don't know." He shakes his head. "One minute he was with us and the next he was gone."

My jaw clenches in anger but I keep my mouth shut. I'll deal with Marco later.

"Who do you think did this?" Axel asks as he turns, accidently hitting a pothole.

Roxy groans in my arms.

"Watch the fucking road," I hiss, and I readjust her in my arms.

Axel winces. "Sorry."

Taking a deep breath, I let it out slowly. "This has Zade all over it," I mumble under my breath.

After several minutes of silence, I can't take it anymore.

"I should have already fucking marked her," I roar out.

"No one can blame you for taking your time. She's made it clear that she wasn't interested." He says as he comes to a stop in front of the clubhouse. "Let me grab the door for you." he throws the car in park and jumps out. Axel runs over to my side and opens the door. As I slowly get out of the car trying not to jostle her too much, he puts his hand on the top of her head, making sure I don't accidently hit it against the roof.

"Thanks," I mumble as I clear the car.

Wordlessly he runs forward and unlocks the clubhouse door before swinging it open for me. Stepping inside I take her straight to my room and slowly lower her to the bed.

"What can I do?"

Leaning down I take off Roxy's shoes before sitting on the edge of the bed.

"Find out where the fuck Marco went. All hands on deck. After we get the all-clear on Roxy we figure out a plan."

The front door slams shut and Axel and I both tense, turning toward the door.

"Let me in," Hannah demands as she pushes Axel out of the way.

She dives toward the bed and I grab her. "Stop," I demand. "Not until doc comes and tell us what's wrong."

"She's my cousin," Hannah hisses as she hits my chest.

"She is, but like you said we don't know what all is wrong and until we do no one is touching her."

"No one, but you," she sneers.

A clearing of the throat catches our attention and makes us look toward the doorway.

"May I come in?" Doc asks.

"Of course." I nod, stepping to the side with Hannah giving him room to check her over.

"Whoever did this sure did a number on her," he murmurs as he takes a pair of gloves and some other things out of his bag, sitting them on the nightstand. "Let's see what we're working with here shall we? Roman, can you come lift her shirt so I can inspect her ribs, please?"

Stepping forward I do as he asks, and I watch as he methodically runs his hands over her ribs. My jaw clenches at the bruises forming and I have to look away. I hate seeing another man's on her skin.

Slowly he checks her over from head to toe, patching her up as he goes.

"So?" I ask, running my hand over her head.

"She's going to be in pain for a while, but she will be okay."

"Why hasn't she woken up yet?"

"Her body shut down because of the amount of pain she was in. She's still out while her body heals. When she wakes up, she will be in a great deal of pain."

"Thank you," I rasp as I stare at her.

"You're welcome. Call me if you need me but your girl should be fine." He says, resting a hand on my shoulder.

Doc packs up his bag and Axel steps forward. "Let me walk you out and get you your money. We appreciate you coming out here on such short notice."

As they walk out of the room Hannah and Blaze step forward. Hannah grabs Roxy's hand and holds it between the two of hers. "Whoever did this has to pay."

"And he will."

The sound of steps have us turning toward the door and we see Marco standing at the doorway looking pale. "What happened?"

"Where were you?" I ask, ignoring his question.

"My mom called. I must have missed what happened." He says, licking his lips as he shuffles side to side. "Is she okay?"

"She will be." I tell him knowing that he's lying.

I don't know what he is mixed up in, but my gut tells me it's something serious. I don't want to question my best friend, but after tonight, I'm not sure I can trust him anymore.

"What do we do now?" he asks as he takes a step into the room.

"Now we wait for her to wake up and tell us everything she remembers." I say, turning my back to him.

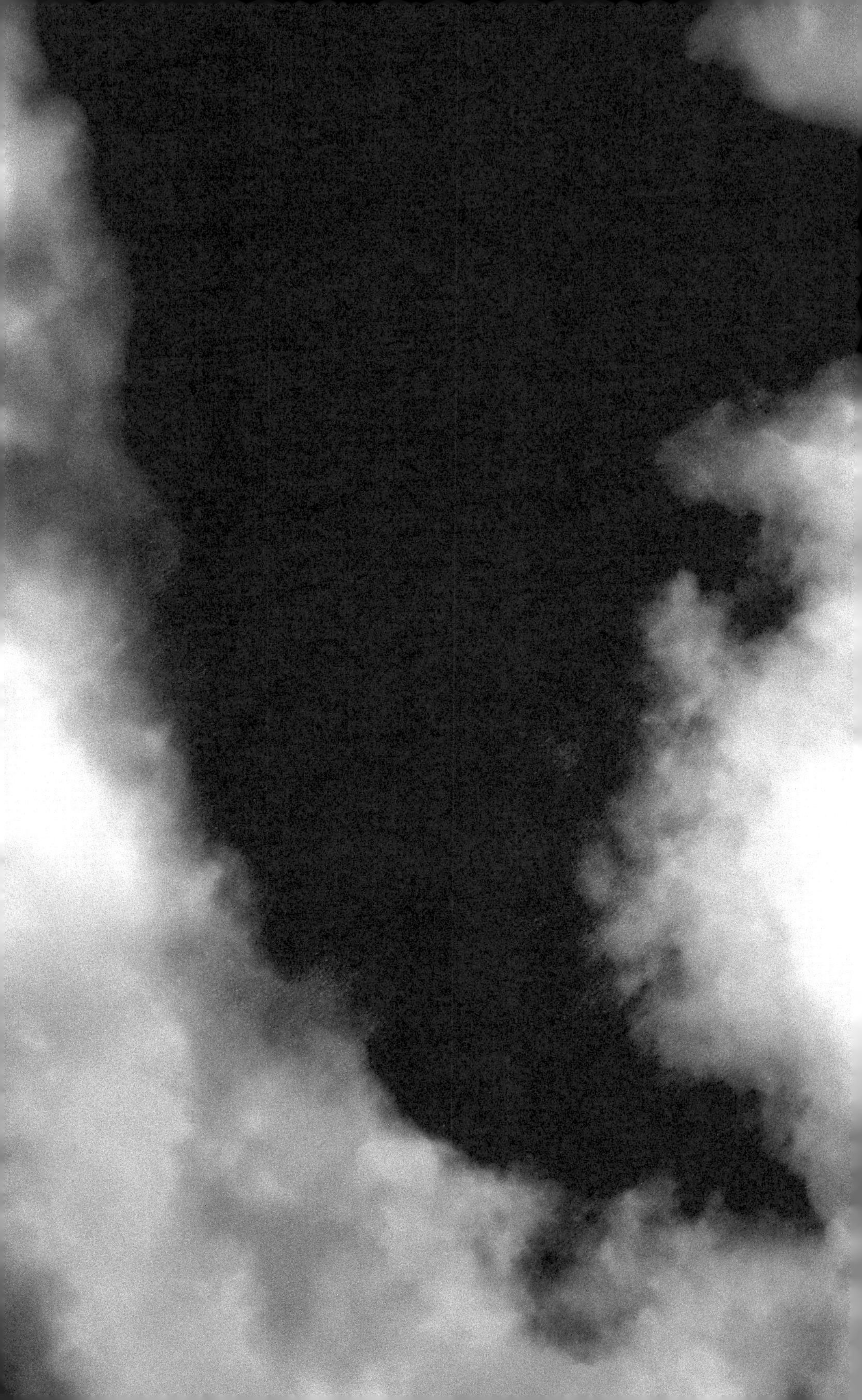

CHAPTER SIXTEEN

Roxy

"Roxanne," Hannah's voice calls me out of the darkness.

I'm no longer laying on the ground. Instead, I'm lying on something softer.

Opening my eyes, I squint at the light above.

"Oh good," Hannah mutters before saying louder. "Rome, she's awake."

I try to sit up, but Hannah stops me with a hand on my shoulder.

"Wait."

Then she steps back and Roman fills her place.

He looks different. Like he hasn't slept, which is odd because I swear the man never sleeps.

"How are you feeling, kid?"

"Fine," I manage to say through my sore throat.

He reaches out, gently running his fingers down my cheek. "You don't have to be strong right now. I need to know how you really feel so I can take care of you."

My heart beats faster at his words. "I'm sore, but I'll be okay."

"When you feel better, you'll be getting your mark."

I gasp, sitting up against his protests. My ribs ache, but I breathe through it.

"What do you mean I'm getting my mark?"

"You weren't protected. With my mark, you'll be protected. No one will hurt you ever again."

"You can't promise that. Hell, you could be the one to hurt me then. I don't want to be marked."

"Why not? Tell me why you won't take the mark." He asks as he paces, running his hands through his hair.

"I don't have to tell you shit."

"Either tell me or I'll knock your ass back out and put my mark on you anyway."

"Really? Against my will?" I ask, shocked.

He shrugs. "Your safety is more important than your will."

I scoff. "You really want to mark me even with my ties to Soulless? Doesn't that bother you?"

"Nothing will change my mind." He shakes his head. "Roxanne, you're the best driver this side of the country. You think I didn't know who you were? That I didn't look into you when Hannah said her long lost cousin from Cali wanted to move in?"

I swallow hard. "Is that why you hated me?"

He shakes his head no. "I spoke with Ross before you came out here. He asked me to keep my eye on you. I did it out of mutual respect."

"Wait. Crews mix?" I narrow my eyes.

"They don't usually. However, you were in danger out there. I don't know anything else other than that, but Ross wanted you to have protection so he reached out."

"Okay, so you know that. Do you know he refused to let me be a part of his shit? They actually refused to let me in."

He rubs his face before nodding. "I figured as much when you didn't have a mark. I figured something happened when you refused to even acknowledge they were your family."

I let out a humorless laugh. "I was never family to them. Just a pawn to use. I see that now. After watching how you guys are together, I know I never had that there. They didn't mark me because I wasn't good enough for them."

"I can't say why they didn't mark you, although I have my suspicions. I can say that you are better than them. Better than us. I haven't withheld the mark because of any other reason than you have not seemed to want it. I would have given it to you back after you went into Zade's. Now you don't get a choice. You are getting my mark."

"Why? Why me?"

"You're family. It's as simple as that. Even if you don't get the tattoo, you'll still be family. The mark isn't what brings you into the fold, kid. You've already been in. The mark is a protection."

"Wait. I'm already in?"

He smirks. "You think I let people who aren't in drive my car let alone race it?"

I smile widely. "It is a nice car."

"You look good behind the wheel. Maybe I'll give it to you and get a new one. I don't think I could ever look that good in it."

I roll my eyes, wincing in pain at the movement. "You don't have to butter me up. Can I think about the mark?"

He nods. "Take these and rest."

He hands me two pills and a glass of water from the nightstand. After I take them, I settle back into the bed.

When he settles into the bed next to me and pulls a laptop onto his lap, I smile to myself. Then I let sleep take me.

ROMAN

Ignoring the laptop on my lap I look down at Roxy and watch her sleep. Running my hand over her hair I can't help but think how beautiful she looks while sleeps even while beaten and bruised.

"I can feel you staring at me like a creeper," she rasps, making my lip twitch. "I don't think I'm up for a quickie right now." She winces as she reaches to touch her ribs.

"Yeah, sex is definitely off the table for now," I murmur. "When you're ready, I need you to tell me exactly what happened."

Roxy reaches forward and grabs my hand. Looking down I see my fist was clenched on my stomach.

"You can't do anything about it." She shakes her head.

"Excuse me?" I ask calmly despite my racing heart.

"It was Zade. He knew who I was. Told me how you couldn't retaliate because I'm not marked," she says, licking her lips.

Letting her go I lean over and grab a glass of water with a straw from the nightstand. "Here. Take small sips," I tell her as I bring the straw to her mouth.

Roxy takes a few sips before smiling at me. "Thanks."

"What else did he say?"

"He wanted to know why I ended up at his shop. Asked what I was looking for. Pretty much what you would expect." She shrugs then hisses as she grabs her ribs.

"Careful," I murmur. "I'll fucking kill him."

"You can't," she says calmly.

"Why the hell not?"

"Like I already said before, I'm not marked. By retaliating you would be putting not only your life at risk but everyone else's too. I'm not worth it, Roman. He might have beat the shit out of me but he didn't break me. I'll heal."

"Bullshit," I hiss. "You are worth it Roxy and it's time you start accepting it. I know what I said before, but every time you hiss in pain, it only makes me more sure that I don't give a fuck about the rules. Let them come for us. We can take them."

When she doesn't respond, I look down at her. Her eyes are glassy, almost as if she is about to cry. My chest tightens at the thought.

Taking a deep breath I hold it in for a second before releasing it. "Are you in pain?"

"Some," she says reluctantly.

"Okay, I'm going to sit you up a little more, then I need you to eat some crackers before I give you some pain pills."

I set my laptop off to the side and help Roxy adjust. With every wince I can't help but feel like I've been shot. I wish I could take her pain from her. Leaning over to the nightstand I grab a sleeve of crackers and hand them to her.

"Please for the love of God don't watch me eat." She mumbles as she takes a bite of a cracker, making me chuckle. "How long have I been out?"

"You've been out for about eight hours."

"Fuck, what about work." She groans.

"Julio knows what happened and I'm keeping him updated. You don't need to worry."

We sit in silence until I see her starting to doze off.

"Here," I say, grabbing some Tylenol. I shake some out of the bottle and hand them and the water to her.

"Thanks." She sighs as she hands the water back to me.

"You're welcome." Setting the water down, I move back and begin to play with her hair.

"That feels so good," she mumbles as she doses off.

"No one will ever get to you again," I whisper to myself as my eyes grow heavy and sleep claims me.

"HEY," SOMEONE SAYS as they touch my shoulder.

Opening my eyes the first thing I see is Roxy's hair. As I roll away I realize that while sleeping I got as close to her as I could.

"What's up?" I rasp, rubbing a hand over my face.

"The guys are all here and want to talk," Hannah says, biting her lip.

"Okay. Give me one minute?"

"Sure, we're out in the living room when you're ready," she says softly before walking out of the room shutting the door behind her.

Groaning, I get up slowly to make sure I don't wake Roxy before walking toward the bathroom to take care of my business. Once done I check on Roxy one last time. As she breathes steady I lean down and press a kiss to her forehead before walking out.

Shutting the door behind me I hear the soft murmurs and walk toward the living room.

"Hey," Axel says when he sees me. "I made you a cup of coffee, I figured you could use it."

"Thanks." I smile as I grab the cup off the table in front of him and take a drink.

"How is she?" Hannah asks nervously.

"She's in pain, but other than that, she is better than I thought she would be. She's strong."

Hannah instantly relaxes. "Good."

"Did she say anything?" Marco asks.

I turn and look at my best friend. My right-hand man and can't help the anger that takes over. "She did." I say watching him carefully.

"What did she say?" Blaze asks as he pulls Hannah into his lap.

"It was Zade."

"Of fucking course it was." Axel says as he pounds his fist into his hand. "What do we do now?"

"Roxy wants us to do nothing."

"What?" Everyone explodes at once.

I raise my hand, silencing them. "He told her that we couldn't retaliate where she isn't marked without putting the entire crew's lives on the line."

"So the fuck what!" Blaze hisses.

"What's your plan?" Axel asks.

"As of right now my plan is for her to heal a little more and then I'm taking her to get marked whether she likes it or not. After that we will figure everything out. In the meantime we need to be on high alert. The races are canceled. I can't be in two places at once."

"We need the money the races bring in," Marco grits out.

"We have more than enough money to take some time off. It will be fine."

"Whatever. Are we done here?" he asks.

"We are."

"Later," he says before turning and walking out.

I don't know what the fuck is going on with him lately but I'm going to find out. Just as soon as Roxy is okay.

She's my priority now.

CHAPTER SEVENTEEN

Roxy

A week has passed since the incident as I've taken to calling it. Roman hasn't said much else about it to me other than he was taking care of it. He can't do much, but he has been here with me almost every day. When he's not here, he leaves one of the others with me.

Marco has been here making me laugh. Hannah binge watches television with me. Axel doesn't talk with me as much, but it's a comfortable silence now that I've gotten to know him. He lets me sit and read while he plays on his phone. Then there's Blaze. He likes to bicker. At first it annoyed me, but now it's endearing. It's like a game we play.

That's how Roman finds us when he comes back from wherever he went today.

"You're just saying that because I like the red power ranger. If I liked the pink one then you'd say you preferred red," I bite at him.

"That's not true. Pink really is the best ranger. Not only is she hot as hell, but she's a woman and can kick ass. There's nothing better than that."

"So you're saying she's better because she has tits?"

"No. I'm saying she's better because she's strong and badass."

"So in your mind women are weak. She gets praised for being strong only because she is female and we are weak. Is that what you're saying?"

He thinks for a moment then smirks at me. "I guess that is what I'm saying. The others I expect to be able to kick ass, but when she does it's extra special."

"If I wasn't under strict orders not to hurt myself, I would come over to that couch and kick your fucking ass and show you what a badass woman is really like."

He chuckles, holding up his hands. "I'd love to see you try."

"Enough you two," Roman says harshly as he comes into the room.

"I'm going to kick his ass someday," I mutter.

Roman smirks. "Don't worry, kid. I'll make sure to put my money on you."

I smile before sticking my tongue out at Blaze.

"Very mature," he teases, but then sticks his out back at me.

That's what I love about Blaze. He reminds me of the brother I never had. He always infuriates me, but then he makes me laugh. He acts silly with me and isn't scared to push my buttons. I also know that the second someone else stepped to me the way he does, he would annihilate them. Such a wonderful relationship to have.

Roman sits on the couch next to me, drawing my attention to him.

"What's up, honey bunny? Long day at work?" I ask sarcastically.

He glowers at me. "Honey bunny? Really?"

I shrug. "You're always calling me kid. I'm trying to find an equally annoying nickname for you."

Truth is, I don't mind being called kid as much anymore. It used to bother me because I felt like it was an insult due to my age. All of them are older than me, but the more I hang out with Roman, the more I realize he means it as a term of endearment. Besides, he is the only one who calls me it and I've never heard him call anyone else it. It feels special.

"You'll have to try harder than that, *kid.* Honey bunny just makes you sound like you want to ride my cock after making my dinner."

I smack his chest making both men laugh.

"There will be no cock riding, thank you very much."

He shrugs. "Offer's always on the table."

Blaze's phone starts to ring.

"Hey. Roman's here. Yeah I'll be right there."

Blaze jumps up. "Hannah's car won't start. I'm going to go get her."

Blaze stops next to me, leaning down to press a kiss to my head. "Catch you later, brat. Maybe you should watch the Power Rangers again so you have better taste."

"Asshole," I call to his retreating back.

"You love me," he calls back.

I glance over to Roman, seeing a smile on his face.

"What?"

"He likes you. Blaze doesn't like many people."

I shrug. "He's like the annoying brother I never had. I like him too."

Roman's smile grows wider. "He can be like a gnat sometimes, but when he cares about you, he does so fiercely."

"I feel like that's a trait of all the inner circle."

He nods. "I do tend to only recruit the most loyal into the inner circle. The ones I can trust the most."

"Well I feel honored that you let me tag along."

He raises a brow. "Sure. You're just tagging along. We will go with that."

I shake my head at his response, but my heart warms. He basically told me he felt like I was already in.

Why am I fighting this so much?

Freedom. That's why. I thought I wanted the ties back in California but having this freedom has been nice. For once I've made decisions that only benefited me.

"Rome." I use his nickname.

"Yeah?"

"If I get the mark, would you still let me leave if I wanted to? In the future?"

"Would you want to?" His voice is softer.

"I'm not sure, but I think I'd like the option."

"Did the Soulless not allow their members to leave?"

"Honestly, I was kept out of their business, but it did seem like they never did."

He stays silent. "If you ever wanted to leave, I wouldn't hold you back."

The way he phrases it almost seems as if there should be a but at the end. Still, his words offer me some comfort.

"Okay." After taking a deep breath, I turn to him. "I'd like to get my mark."

The corner of his lips twitch as if he wants to smile, but he keeps his emotions in check. "Are you absolutely sure? This is permanent. You may not be welcome in some areas because of the mark."

"I'm sure. I know it's only been a couple of months, but this place already feels more like home than the place I actually grew up. I feel like you guys are actually my family. I haven't had that before. It's an adjustment, but it's not unwelcome."

"Alright. Then I'll take you tomorrow to get your mark. Most members get a celebration when they get theirs. Do you want one?"

I smile at him. "No celebration needed, but I wouldn't mind a night at the races."

He shakes his head. "You're something else. I'm letting Marco handle the races this weekend, but next weekend I'll take you."

"Can I race?" I give him my best puppy dog eyes.

He shakes his head. "I'd like you to heal a bit more, but maybe I'll race for you. Would you like that?"

"I would love that," I say, thinking about the last time I saw him behind the wheel.

"Then it's settled. Now what do you want to do for the rest of the day."

That's how I ended up curled up on the couch watching shows about building cars with the single sexiest man I've ever met.

ROMAN

WITH EACH NEW episode Roxy fidgets more and more.

"You good?" I ask after the fifth time before the first commercial break.

"Yeah, sorry. My ribs are starting to hurt." She winces.

"Why don't we call it a night and you go to sleep."

"I don't want to…"

"How about you lay down on the couch?" I say, offering a compromise.

"Are you sure?"

"As long as you're comfortable." I shrug.

Roxy scoots down on the couch, then curls up in a ball resting her head on my thigh. Instinctively my hand goes to her hair tie and I pull it out, running my fingers through her hair.

Roxy groans as she buries her head into my thigh and I can't help but think of what else she could be doing with her head right there.

Let her heal first, jackass. I chastise myself.

"That feels so good."

"I hope so."

"Have you always been a hair man?" she asks while staring at the TV.

"Can't say that I have."

The show comes back on and we both fall silent as we watch. The silence should be awkward but it's not. I don't know the last time I was this relaxed.

As another episode ends and the next show starts Roxy rolls onto her back and looks up at me. "You can't be comfortable."

"I'm okay." I tell her as I watch her lick her bottom lip.

"You could lay down with me." She shrugs as if it's not a big deal that this is the first time she's asked for me to touch her. Hold her.

"You sure?"

"I mean, as long as you'll be comfortable I have no problem with it." She shrugs before sitting up then standing. "I'm going to go to the bathroom. I'll be right back."

I watch her walk away as I stand and stretch. Pulling my phone from my pocket I check to make sure that no one has tried to get ahold of me. Once I see that I have no notifications I drop my phone onto the coffee table and lay down on the couch.

The bathroom door opens and I hear Roxy walk down the hall, toward me and my heart beats a little faster.

"Come here," I say to her as she stands at the end of the couch looking at me nervously.

She sits on the edge of the couch and lays down in my arms. My front to her back as she faces the TV.

As she settles in I can't help, but close my eyes, loving the way she feels in my arms. The way her head tucks perfectly under my chin as my body curls around hers. With one arm under her head and the other wrapped around her hip I can't help but wonder what it would be like to do this every night. Fall asleep with her like this every night.

What the hell is she doing to me?

After who knows how long I feel her breathing settle letting me know she's fallen asleep. Reaching up I grab the blanket from the back of the couch and spread it over us as carefully as I can without waking her. Kissing the back of her head I shut my eyes and drift off to dreams of her and what our future could possibly hold.

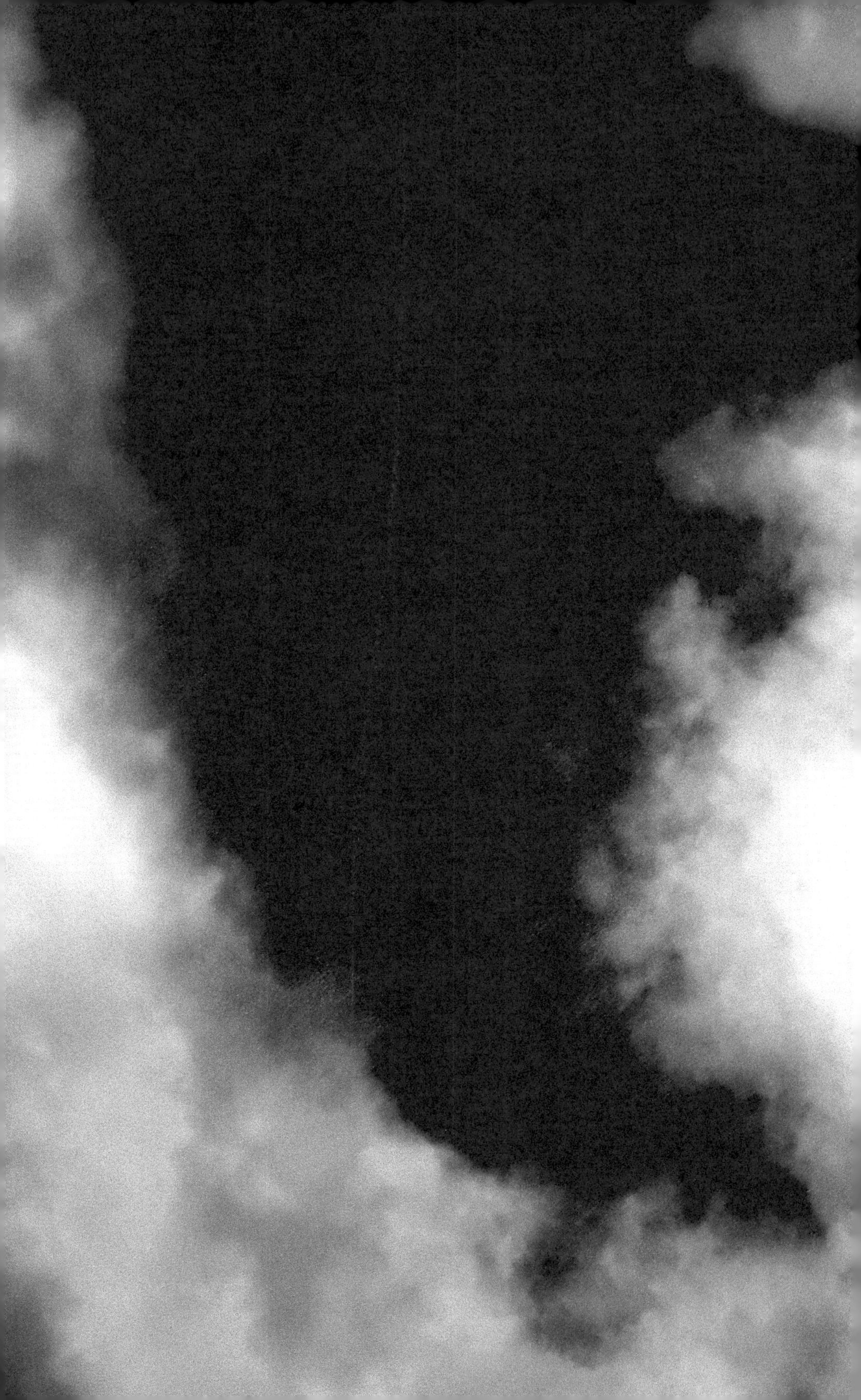

CHAPTER EIGHTEEN

Roxy

"Roman, my friend. What can I do for you today?" The man greets us as we walk in the door.

"Roxy here is getting her mark." Roman wraps an arm around me as he smiles down at me.

"Wow. Congratulations. Welcome to the family."

The man shows his own mark, not quite as intricate as the core group, but showing he is indeed family.

"Thank you."

"Come on back. Where do you want it?" the man asks as he leads us through the shop.

"Um…" I look up at Roman.

"You can get it anywhere, but I suggest somewhere it is easily shown. It's the best way to be protected."

I nod. "Can I get it on my wrist?"

"If that's what you want." Roman turns to the man.

"Jeremy, the woman would like it on her wrist."

He gestures to the chair. "Well sit on down then."

Roman walks over to Jeremy as I settle in and whispers in his ear. When

Jeremy's eyes widen in surprise, I narrow my own.

"What are you whispering about?" I meet Roman's eyes.

"Nothing you need to concern your beautiful head about."

"Sure. I bet you told him to make it as painful as possible."

He smirks. "Nah. I bet you get off on the pain."

"Asshole," I murmur.

"Okay, I'll have to clean your skin then sketch the tattoo. Is that okay?" The man asks me, his demeanor changing completely.

Before he was friendly, almost joking. Now he is more serious. He even seems a little nervous.

"Do whatever you need to."

Roman pulls a fold out chair over next to me taking my other hand in his.

I quirk an eyebrow. "What are you doing?"

"Holding your hand."

"Why? I'm not scared of a tattoo."

His lips twitch as if he wants to smile. "Hush now. Let's talk while he works."

"What do you want to talk about?"

"You. I barely know you. What did you do back in California?"

I feel the cool wipe of the alcohol pad on my skin. When I turn to look, Roman squeezes my hand, drawing my attention back to him.

"I raced. I already told you that."

"That's it? Hannah said you went to college."

I chuckle. "I did. I got a stupid ass business degree I'll never use."

"Why did you do it then?"

It's on the tip of my tongue to tell him the truth, but I don't. Even if I only went for Ross, it doesn't matter anymore.

"Something to do I guess. Isn't that what you're supposed to do after high school? Go get a pointless degree and put yourself into debt?"

He absentmindedly starts to stroke my hand as I feel Jeremy begin to draw on my skin.

"Are you in debt?"

"No. I managed to figure a way around that." I don't add, *because Ross paid for it.*

"Good. Do you want to use your degree?"

"I've never really thought about it."

"What do you want from your future? I suspect you don't plan to work as a server for the rest of your life."

"No. Not really. I enjoy racing, but I guess that's not really a career either."

"You have plenty of time. You're still young."

"Is that why you call me kid?"

"Well I am five years older than you."

"Don't you know that men mature slower than women. If we go by maturity age I'd bet I'm actually older than you."

He chuckles. "Maturity is gained by experience. Trust me, my experience outweighs yours."

"Don't bet on it. You don't know my past."

"As you don't know mine."

We are silent for a moment, both staring at each other. His eyes flitter with suppressed emotions. Surprise, adoration, caring, heat, but as quickly as I see them, they disappear, making me question if I ever saw them in the first place.

"Now that you have your mark, are you planning to stay?"

I bite my lip. "Do you want me to?"

"I always want my members close. It's easier to protect them that way."

My heart drops. Of course. I'm a member, nothing important to him. I'm surprised he even brought me here. I should have asked Marco to bring me.

Here I am letting myself fall further for him, but he's not on the same page. I'm not even sure we are in the same book.

I think back to the way I felt in his arms last night. Did he do that because he wanted to or did he do it out of pity?

"I haven't decided yet." I cast my eyes down to look at our joined hands.

I want to pull back now, the warmth from his hand no longer comforting.

"Hey," he whispers, placing a finger under my chin to bring my gaze up to his. "What just happened?"

I shake my head. "Nothing. I don't like thinking about my past or future. I'm more of a here and now girl."

He lets out a deep sigh. "Roxanne…"

"I'm ready to start with the tattoo gun. Do you want to look at it first?"

Jeremy asks.

I go to turn my head, but Roman's hand cups my face. "Do you trust me?"

I think his question over. Do I? To a certain extent I do, but can you ever really give someone one hundred percent of your trust.

"Yes," I tell him, deciding to keep it simple.

Today, I trust him. With this I trust him.

"Don't look. I want it to be a surprise."

"What if he messed up the stencil?" I ask.

He smiles. "I'll make sure it's perfect. Hold on."

He stands, looking at my arm. I'm itching to look at it, but he asked me to trust him. I can give him this. It doesn't matter anyway. I've already decided to get the mark. Seeing it drawn on my skin is no different than seeing it permanently attached to it.

Roman comes back, gripping my hand again. "You ready?"

I nod as I hear Jeremy turn on the tattoo gun.

The first touch to my skin startles me, but the soothing feel of his thumb caressing my hand distracts me.

"Tell me something about you Roman," I ask him after a few moments.

"What do you want to know?"

"Anything. Something real. Not crew related."

He freezes so long I'm not sure he plans to answer. He glances at Jeremy before looking back at me.

He leans in, brushing his lips against my ear. "I can't reveal all my secrets in public."

I let out a heavy sigh. He leans back, looking at my face. I'm not sure what he sees, but it does something to him.

He cups my cheek, holding my head in place as he whispers into my ear. "My favorite color is blue. My favorite food is steak and potatoes. I don't really care for television. I've never had a long-term girlfriend. I never went to college. Is this good enough or do you need more?"

He whispers the words almost harshly, but they still warm me. He still shared with me.

I turn my face, pressing a chaste kiss to his cheek.

"Thank you," I whisper.

When he pulls back, his eyes are dark. He nods once, settling back in his chair, his hand taking mine again.

"What can we talk about?"

He smirks. "Superficial shit."

"Okay. How about that sexy ass car you have?"

His smile widens. "You like my Chevelle?"

"What's not to like about it? It's a sixty-nine right?"

"Yep. Mostly original."

"I could tell. It's damn nice car."

"You know, that's what made you stand out that first night."

"What?"

"At the races. All the other girls were trying to get the guys' attention, but not you. You were walking from car to car looking under the hood."

I wince a little as the needle hits a particularly sensitive area. "I'm not most women."

"I know. You looked at my car that night."

I smile. "I remember. I was warned to stay away from it, but I couldn't help but get a closer look."

"I had to send Axel over to chase you away. Before he got to you, that dickweed Jordan stole you away. I wanted to rip you from his arms."

I laugh remembering that night. "That seems like so long ago."

"Time flies when you're having fun."

I shake my head. "That's what we are calling it? Fun?"

"If you only dwell on the negative in your life all you will ever feel is negative. Sure shit has gone down. It hasn't been perfect, but life is imperfect. I prefer to think of the positives. Like the fact that I won that race that night. That night brought you into our world. Now you're sitting here getting my mark and becoming a permanent fixture in our family. That's what I would call fun."

I swallow hard. His words touch me somewhere inside my chest, breaking down my already crumbling walls.

"That's an interesting way to view life."

"I can focus on all the hurt in my life. The ways shit went wrong, but is that really living? Living in the past and only focusing on the pain?"

My eyes prickle. "No. It's not."

That's how I've been living though. Angry at Ross for sending me away.

Focusing on the life I lost instead of enjoying the life I still have. I used to think that the Soulless were my life. I lived each day to do whatever I could to prove to them that I was an asset. So they would let me finally become one of them. When they sent me away, I was shattered. I didn't want to admit it then, but they broke part of me.

I didn't realize it, but the Shadows have been slowly putting me back together. Roman has been.

He's still an asshole, but it's like I'm seeing him in a whole new light. I wasn't lying when I told him I don't like thinking about the past or future. I really do prefer to live in the here and now, but maybe he does too. Maybe he prefers to live in the moment and make positive memories.

Thankfully, he reads my mood, letting me lose myself to my thoughts. He doesn't leave my side though. He sits there, holding my hand, tracing a circle over and over with his thumb.

Even when his phone rings, he doesn't let go. He sits there with me until the tattoo artist is done.

"Alright, it's done. That wasn't so bad was it?" Jeremy asks.

I shake my head. "I was lost in my thoughts. I didn't feel a thing."

It's the truth too. I was so focused on processing everything that I forgot he was even there.

"Want to take a look?"

I glance over at Roman. He smiles encouragingly at me.

I pull my wrist up, turning it so I can see it properly.

I smile.

There is an outer circle of intertwined lines in an intricate design, much like I've seen on others. In the middle, the symbol for the Shadow crew is the focus, but around it is another intricate design. Then right there, above the symbol, is the letters "RC" with a feminine looking crown.

"It's beautiful. I don't think I've actually looked at any marks up close before," I tell him.

I hold it out for Roman to look.

He swallows hard as he takes my arm, caressing the side of it gently. "Perfect. Like I told you."

I roll my eyes. "I said I trusted you, didn't I?"

"You did."

"Thank you Jeremy. How much do I owe you?" I ask him, fully prepared to pay my way.

He shakes his head. "Crew business is on the house."

"What? No, you deserve something for your work."

"I get everything I need from the crew. Come back anytime, Roxy."

I want to argue, but one look at Roman and I know I won't win. This is the way it is.

"Fine, but if you ever come over to Julio's your meal is on me. Got it?"

He smiles. "Of course. Here's a care kit. It has instructions in it on aftercare, but I'm sure Roman can help you."

"Thank you." I accept the bag from him, ignoring the knowing gleam in his eye.

He has it all wrong. He thinks Roman and I are something, but we aren't. I'm just another soldier on his team for now.

Roman holds the door as he leads me out to his car.

"Can I drive?"

He lets out a rough laugh. "Not in your wildest dreams, kid."

I roll my eyes, but I knew that would be his answer. He might let me race it, but when he is in the car, he would never be a passenger in the day-to-day life.

Still, as we drive away, I think about how nice it was today. To be with Roman like that. Learning more about him.

Fuck, my mind is messed up, but I almost felt like today was a date.

ROMAN

"You hungry?" I ask as I pull out of the tattoo shop.

"I could always eat." Roxy shrugs.

Reaching over I grab her hand, weaving her fingers with mine and resting them on my thigh.

"Can I take you somewhere?"

"Sure."

Looking down I can't help but be turned on seeing my mark on her skin.

Yeah, I probably should have told her what the mark means, but honestly, I'm not ready to say it out loud.

She's mine.

She's loud, mouthy, brash, and gives zero fucks. I couldn't think of a better person to rule at my side. And if I can't have her then no one else ever will.

As I drive down the road Roxy hums along to the song on the radio. The coffee shop comes into view and I start to slow down.

"You game with getting sandwiches and drinks to go?"

"Works for me." She pulls her hand out of mine and I instantly want to grab it again.

I park the car and we both get out. I jog forward and open the coffee shop's door before she can.

"Thank you." She smiles softly as she walks past me.

While we wait in line out of the corner of my eye I catch Roxy looking down at her mark with a small smile on her face.

Would she be smiling like that if she knew that mark tied her to not only the crew but to me too?

"You going to order?" Roxy asks, pulling me out of my thoughts.

I step up behind her, resting my hands on her hips as I place our order and pay. Moving us off to the side we wait for our order.

"This place is cute." Roxy says softly.

I look around and see the shop through her eyes. The chairs that look comfortable for a nap and the warm colors on the walls with pictures of landscapes scattered on the walls.

"It is."

"Roman and Roxy?" the barista says as she places our order on the counter.

Stepping forward I grab the sandwiches as Roxy grabs the coffee.

"You two have a great day."

"Thanks. You too." Roxy smiles at her.

Walking to the door I open it, letting Roxy walk out first. Stepping around her I hustle to the car and set the sandwiches on the roof of the car and open her door.

Roxy leans up and kisses my cheek. "Thank you," she says as she gets in.

Grabbing the food I hand it to her. "You're welcome," I say as I shut the door.

Walking to the driver's side I look up and down the street. I don't know why but today feels a little different and it has me on edge. Getting in the car I look over and laugh seeing that Roxy has already started in on her sandwich.

"What, I'm hungry," she mumbles over a mouth full of food as I pull out of the parking spot.

"We will get to our destination in ten minutes," I tell her as I start to drive.

Before I know it I'm pulling into the drive-in movie theater. I pay the employee working the gate and pull in and find a spot to park.

"Wait, Drive in movie theaters are still a thing?" Roxy asks as she leans forward.

"They are." I nod as I park.

Reaching down I adjust my seat, making myself comfortable.

"What are we watching?"

"Honestly, I never even looked." I frown as I take a drink.

"Well then I guess we will both be surprised then, huh?"

I turn, grabbing my sandwich. "So tell me something about you, Roxy," I say as I unwrap my food.

"What do you want to know?" she asks, throwing my words from earlier back at me.

"I want to know everything."

"My favorite color is red. I hate mayo, and I've always wanted a dog."

"Then I think you should get a dog."

"Maybe someday. Once I'm settled. Until then it wouldn't be fair to me or the dog." She shrugs.

"I've never really thought much about owning an animal."

"No? I thought for sure you could be a fish person." She smirks.

We don't even realize that the movie has started until the speakers go crazy up front, making her jump.

"That caught me off guard." She laughs making me smile.

Once we both finish eating, Roxy slides over the center to settle into my lap. I almost stop her when she winces in pain, but once she is fully relaxed in top of me, I hear her let out a sigh of contentment.

Something about that speaks to a part of me I didn't know existed. I'm satisfied knowing she is content being with me.

I couldn't tell you a single thing that happened in the movie that night. What I can tell you is the way Roxy's hair smelled. How it felt when her body vibrated against me as she laughed at the movie. How I felt completely at ease when she looked back at me, pressing a chaste kiss to my lips.

"You ready to get out of here?" I murmur against her temple when the movie credits start to roll.

"Yeah, I should probably go home and get some sleep," she says, biting her lip.

"You could always come back to my place you know…" I trail off.

I've never had anyone at my house other than the core group. No one else has ever slept in that bed, but me. I really want Roxy to be the first and last one next to me.

Sliding off my lap, she settles back into the passenger seat. Starting the car, I wait for her answer.

"Maybe tomorrow." She says softly as I pull out of the theater.

I give her a tight smile, not wanting her to see my disappointment.

The drive back to her place goes by faster than I would like and before I know it I'm pulling into her driveway. As I reach forward to shut the car off Roxy reaches over and rests her hand on my forearm.

"I'll just jump out. I'll see you soon." She rambles before leaning forward and kissing the corner of my mouth.

As she pulls away I reach forward and grab her, pulling her back into me. I kiss her like I've wanted to all day. I nip at her bottom lip before pulling away slowly. Roxy looks dazed and I can't help but smile.

"Before I forget, I have something for you." I tell her as I reach for the glove box. Popping it open I grab the black box and hand it to her.

"What is it?" she asks, slowly taking the box from me.

"Open it once you get inside. But I want to see you wear it."

"Roman…" she says full of suspicion.

"Call me if you need me."

"I won't." she smirks as she slides out of the car. "Later." She says as she shuts the door.

I watch as she bounds up the front steps to Hannah's front door and watch her slip inside.

Leaning my head against the headrest I can't help but smile.

Today was a good day.

CHAPTER NINETEEN

Roxy

"I'm going to get out of here," I tell Janet.

"Go on girl. Your ride is already here."

I shake my head at her. She's been scoping out the guys sent to pick me up. Ever since the attack, Roman always sends someone to bring me home so I don't have to walk or try and catch the bus.

Sometimes it's Hannah, but most of the time it's a random person I've never met.

As I walk out the front door, I stop short.

"Marco?"

He turns, smiling at me. Fuck if he isn't gorgeous. I have to admit, there is something in the water here. Between Roman, Axel, Blaze, and Marco there isn't enough good looks for the rest of the general population.

Hell, even their other guys are attractive, just not on their level.

"Hey, pretty girl. You ready to get out of here?" Then he gives me that smile.

That fucking panty dropping smile that I'm sure bring weaker women to their knees. If I wasn't so fucked up over my feelings for Roman, I could see myself giving into this man.

"What are you doing here?

"I figured you might like a friendly face."

I walk over to him, smiling. "That's kind of you."

He pulls me into a hug, pressing a kiss to the top of my head. "Don't go letting anyone hear you say that. You'll ruin my image."

"I suppose I can keep it under wraps. Well, chauffeur. Where is my ride?"

He smiles. "How do you feel about bikes?"

"Like bicycles? Not really my thing, but I mean you'll be the one doing all the work."

"Smart ass. I have a Ducati Panigale."

I already knew this, but I have yet to ride on it with him. Since I try to avoid being alone with him, we are almost always in one of the other guys' cars.

"Cars are more my thing, but I wouldn't say no to a ride on a machine like that."

He reaches down, grabbing my hand to pull me over to the bike parked at the curb. Then he picks up a jacket sitting on the seat, handing it to me.

"Here. I grabbed my extra jacket for you. It might get cold."

I give him a grateful smile. "I'm sure I'd be fine, but thank you for thinking of me."

I shrug the jacket on before doing the same with the helmet he offers me. Then he mounts the bike, helping me on behind him.

When he starts it, a jolt goes through my body. There is something sexy about the purr of an engine underneath you. I may have to reconsider my position on bikes.

"You better hold on."

I wrap my arms around his middle, plastering myself to his back as he takes off. I squeal at the exhilaration I feel running through my blood. Once he is on a straight road, he opens the engine really pushing the limits of the bike.

I smile to myself at the feeling of freedom I find. He takes several turns, his body vibrating with laughter every time I squeal or squeeze him tighter. Finally, he slows down, pulling into the parking lot of a park.

He helps me off the bike, taking my helmet.

"What are we doing here?"

He shrugs. "I figured you might not be in a hurry to get home. I used to come here a lot when I was a kid."

"Are you sharing secrets with me, Marco?"

He gives me an embarrassed smile. "Would you care if I was?"

"Not at all. Your secrets are safe with me."

We head into the park, walking side by side in silence. When I see the swings, I turn toward them, taking a seat.

He sits on the swing next to me.

"What was your favorite thing to do here?" I ask him.

"They used to have a merry-go-round. They got rid of it years ago. It was too dangerous."

"A merry-go-round like with horses and shit?"

He laughs. "No. It was a circular metal contraption that had rails on it. You would run as fast as you could to get it to go in a circle then you would jump on, holding onto the rails as tight as you could so you didn't fall off. I can't tell you how many times I was flung off. My sister too. I would get in so much trouble when she would end up crying, but she always wanted to play on it with me."

"That does sound dangerous, but I have a feeling you're a risk taker."

"I am. Susie was always a follower. She wanted to do whatever I wanted to do. It's why I would be the one to get in trouble even though she made her own choice. Mom used to tell me if I made better choices she would follow. Like I was her role model."

"Is she younger?"

"Yeah. She's three years younger than me."

"I don't have any siblings so I can't really tell you if your mom was right."

He shrugs. "What was your favorite part of the park?"

I give him a sad smile. "I never spent much time at parks, but I always liked the swings. The feeling of wind in my hair always made me forget about what was going on around me."

"Ah. Freedom."

"Yep. I got that same feeling on the back of your bike there."

He gets up, moving behind me to push me gently. "Like this?"

I laugh. "Yes. Like this."

"You're beautiful."

I blush at his admission. "You're not so bad yourself."

"I haven't had any complaints." He laughs.

"I'm sure you're a real lady killer."

I glance back at the bright smile on his face. "My mom would say I've left a broken heart or two in my wake. I'm not that man anymore though."

"No? With as flirty as you are, I would have assumed you were dead set in your playboy ways."

"I have a flirty personality. I won't deny that, but if I found the right one, I wouldn't have a reason to look at another."

"Well for your sake, I hope the woman is feisty as fuck. She will need to be to deal with the attention you get."

"Oh she will be. She would have to be to deal with my shit."

"Fuck, she'll need to be a goddamned saint to deal with you."

He grabs the side of the swings stopping me abruptly. "Hey. You don't think I'm worth it?"

I smile, shaking my head. "I never said that. I think you're a great guy. You just need some TLC to turn you into an even better man."

"How do you feel about TLC?" he asks, bringing his face closer to mine.

My heart starts pounding in my chest. Fuck.

All my mind can think is *abort mission.*

I lift my hand up to grab the chain to steady myself.

Marco's eye flits to my arm briefly then back to me. Then he freezes. Turning to my arm, he reaches out to gently touch the still tender flesh.

"When did you get this?"

"Two days ago. I figured Roman would tell you. He took me."

He shakes his head. "He hasn't mentioned it."

He studies my tattoo for a moment before turning back to me, sadness swirling in his eyes.

"Do you care for Roman?"

I bristle at his question. Is this some test?

"Why?"

"I'm curious. I didn't realize you would accept his mark."

"I wasn't sure I'd accept it either, but here we are. It's not a big deal. Unless you didn't want me part of the crew."

My heart hammers in my chest. I never considered that the others wouldn't accept me.

"Of course not. I already thought of you as crew. You know that. I'm just surprised."

He forces a smile on his face before stepping back.

"To answer your question. I've grown to care about all of you. We're family now right?"

He nods. "I should get you home. I thought the break would be nice, but I have some things I need to get done."

"Oh. Okay. Well thank you for sharing this with me."

He steps around the swing as I stand up. I let him walk in front of me before following him back to the bike. Before he hands me the helmet, he reaches out, brushing a hand along my face.

"You really are beautiful."

Leaning in he presses a kiss to my cheek before helping me put my helmet on.

I don't know what happened, but the ride back to my house is different than the ride here. I don't feel as free. It almost feels somber. Like something was lost.

After he helps me off the bike with a quick good-bye, I stand outside watching him fade into the distance wondering if somewhere along the way I did something wrong.

ROMAN

"ROMAN!" MARCO BILLOWS through the shop.

"What's up?" I ask sliding out from under the car.

Marco charges forward, making me stand.

"What's wrong?" I demand as he approaches. Ignoring me Marco takes a swing. I step back, avoiding the first punch and grab his fist, stopping the second.

"What the fuck is wrong with you?" I hiss.

"What's wrong with me?" he scoffs, taking a step back. "You put your fucking mark on her!"

I watch as Axel and Blaze stop working, waiting to see if they need to break us up.

"I did."

"Does she even fucking know?"

"All you need to know is that Roxy is marked. The rest is between me and her."

Marco's nose flares as he turns, kicking an oil pan, spilling oil all over the floor.

"You're cleaning that up." I point to the spill.

"Fuck you. All you do is think about yourself."

"Is that right?" I chuckle. "Last I checked I put this crew first. You included." I pause. "What the fuck is going on with you man? This isn't like you."

"You don't fucking know me."

I look at the crazed look in my best friend's eyes and shake my head wondering if he's right.

"Talk to me. Talk to us," I say, nodding toward Axel and Blaze who are slowly approaching. "All this anger you're aiming at me can't just be over Roxy."

"She's too good for you."

"Trust me, I'm well aware."

"What's going on man?" Blaze asks, frowning.

"Nothing is going on," Marco says, not looking at any of us.

His phone goes off and he pulls it out of his pocket. "I got to go," he mumbles as he walks away.

"Is it just me or has something been different with him lately?" I ask Axel and Blaze.

"It's not just you," Blaze says.

"Want me to look into it?" Axel asks crossing his arms.

"Please do." I sigh, suddenly exhausted. Looking around the shop I can't help but be ready for the day to end. "How about we all finish up what we were working on then head out for the day?"

"Sounds good to me," Blaze says, walking away.

Axel lingers next to me. "How far do you want me to dig?" he asks quietly.

"As far as you can."

"I'll let you know," he says, walking away.

Turning back to the car I get back to work. Between Roxy, Marco, and Zade I don't know how much more I can take. I need a fucking vacation.

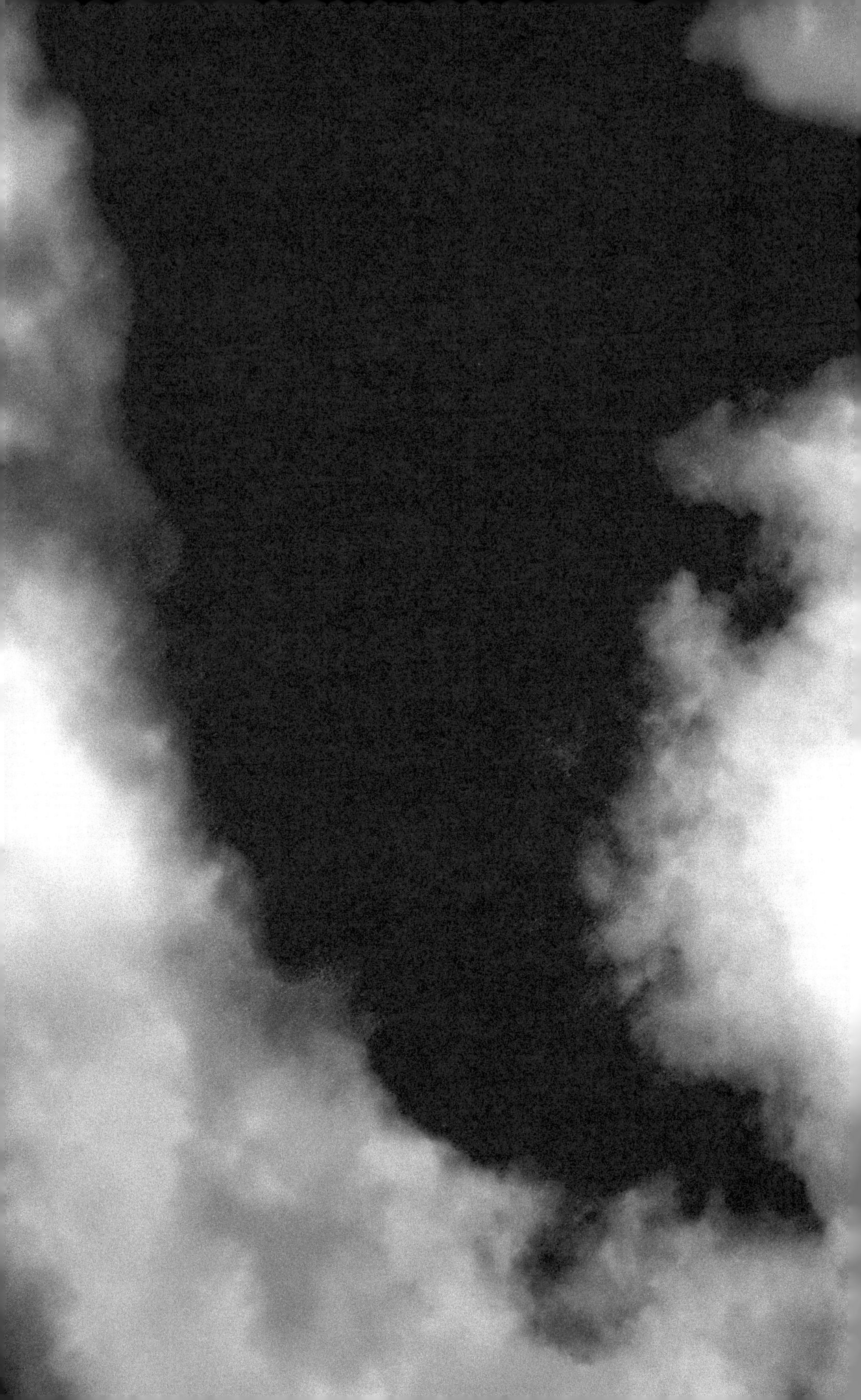

CHAPTER TWENTY

Roxy

Walking through the door after a long shift, all I want to do is relax. Since Marco dropped me off four days ago, I haven't seen him again. Nor have I seen Roman. It's like they are both ghosting me and I don't know why.

While I'm a little miffed about Marco avoiding me, I'm hurt that Roman is doing the same. I thought we were getting somewhere, but now we are back at square one. I feel like a damn yo-yo.

"Roxy? Is that really you?" Hannah calls from the living room.

Toeing off my shoes, I make my way inside to find her sitting on the couch watching a movie.

"Yep. It's me."

"I swear I haven't seen you in days," Hannah complains.

I shrug. "It's been a busy couple of days."

"I heard. Want to watch a movie with me?"

"Sure."

I settle on the couch, not even bothering to change out of my uniform. I smell slightly of Mexican food, but I'm too tired to change. Besides, my feet need a break.

"What are we watching?"

"*Guardians of the Galaxy.*"

I smile. "Chris Pratt. Yum."

She giggles. "Right? Anyway, how have you been?"

"Fine. Trying to stay out of trouble."

"I'm surprised Roman let you go back to work."

I narrow my eyes. "He doesn't dictate what I do."

She looks shocked. "I mean I thought you took the mark."

I shrug. "I did. What does that have to do with anything?"

"That means he's now your leader. You can't go disrespecting him or ignoring his commands."

I roll my eyes at her. "Crew or not, I won't let him dictate my life. What's the worst he can actually do to me?"

"Um, kill you? You do realize that's the punishment for betrayal in the crew right? Fuck did he tell you anything before he let you take the mark?"

"Not really. He said it would protect me, but that it would also mean I was crew and I would have to follow some rules, but we never really went over them." I frown, wondering what exactly I agreed to.

You should have asked more questions.

Except that all thoughts flee when I look into his eyes. Fucker is too sexy for his own good.

Hannah shakes her head. "Such a fucking man. Well, let me educate you then. Rule number one, what Roman says, goes. It doesn't matter if he orders you to put a gun to my head and pull the trigger. If he asks you to, you do it."

I hold up my hand. "I won't compromise my own morals for him."

She sighs. "I don't think he would actually ever ask you to kill someone, but if he did, you are expected to do it or else face death yourself."

"Noted."

"Like he said. The mark offers you protection. From law enforcement. From other crews. I mean as long as you are around here, it will even protect you from low level thugs. We are pretty well known around these parts."

"I got that already from the several people who told me to not mess with you."

"*Us.* Now you're a part of this, it's us. You're family now. No more being left behind when shit goes down. If you need help, you find a member and they will help."

"What if they don't want to help?"

"Technically, they don't have to, but you're crew. It's the way we run things here. Not every crew is like us. The Devil's Den, for example, are rougher. They take the whole death thing seriously. Disobey Zade and you are guaranteeing your death."

"Is that why Roman hates them?"

She shakes her head. "It's more personal than that. We are still a newer club. Roman started this when he was eighteen. It took several years to be recognized, but we are now a crew to be respected."

"You mean feared. A lot of people fear you… or us I guess."

"Some do. Roman has to do things to keep some members in line. Make examples to show others we were serious, but he's loyal. He will do whatever he can to take care of his people. That includes you now."

"Okay, I get that. What else?"

"It's good that you have a job. Usually you cover your bills and then a percentage of what's leftover goes to the community pot to fund activities."

"By activities do you mean like that trip we took?" I ask, thinking about when we made the trip to spy on Zade.

"I do. Also, if a member gets into trouble, it pays their lawyer. Or if their family member becomes ill, it pays the hospital bill."

"I thought you said it protects me from the police."

"It does, but only to certain extents. For example, if you were to travel back home and get into trouble, we don't have a relationship with that police department so we wouldn't get able to get you out so easily."

I never had to worry about that back home. Ross always protected me in that sense.

"I see."

"There are also layers to the crew. You have the lower level, newer members. They handle what we call grunt work. They are errand boys or sometimes security if needed. Then you have the middle members. Those who have proven their loyalty. A lot of them enjoy the benefits of the crew without actually having to do much. They can be as involved as they want to be in the day-to-day stuff, but they are still required to answer the call if Roman requires it. This is the goal of most members. Pay their dues and live an easier life knowing they are protected. They still attend parties thrown by the crew. A lot of them still go to the races and other crew sanctioned events. The next level is upper security. These are our best of the best guys. The ones we trust to protect us or the ones close to us. Then you have the inner circle. That's Blaze, Axel, and me. Then you have the second in command, Marco and the leader, Roman."

"Is that why everyone's tattoo looks different?"

"Yeah. Like take mine," she holds out her arm, showing the tattoo on the inside of her forearm. "I have the traditional border and the internal symbol for the crew, but I also have this intricate design around the symbol showing that I am in the top five. If you look at Axel and Blaze, they have the same tattoo. Marco's is the same except the number two is also there. Roman's has his initials with a king's crown showing he is top dog."

My forehead furrows in confusion. "Wait, what?"

"I know it's confusing. Here, show me yours."

Confusing is an understatement. I followed what she said, but my tattoo is different than hers. It's not simple at all.

I hold out my wrist to her. For a moment, she freezes, then her eyes widen.

"Jesus fucking Christ," she whispers out on a harsh breath.

"What does this mean?"

She looks up at me. "He claimed you."

"What? Like his property?"

"See this." She traces her hand over her initials in the middle of the tattoo. "Roman's initials marking you as his and this"—she presses into the delicate crown marked on my skin— "says you're his queen. He has placed you at the very top right next to him."

My heart stops. "Why the fuck would he do that?"

She seems as surprised as I. "I don't know..."

I grit my teeth. "So what does this mean?"

Her mouth opens and closes twice before she's able to spit it out. "It means you are the single most important person in the crew now. You command us like him. You might as well be one."

I take a deep breath, trying to control my emotions. They are going haywire. I'm angry that he marked me in this way without telling me its meaning. I'm upset that I had no clue the power he has given me without my knowledge. I'm furious at the target he has painted on my back from his enemies. As if this mark makes me important to him.

I'm so important to him that I haven't seen him in almost a week. Haven't heard a peep from him either.

With all the anger, there is also a small part of me that warms at the knowledge. That maybe this means he feels the same sparks that I do. That he may want to explore them.

"Where is he?" I ask calmly.

She widens her eyes. "What are you going to do?"

"I want to talk to him."

"This isn't a good idea."

I chuckle. "Didn't you just basically say I'm your boss? Tell me where the fuck he is."

She swallows hard. "The clubhouse. They are having a meeting. You shouldn't interrupt."

"Why aren't you there?"

She heaves out a heavy sigh. "Roman wanted me here for when you got home. As an added layer of protection for you."

My heart clenches at her admission.

"Wow. So even our relationship is dictated by him. Good to know."

I stand from the couch, heading toward the door. Hannah follows behind me.

"It's not like that. He didn't ask me to be your cousin or your friend. He only asked me to be here, which I would have done anyway. I don't care about the meetings. I only go when he needs me to. I would rather be here hanging out with you."

"I can't deal with you right now. I need to go confront a sneaky asshole."

"Be careful, please. Do you want me to come with you?"

I shake my head. "I can handle this on my own."

"Take my car at least," she hands me her keys.

I nod my thanks before heading out.

The drive didn't calm my emotions. If anything, it made it worse.

All I kept thinking was why? Why tie me to him in such an intimate way when he keeps pushing me away? Up until I was jumped, he ran hot and cold. Now he's more bearable, but I wouldn't exactly say I'm his favorite person. Add in the fact that he gave me his mark and took me out on what I felt was a date, gave me a necklace I can't convince myself to take off, then ghosted me for the next six days and I don't know what to fucking think.

When I get to the clubhouse, I don't hesitate. I walk right up to the front door, but a man steps out in my way. I don't recognize him.

"Move," I growl at the man.

"I'm not supposed to let anyone in. Not even a fine ass like yours."

I flip my wrist around, showing him my mark. "Do you know what this mark means?"

His eyes widen as he notices the initials in the center.

"I can see you do. This means if I want in this door, you will step the fuck aside and hold the fucking door like a gentleman."

He swallows hard, nodding. "Sorry, ma'am. Here you go."

He opens the door without meeting my eyes.

I don't waste another second on him. I fly into the house and into the dining room where they have a table set up.

When I walk in, the man talking pauses, eyes wide when he sees me. I recognize Axel, Blaze, and Marco, but none of them concern me. My eyes are for one man only.

"Have you lost your fucking mind?" I grind out through my clenched teeth.

Roman narrows his eyes at me. "This is not the place or time for your tantrum. Go home."

"Oh? Who is going to make me?" I ask him, walking right over to where he is now standing.

"You don't want to test my patience, kid. Back the fuck down."

"Or what? You'll con me into some other stupid fucking plan you have going? Fuck, you're an idiot."

"And you're a child. Go home and come back when you mature."

My hand reacts before I can think. The sting on my palm makes me wince as I look at the now red imprint on the side of Roman's face.

For a brief moment, I see my death. He is going to kill me for this. Not only did I hit him, but I did so in front of his men.

This is how I go.

"*Out,*" he growls.

On instinct, I move to heed to his demand, but his hand reaches out, grabbing me as he spins, pinning me to the wall.

I hear shuffling behind him, but my eyes are locked on his. One hand on my throat pins me to the wall while his body is pressed against mine.

My blood is pulsing through my body both in fear and exhilaration. It's the same high I get when racing. The thought that one wrong move can end my life, but all the right ones can lead to victory.

Roman leans in, biting my neck making me gasp, before kissing the same spot.

A throat clears from behind him. He looks over his shoulder. My eyes follow as I see Marco standing at the other end of the table.

"I said out. Make them wait for me outside."

Marco nods, his eyes flickering to mine as if to ask me if I'm okay. I don't give him anything. Instead, I bring my eyes back to Roman.

Once we hear the door shut, Roman presses his nose against mine.

"What the fuck do you think you're doing waltzing in here like you fucking own the place? Do you know what you've interrupted?"

I attempt to shake my head, but his hold on my throat tightens slightly, halting my movements.

I swallow hard. "What were you thinking? Giving me a permanent mark tying me to you?"

"Do you remember what I told you before? That if you hit me again there would be consequences?"

"You said you'd kill me. Do it then. I'm not afraid of death."

It's a lie. I most definitely am afraid to die, but I refuse to cower under him.

"I should kill you. Not only did you throw a tantrum, but you hit me in front of my men. What are they going to think?"

"That the woman you chose to wear your mark is not weak and will not bow to anyone."

His eyes flare. "You're playing a dangerous game, Rox. Fuck, you *are* dangerous."

"I know I hit hard, but it will hardly kill you."

His chuckle is dark. "You have no idea."

His hold loosens slightly. I take the opening, bringing my knee up to hit him in the balls.

He moves slightly at my movement, throwing me off my mark, but it's enough to give me some leeway. I quickly slip from his grasp and start heading to the door.

"What are you doing? Running away like a child?" Several long strides has him at my side. He grips my arm, turning me back toward him. His grip is tight almost to the point of pain.

"You demanded my attention tonight. You have it. You're pissed. We don't do this whole running off thing. If you're pissed, you stay and we fight it out until you're no longer pissed. There's no escaping me now." His finger brushes down to my wrist as his thumb brushes over his mark there. "I gave you a choice and you chose to commit. That means you stay and you fight. You don't leave when shit gets tough."

"I wasn't leaving forever. I'm done with this conversation."

He backs me up until my ass is pressed against the edge of the table. In a quick movement, he picks me up until I'm sitting on the edge.

"We don't walk away from each other angry. We solve our shit and move on. You have two options. We can fight this out or we can fuck it out. Which do you want?"

At his words, my body heats. Liquid floods my core at the thought of fucking this man, but I refuse to give in to him now. That's what he wants.

"Fine. Why did you give me your mark?"

"To protect you."

"The crew mark would have done that," I remind him. "You didn't have to give me *your* mark."

He's silent so long I almost don't think he is going to answer, but then he speaks. "The crew mark gives you a level of protection. It says that by attacking you, they run the risk of retaliation. Having my mark gives you an added layer of protection."

"How so?"

He reaches out with one hand threading his hands into my hair. The next second, he pulls my hair roughly to the side as he bends down to my neck, nipping the skin.

My body lights up at the sensation. My mind clouds for a second before I remember what we were talking about.

I try to push back on his chest, but he doesn't move.

"We are fighting this out. Not fucking. Tell me."

He growls. "It means if one single hair on your head is harmed, I would burn down the world to avenge you. Leaders only get one mark. There's no harem of women under protection. It's sacred. You only get one."

My thoughts race. I go to ask him why, but he leans up, pressing his lips to mine in a hard kiss. When I don't react right away, he nips my bottom lip, making me gasp, opening my mouth to his.

At first, I try to push him away, but the deeper he kisses, the more I melt into him. I'm finding it harder to hang on to the anger when pure ecstasy is filling my veins. Especially when I know how amazing he can make me feel.

He finally breaks the kiss only to trail kisses down my neck.

"That mark means that you're protected from everyone, even me. Don't abuse your power, kid." His whispers against my skin cause me to shiver.

"Stop," I tell him, going against my very willing body.

I need a second to think.

"I have a reputation to uphold.," he murmurs, tightening his hand in my hair.

There is a burn of pain, but also something so primal about it.

"You haven't earned the right to touch me," I breathe out.

He smirks as he trails his free hand up my thigh. "Really? What about on the porch? Or the night in my car? You really want me to stop?"

My breath hitches as his fingers find my core. I knew I should have changed out of my skirt before I came here. I can't even shut my knees with him standing in between them.

His finger brushes once over my center, making my body quiver with need. "Yes."

His hand in my hair moves to his other, ripping the center of my underwear open.

I gasp. "I meant yes, I want you to stop."

His eyes are full of heat and promises. "I'm not sure I believe you. You're fucking soaked."

Before I can respond, one of his hands grips my hips as his other brushes my clit, making my eyes roll back. Then he shoves a finger inside me, making me moan at the intrusion.

He adds a second finger quickly, thrusting inside me as his thumb rubs circles over my clit. My moans become louder, more desperate. I want to hate myself for reacting this way. I want to push him away, but my body has taken over. It wants this release more than it needs its next breath.

I can feel my body building up to release, my hips grinding against Roman's hand with wild abandon.

Suddenly, he removes his fingers.

I blink up at him in confusion.

He smirks. "To be continued when you decide I've earned it."

I want to cuss him out, but my mind is still fuzzy. Roman hasn't moved yet. Instead, I watch as he brings his hand up to his mouth and licks each finger that was inside me. My body burns as he moans at the taste.

"Divine. I cannot wait to get my mouth on you again."

He steps back, a very noticeable bulge in his pants. I almost beg him to finish what he's started, but the cool air on my center brings a moment of clarity.

Roman moves his hands to my hips, pulling my now ruined panties off before pocketing it.

He winks at me. "For later. If you want to continue this discussion, feel free to go to my room. Otherwise, I have a meeting to finish."

He pulls me off the table, pressing my skirt down to make sure I'm covered.

When I don't move right away, he chuckles.

Then he walks me over to the door.

Once at the door, he grips my neck again, pulling me closer to his face. "Be a good girl."

When he leans in to kiss me, I press forward, biting his lip until I can taste the metallic taste of his blood. He took something from me here, so I'll take something from him too.

He smirks, pulling back to touch his finger to his lip.

He presses another hard kiss to me. "Run along now."

He opens the door, shutting it behind me.

I expect to see all those men waiting outside, but the only person there is Marco. I smooth my hand down my hair, my cheeks heating with a blush. There's no doubt in my mind that Marco knows what happened.

"Are you okay?" he asks, his eyes taking in my skin.

I give him a small smile. "I'm fine. I should go."

The disappointment in his eyes causes a pang to hit my gut.

Instead of dwelling on it, I walk away.

ROMAN

LEANING AGAINST THE door I take a deep breath trying to collect my thoughts. Roxy turns me on like no other but she also infuriates me. Why does she have to be so fucking mouthy?

Because boring girls aren't your speed, I think to myself.

Pushing off the door, I walk toward the back of the clubhouse and slip out the back door. I see all the guys gathered around a bonfire.

Everyone except Marco.

"Everything good, boss?" Blaze smirks.

"Everything is fine. Where's Marco?" I ask.

"Right here," he calls out as he rounds the corner of the house.

"Good, now where were we?" I ask the group of men.

"We were about to discuss the next race and if you wanted to invite any other crews. Kind of like a coming-out party for Roxy as your woman," Axel reminds me.

"That's right." I nod. "Let's do it in two months. Invite Soulless since she knows them."

"Why wait so long?" Marco asks.

"Hopefully things with Devil's Den will settle down. Plus, it gives Ross and his crew enough time to plan to travel out here."

"Warm Roxy up to the idea of a party too," Blaze jokes, making the guys laugh.

"Don't worry about Roxy. Leave her to me." I smirk. "Speaking of Devil's

Den, do we have an update?"

"No." Axel shakes his head. "And I won't lie, it's starting to piss me off."

"Whatever we do, we have to be smart about it," Marco says thoughtfully.

"I'd like to get my hands on them for what they did to Rox," Blaze says, cracking his fists.

"You and me both. We will get our revenge soon enough."

"Damn right we will," one of the guys mutters.

"Anything else?" I ask. Everyone shakes their heads. "All right. Get out of here and be safe. I'll see you all soon."

One by one, the guys take off toward home. Once everyone is gone, I walk through the clubhouse and shut off all the lights before locking up. Walking toward my car, I pause as I see Axel leaning against the door.

"What's up?"

"We need to talk."

"You found something?"

"I found something."

"That bad?"

"Worse," he says gravely.

"Lovely," I mumble to myself. "All right, tell me."

CHAPTER TWENTY-ONE

Roxy

"Hey there, brat."

I roll my eyes at Blaze as he leans against the wall outside work. I'm just glad he isn't making jokes about last night. Once I got home, I finally admitted to myself how childish I was by bursting in there the way I did. I, then, also had to admit that I deserved the embarrassment I felt from the way Roman left me.

"You're such an ass." I roll my eyes at him.

He shrugs. "I know. Boss man wants to see you."

I chuckle. "Who says I want to see him?"

"Unfortunately, I do not have the option of denying him, so please don't make me wrestle your ass into the car."

I hold up my mark. "I don't know. From what I hear, this is a pretty powerful thing. You willing to go against it?"

He shakes his head, running his hand down his face. "Listen, that gives you power for sure, but Roman called a meeting. It's best if you're there for it."

"You just had a meeting last night." I remind him.

"Yeah, well shit popped off overnight. There's another one."

"What kind of meeting?"

"The kind where he reveals shit you've been in the dark about. Now come on."

He reaches his hand out. I huff out a sigh.

"Better be fucking worth it. My feet are killing me."

"Now what you really should do is use that little power play you just pulled on Rome. I bet he'd massage your feet all night for you."

He holds open the passenger door for me.

"You think?"

He grins. "Play up the pain. 'Oh my feet hurt so bad I can barely walk.' Maybe a few fake tears. Oh, I got it. Let me carry you into the house. He will go total caveman on you."

I slide in the seat. "Unlikely."

I shut the door without waiting for his response. When he gets in the driver's side, he continues the conversation anyway.

"After yesterday, I figured you would be down for that."

I chuckle. "What do you think happened yesterday?"

"Well, you were all badass and interrupted our meeting, thank you for that by the way, and handed Rome his ass. Then he gave it right back to you in the form of an orgasm and let you walk away happy. Seems like you'd be okay with him being handsy."

So much for not bringing up last night.

I scoff. "He did not give me an orgasm. He was an asshole then basically told me to leave."

"That asshole didn't even give you the big 'O?' Don't worry, little sis. I'll beat his ass for you."

"Ew. Do not use sister in a sentence with the term 'O.' Isn't he your boss?"

He shrugs. "Semantics. He should make sure you get pleasured before himself. If he doesn't then he doesn't deserve you."

I chuckle. "That's almost sweet I think. Besides, he wasn't pleasured either."

"Ah. So it was some kinky game you guys are playing. Got it."

"No. When the fuck did this conversation get so off track?"

"You're the one denying your pootang power on my brother from another mother."

"Jesus, you never give up, do you? Do you even listen to the bullshit that spews from your mouth?"

"Yep. Sometimes I even make myself laugh. It's a great trait to have."

I shake my head. "Moving on, what is this meeting about?"

"Honestly? I have no idea. He said there have been new developments on the Devils. That's what we were working on yesterday."

"Why wasn't I there yesterday then?"

"You are moody today. I don't know. Maybe ask your boyfriend."

"He's not my boyfriend. I'm not even sure we are friends."

"For someone not claiming to be his girlfriend, you sure are quick to throw around his mark."

I grit my teeth. "I didn't know it was his mark when he took me. I didn't choose this."

Blaze barks out a laugh. "He fucking marked you without telling you the meaning? Wow, Rome can be dense sometimes, but fuck was that the dumbest shit he could do. Make him work for it, Rox."

"Work for what?"

"You. Make him work for you. He deserves a little havoc in his life after that stunt. I thought you were playing hard to get after taking it, but fuck. Rome never does anything half-assed I guess." He shakes his head.

"I am so confused right now. I'm not making him work for shit because we aren't together."

"He wants to be though. That's why you need to make him work for it. Make him see that you won't roll over. You stick up for yourself. Fuck, want me to teach you some defensive moves? That way you can fend him off when he can't keep his hands off of you. I'm sure that will be sooner rather than later. The guy always has his eyes on you. Ever since the day you walked into the races. Fucker didn't even know then that he was a goner."

"Are you done spouting bullshit? Roman is an idiot, sure, but he hasn't even made a move on me." I lie.

Fuck. Does Roman want me as more than a fuck?

"Keep fooling yourself, sweetheart. I'm trying to help you out here. Remember, I'm your brother. That's what big brothers do. We watch out for our baby sisters."

"I'm not a fucking baby."

"No, but you're younger than me. Hey, maybe I can marry Hannah and you can be my cousin. You think Hannah would go for that? Fuck, maybe not. She's as much of a playgirl as I am a playboy, but maybe that's why we work."

"Excuse me? Are you sleeping around on my cousin?"

"We aren't fucking. We are friends. It's not like that." He waves away my question.

"Fuck, you guys are crazy. I'm not getting involved. That's all on you guys."

"Good. Smart. Stay out of it. Anyway, so back to Roman."

"Fucking what, Blaze? There's nothing going on. He has been an asshole from the very first moment I met him. I don't want anything to do with that toxic bullshit. I refuse to let him treat me like shit. He wants some meek and demure chick? Well he tatted the wrong one."

"Whoa," Blaze says at my blowup. "No one would ever confuse you with being meek or demure. Trust me. I think that's why he likes you. You push him. You don't give in. Honestly, you're him with tits and an ass."

"Jesus fucking Christ, Blaze."

"What? I mean, you're like my sister, but like not. I can say that."

"You are a fucking mess is what you are. Can we not talk about this shit anymore? You're giving me a headache," I say, rubbing my forehead.

"Sure thing. We are almost there anyway."

The last several minutes of the drive, Blaze leaves me in peace, instead humming to the low music on the radio.

When he pulls into the driveway of the clubhouse, he grabs my arm before I can get out.

"Last chance. You sure you don't want me to carry you in there?" He wiggles his eyebrow.

I punch him in the chest. "Asshole."

I step out of the car, not waiting for him to follow me. Walking inside, I see many of the same faces from the day before, but also several more that I don't recognize. Seeing Hannah, I make my way to her.

Blaze walks in seconds behind me, his eyes scanning the room until he finds me. Then he smiles big.

"Hey, Rome," he calls out.

What the fuck is he doing?

Rome walks in from the hall, making his way to the head of the table while the rest of us mill around.

"Your girl's feet hurt. You should take care of that for her." He winks at me.

"I'm going to fucking kill you, Blaze." I glower at him.

Roman comes toward me, pulling me to where he was headed, making me sit in his seat. He grabs another chair, pulling it next to mine.

Then he leans in and whispers, "Do you need anything? I have some painkillers."

"I'm fine. Blaze is being Blaze. Ignore him. I fucking do."

He shakes his head, reaching down to place his hand on my thigh. "If you insist."

Turning to the room, he clears his throat. The voices quiet down.

"Take a seat."

As everyone settles down, I can feel their eyes on me. I'm no longer just Roxy. No, now I'm the boss's girl.

Fuck, this sucks.

"We had a development overnight. We intercepted some communications from the Devil's Den about a shipment they are transporting. We believe this shipment is stolen parts from our town. We are going to run our own mission, taking these parts back. We need at least one man from the crew alive to record a message as proof. Once we have it, we can make our next move."

A man I don't know raises his hand. "What if they retaliate?"

Roman speaks up again. "I'm sure they will. We will be hitting them where they have been making their money. My source tells me that since they were banned from many of the races around the state and some in California, they have had to resort to other means to keep shit up and running."

A different man speaks up next. "Is this the best course of action for all of us?"

I tense, waiting for Roman to explode, but he doesn't. Instead, his thumb begins to caress my leg. "That is always the concern. What move is the best to make for the crew? Should we do nothing and let it fester? Should we attempt to set them up with the authorities? Or should we handle it ourselves? I'm a firm believer that it won't get done right unless you do it yourself. I don't want to trust this with anyone, but my family. If any of you truly feel this is something you do not wish to participate in, then I understand. I will pardon you from this mission as the dangers are grave."

The second man that spoke speaks again, "Of course I'm in. Family first. Always."

Roman nods his appreciation.

"Are there any more questions?"

When no one speaks up, he continues, "Three days from now. That's when we hit. Everyone will get their marching orders separately. Keep your orders to yourself. Don't speak of them to anyone, not even another Shadow. Don't even tell your fucking cat. Understood?"

When they all nod, he dismisses them. "Thank you for coming. We will talk in a couple of days."

He stands, so I stand with him. When he slips his hand into mine, pulling me along with him, I follow. Then he introduces me to everyone as they say their goodbyes to him.

The level of respect is astounding. Not only for Roman, but for me. They blindly trust me because Roman told them they should.

It's a heady feeling.

When the last of them leaves and it's just the core group, Roman turns to them.

"We're going to my place."

No one argues as he pulls me out the door. I don't miss the wink Blaze sends me though.

Asshole.

When we get to his car, he opens the door for me.

"What if I don't want to go home with you? I'm still mad at you." I cross my arms over my chest.

He grips my shoulders, pulling me into his chest for a hug. Then he kisses the crown of my head.

"Please don't be difficult tonight." He lets out a sigh. "Shit is about to pop off and I really could use a relaxing night before it does."

Pulling back, I look up and see the mask he normally wears is nowhere in sight. Instead, I see the real Roman. The one who has the weight of the world on his shoulders.

I nod before turning to get into the car without saying a word.

I can give this to him. For tonight.

The ride to his house is silent. He doesn't live far from the clubhouse though, so it's a short ride.

Once we arrive, he comes around to open my door for me. Before I can stand, he bends down to pick me up in his arms.

"What are you doing?" I ask, wrapping my arms around his neck.

"Your feet hurt. I'm helping with that."

I snort, but don't stop him. My feet really do hurt, but I also want to give him this. If this makes him happy, then I can take it for the night.

Once at the door, he types in a code on a pad before I hear the lock disengage. Then he opens it, walking me inside to set me down on the couch. He doubles back, closing the door before heading into the kitchen.

"You want something to drink?"

Making a rash decision, I admit to myself what I really want.

"No."

Standing, I pull off my uniform before pulling off my bra and panties.

Then I walk toward the kitchen, finding him at the fridge.

"Rome, will you take me to bed?" The sultry tone of my voice surprises even me.

He spins, his eyes widening as he takes me in. The bottle of beer in his hand slips from his grip, shattering on the ground.

"Roman." My voice now laced with concern.

He steps over the mess, stalking toward me. Once he clears the kitchen counter, he toes off his shoes before he is at my side. Then he picks me up, my legs wrapping around his middle.

"You are so fucking gorgeous and all fucking mine."

His words hit me in the chest, but before I can respond, his lips are on me. As he kisses the life out of me, he starts walking. It's not until my back hits a soft surface that I realize he has taken me to his bed, just like I demanded.

Pulling back from him, I bark out my next instruction. "I need you naked. Right now."

He smirks at me. "So bossy."

I give him my own smirk back. "From what I hear, this fancy mark I have means I can make demands. Now, naked Roman."

He salutes me with a laugh before pulling his clothes off.

Once he is back against me, he presses kisses to the corner of my mouth. I thrust my hips at him, needing him inside me.

When the head is finally at my entrance, I angle up to take him inside.

"Fuck, Rox. You feel fucking amazing, but we need a condom."

He pulls back, making me whimper, but I appreciate that he is in control enough to remember that neither one of us is ready for a kid. Fuck, we can't even decide we are a thing.

I wait impatiently as he reaches into his nightstand to pull the condom out before tearing it open and rolling it onto himself. Then he is back at my entrance.

Instead of roughly thrusting in as he has in the past, he slides in nice and slow. As he continues a languid pace, his hand reaches up to tangle into my hair. His forehead rests on mine as I wrap my legs around his hips.

"Rome," I moan as I feel myself slowly climbing.

This is different. The times before were like a current, dragging me higher so quickly I could barely register what was happening as I cascaded over the edge.

This time is slower. More sensual. He is in no hurry to finish this, yet I feel this is even more erotic. As if the slow pace allows me to feel every minute movement he makes. Like the way his dick twitches when I take a deep breath, clenching around him.

My eyes meet his as my chest starts to feel heavy with emotion. This is not just sex. This is more than that.

I don't know what it is, but I don't want to stop it. I'm tired of fighting it.

As I climax staring into his eyes, I finally let go.

I'm his.

ROMAN

FEELING ROXY CLENCH around me is one of my favorite things in the entire world. Especially when I'm making love to her because have no doubt, that's what we just did.

After she came all over my cock, I let myself release inside her.

Fuck, when I slid in bare, it was all I could do to stop her. I wanted to feel her like that. It was more intimate that anything we have ever done.

Still, I stopped us. I want to fill her up until she is impregnated with my baby, but we need to settle shit between us first.

She's not ready to hear it, but I love her. I have for a while now. If she was being honest with herself, she loves me too. I can see it reflected in her eyes.

Still, she pulls back. That's okay though. We have nothing, but time.

As she lays on my chest in the aftermath of the best sex of my life, I twirl her hair between my fingers.

I want this every single day of my life. My feelings for her are so big that I would give up the crew for her without a second thought. She's it for me.

After several moments of silence, I decide to give her what has been plaguing me.

"I think we have a rat in our midst."

The words are a whisper, but the way she tenses tells me she heard.

"Like in the club or in this house?"

I shake my head. "In the club. Someone has been feeding information to the Devil's Den about places to hit and our activities."

Leaning her chin on my chest, she looks up at me. "What are you going to do?"

I give her a sad smile. "This plan isn't a real thing. It's a smokescreen. We are hoping the rat runs to them and tells them we have a line on their shipment, but there is no shipment. We made it up. Either way, the day of the mission, each member will get a different location to go to. The rat won't go to theirs. Axel has eyes on each one. I'm not sure what they will do, but we will catch them either way."

"What will you do when you catch them?"

I brush a piece of hair from her face. Fuck, she is beautiful.

"We will interrogate them then use them to send a message."

She swallows hard. "You'll kill them?"

"We have to, baby. If we let them go, it would be seen as a weakness. We have to nip this in the bud before others defect. I don't know what the Devil's Den offered, but to see one of my own stray breaks my fucking heart."

She presses her face closer to mine, kissing my lips gently. "You are an amazing man, Roman Carter. You care about your people. Whoever strayed, that's not on you. That's on them. I know you. You wouldn't have given them a reason to leave. They should've come forward as soon as the Devils approached them."

Cupping her face, I press my lips back to hers. "This is why I chose you. I know you didn't want my mark, but I'm glad it's you. Thank you for being here with me."

"Of course." She settles her head back on my chest as I go back to playing with her hair.

After several minutes of silence, she asks, "Do you have a suspicion as to who it is?"

My heart hammers in my chest.

"I do."

"Who?"

"I don't want to speak it into existence. I'm praying to God I'm wrong."

Her breath catches. "It'll be okay, Rome. No matter who it is, we will handle it."

"We?" I tease.

I can feel her smile against me as she presses a kiss to my chest. "You gave me your mark. That means we are a team now. Isn't that right?"

"That mark means you're mine," I growl.

"It also means *you* are mine. Don't forget that."

My dick twitches at her declaration. I fucking love that she just claimed me like that.

Flipping her over, I press a hard kiss to her lips as I settle between her legs.

"Fucking right, that makes me yours."

She giggles. "Again, Roman?"

"I can't get enough of you."

Shaking her head, she says, "You're insatiable."
Then she pulls me closer.
Fuck, I love this chick.

CHAPTER TWENTY-TWO

Roxy

I pace the floor, waiting for an update. Roman didn't want to leave me here alone, but he needed as many people as he could get. I should be there with him too, but I understand why he asked me to stay back. I would be a distraction to him. I don't want him to get hurt for my own foolish pride.

A knock at the door causes me to pause. I look down at my phone, not seeing any missed called or texts.

I make my way to the door, peeking out the peephole. My anxiety melts away when I see him.

Throwing open the door, I greet him.

"Marco, what are you doing here?" I ask hesitantly.

Roman told me all the guys were on a job and not to leave the house or open the door for anyone, but it's Marco. I can't not open the door for him.

"I finished early. Do you want to go for a ride with me?"

I smile warmly at him. "Sure. I should let Roman know though."

He shakes his head. "I already told him. Come on."

He reaches his hand out. I slip mine into his easily.

As we walk to his bike parked in the driveway, I notice the slump in his shoulders. When he turns to help me put the helmet on, the sadness in his eyes punches me in the gut.

"Is everything okay?" I place my hand on his arm.

His smile is somber. "It will be. Come on."

Marco pulls off his jacket offering it to me. I smile at him. Always considerate.

I climb behind him, wrapping my arms tightly around him, pressing my body against his in a hug. I feel like in this moment he really needs it.

He reaches down to squeeze my hand before starting the bike and taking off. This time I don't feel the freedom. I don't feel the light heartedness or the exhilaration. Instead, I feel like there is a weight on us. A dark cloud looming overhead ready to pour its sorrow down.

I recognize the park as soon as we pull in. He helps me off the bike, not letting go of my hand. Then he leads me over to the swings, gesturing for me to sit as he grabs the swing he sat on before.

I want to say something, but I feel like he might need this moment. Just a moment of silence with someone he cares about.

I don't know how long we sit like that, but when he eventually speaks, his voice is flooded with emotion.

"I met Roman on this playground twenty years ago. It was always me and Susie, but then Roman came. We would take turns being the runner on the merry-go-round so the other could get the full experience. When Susie would get hurt, he would help me care for her. He became my best friend and Susie's other brother. He became family. When he started the Shadows, I understood why he did it. He made a place where he could better protect his family and that included us. You see, Mom worked a lot. My dad ran off shortly after Susie was born. It was just us three. Roman had a similar background. He didn't have much at home, so he made a home for us. Then Axel and Blaze came. Then Hannah. Now you. He only ever lets those he trusts the most in the inner circle. Until you, he hadn't let anyone in for a really long time."

I go to say something, but he shakes his head.

"Let me get this out. It's hard enough."

"Okay." My voice is almost a whisper.

"I'm telling you this because I want you to know where I was coming from. Roman has always given up everything for us. For his family. He has never once taken a second look at a woman. He always vowed he would never give his mark because that would give that person power over not only him, but his whole family and he could never see himself trusting someone that much. That's why he is going to need you."

My mind is racing with his words. What is he saying? My stomach drops when his voice falters. He looks up at me with watery eyes.

"I fucked up, Rox."

I move off my swing to stand in front of him, pulling his head to my chest as I stroke his hair. "It's okay. We're a family. We can fix this. Whatever it is, we will get through it."

"It's not that simple."

"It is. Family forgives. We heal."

He lets out a humorless chuckle. "You're perfect. Do you know that? You're the perfect woman. As quickly as Roman fell for you, I fell for you too. You didn't see me though. I was angry about that. He marked you before I even really had a chance. Then I found out he didn't even tell you the real reason for the mark? Fuck, I never wanted to hurt my best friend more than I did that day."

My heart starts beating frantically in my chest.

No. Why would he admit this now?

"I'm sorry," I whisper.

I'm being honest too. I'm not sorry for my feelings for Roman, but I am sorry I couldn't feel that way toward Marco. That I couldn't give him the love he deserves because my heart had already been stolen by another.

"Don't be. You chose right. I'm not worthy."

"Yes, you are." I grip his face in mine, leaning down so we are eye to eye. "You are worthy of love. You will find it. I'm sorry it wasn't me, but you have someone out there that is perfect for you."

He reaches up, cupping my face. "I never even got to kiss you."

Before I can pull back, he presses a quick kiss to my lips.

"Marco," I start, but he interrupts me.

"I had to. Just once. Roxy, the Devils took my sister. They have Susie. They have had her for months now and I can't get her back. I've been doing everything I fucking can, but I can't get her. I fucked up."

"What? We need to call Roman. He will know what to do. What the fuck are we doing sitting here?"

"Roman knows… Now. Listen, I'm telling you this because I know you. You're going to blame him, but I wanted to talk to you. To tell you not to. He loves you. Don't give up on him. This has to happen, Rox. He doesn't have a choice. There's a code we live by. I broke that code and I need to face the consequences."

"What are you talking about?"

I hear him then. The distinct purr of Roman's engine. He's here.

Glancing over my shoulder, I see his headlights as he comes screeching to a stop.

"Remember what I said, Rox. He loves you even more than I do."

Then Marco pushes me back to stand next to me.

Roman jumps from the car, striding to us with purpose.

"Get the fuck away from her," Roman spits, reaching to pull me to his side.

"What the fuck, Rome?" I scream.

He ignores me. "You traitorous bastard."

Marco nods. "They have Susie. I did what I had to."

"You didn't have to do this, man. Why didn't you tell me right away? We could have fucking got her back. Instead you turned rat. How much did you tell them?"

He shrugs. "I wanted to tell you, but they threatened to torture her if they even thought I said something. I couldn't do that to her, Rome. Susie is innocent in all this. She never wanted to be part of it."

"What about your mom? She didn't call me or the cops."

"They let her talk to Mom. Mom believes she is backpacking in Europe with a friend. It was a surprise to her, but not unlike Susie."

"Fuck man. You know what I have to do." Roman paces, running his hands through his hair.

"I know. I'm sorry, brother. I'm so fucking sorry."

Marco breaks down and starts sobbing. I take a step toward him to comfort him, but Roman puts a hand to my chest, stepping into him instead.

He pulls Marco into a hug. Marco clings to him.

After several minutes pass, Roman steps back, pulling a gun from his hip to point at Marco's head.

"Roman, what are you doing?" I try to step between them, but Roman wraps his free arm around my shoulders, pulling my back to his front.

"It's okay, Rox. Remember what I said. He has to," Marco reassures me.

"No, he doesn't. He has a choice. You're family. We don't kill family." My own tears well up in my eyes as I stare at him.

Everything starts falling into place. Marco wanted to say his goodbye to me. That's why he brought me here. He knew Roman would come. He knew Roman would kill him.

"Rome, I need you to take care of them. Mom is going to need you, especially when you tell her about Susie. You need to promise you will do whatever you can to get her back."

"I will. I'll take care of them. I'm sorry it has to be this way."

"Me too. I love you, brother."

"I love you too," Roman rasps.

"Wait." I turn in Roman's arm, looking up at him. "Don't do this. We can let him leave. They can think he's dead. Please Roman. Don't do this," I beg.

"If I don't, someone else will. He can't run. What kind of life would that be? He would be hunted. He would have no one. He would never be able to talk to his family again."

"He would be alive, Rome. Please."

Roman glances up to Marco. "Is that what you want?"

Marco speaks behind me. "I want an honorable death. Rox, I know this isn't what you want, but it's how it has to be. If I don't die, they will think Roman is weak. They will attack you guys more because of me. I could never live with myself if that were the case. Rome, do it. She will forgive you. Do it."

I start to sob. "I won't forgive you. He's lying."

Roman gives me a sad smile. "I know."

Then he pulls the trigger as my body crumples. He holds me to him as my ears ring. My body shakes and convulses.

I don't know how long we stand there, but the whole time Roman holds me to him, letting me cry for the brother we just lost. He whispers words I can't hear and strokes my hair, letting me have my moment.

When I finally start to get myself together, I tense. Then I pull away from him.

Roman's own eyes are teary as he stares at me.

"I won't forgive you for this. We are a family. We do anything for one another. We do not kill each other."

"I understand. Go wait in the car."

I scoff. "Wait in the car? No. I'm fucking leaving."

I start to walk away, but he follows me, grabbing my arm to stop me. "You're not going anywhere."

I shake my head, laughing. "So not only are you a murderer, but you're a liar?"

"I've never lied to you."

"You said you would let me leave if I wanted to. I want to leave."

He tightens his hold. "I said I would never hold you back from leaving. I never said you would go alone. Where you go, I go. You want to leave this place? I go with you. I don't care where we end up. Some mansion in fucking Ireland or some shit hole in Peru. Fuck, let's move to Antarctica. I don't care. You're angry, I get that. Remember what I said before. We fucking fight or we fuck, but we do not fucking walk out."

"This is more than anger, Rome. I fucking hate you. I can't even stand to look at you. You're despicable. The worst human being on this Earth. I can't be around you right now. I'm leaving. I can never trust a man who would put a bullet in his brother's head for any fucking reason. How could I trust you not to do the same to me? I'm leaving. I don't give a fuck what you say. Even if I have to cut this tattoo from my skin, I will go. Let me go."

"No," he growls.

I don't hesitate another second. Catching him off guard, I swing my hand out to hit him in the neck before bringing my knee up to hit him in the crotch. As he doubles over, I take off toward Marco's bike. I shove the helmet on, grateful that he left the keys in the ignition.

For a brief moment, the sorrow starts to creep up, but I push it down. I start the bike, taking off down the road. I don't wait.

ROMAN

Dropping to my knees, I breathe in through my nose and out through my mouth. Looking up I watch the taillights of Marco's bike speeding off. Roxy swerves, making my stomach lurch.

"Fuck!" I roar, looking up at the sky.

My phone rings in my pocket and I reach into my pocket grabbing it.

Axel's name flashes on the screen.

"Yeah?" I answer, trying to sound strong.

"Hey, where are you?"

"What's up?" I ask, purposely ignoring his question.

Axel pauses for a moment. "Did you find Marco?"

"I did," I rasp, looking over at my best friend.

"Did you handle it?"

"It's done," I tell him.

"Do-do you need help?" he hesitates.

"No, I got it."

"Are you sure?"

"I'll meet you and the others at the clubhouse once I'm done," I tell him before hanging up.

Getting to my feet, I stagger toward my best friend. Looking down at Marco, I go through the emotions. I'm hit with betrayal and anger.

"I fucking hate you," I whisper to him.

Leaning down, I get to work, moving his body out of the park.

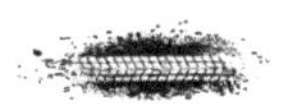

Pulling into the clubhouse, I put the car in park and lean back, shutting my eyes.

Why did I choose this life?

I always knew there would come a time I would have to take a life I just never thought it would be my best friends. Swallowing down the emotions, I get out of the car and walk toward the clubhouse. Looking around, I see everyone has left for the night but the main crew. As I walk in I brace myself for the questions.

Shutting the door, I walk toward the kitchen and come to a stop and stare at Axel, Blaze, and Hannah. Hannah spots me and jumps out of Blaze's lap, running toward me. She runs full force into me, wrapping her arms around me in a tight hug. I'm so tired I don't even have the energy to hug her back.

"Are you okay?" she asks as she pulls away.

"Han," Blaze chastises.

"Shit." She cringes. "Dumb question. Sorry."

"It's okay," I say, patting her shoulder.

We walk toward the table and I take a seat while she sits back in Blaze's lap.

"Have you talked to Rox yet?" she asks.

"Yeah, I'm surprised you didn't bring her," Blaze says.

"Guys…" Axel warns as he looks at me.

"For some reason, Roxy was with Marco. She watched everything go down and couldn't handle it and left." I shrug, reaching for the bottle of whiskey.

"What do you mean left?" Blaze asks, sharing a look with Hannah.

"I don't think she will be back," I say before tipping the bottle back.

Hannah opens her mouth to say something but stops when Axel shakes his head.

"Did Marco say why he did it?" Axel asks.

I nod. "They have Susie. I guess they have for months. He double crossed us to try and get her back." I chuckle darkly. "Too bad he never told us. Maybe she would be home by now and he would be breathing."

"We will handle everything so you don't have to," Hannah says softly.

"I'd appreciate it." I sigh. "Tonight I'm going to drink until I forget. Tomorrow we will figure out a way to get Susie back."

"And Roxy…" Hannah says hesitantly.

"She made her choice," I say, standing. "Now, if you excuse me. I need a shower," I say, carrying the whiskey with me.

I make my way into my room and shut the door. Walking into the bathroom, I turn on the shower. Setting the whiskey on the counter, I grab my phone, setting it next to the bottle and remove my clothes. Once the bathroom starts to I grab the bottle and walk into the shower and sit on the bench. Taking a pull from the bottle, I tilt my head back and replay the evening over again.

Fuck Marco and his secrets. I gave him more than enough chances to come clean and he wouldn't.

Fuck Roxy for running when she should have stayed.

Setting the bottle down, I wash the dirt and grime off before shutting off the shower. Grabbing the bottle, I get out of the shower and dry off. With the towel wrapped around my waist, I grab my phone and walk into my room and sit on the edge of my bed.

Pulling up my contacts, I stare at the naming, knowing that I need to call but not wanting to. Bringing the phone to my ear it rings twice before he answers.

"It's late."

"She's gone," I say emotionlessly.

He pauses. "What do you mean?"

"She couldn't handle club business and ran." I shrug, taking a drink.

"I see..."

"I just thought I should let you know. In case she shows up."

"Thanks for the heads up," he says before hanging up.

Dropping my phone on the bed, I take another drink. Leaning back, I let the whiskey run through my veins and shut my eyes, praying for sleep.

CHAPTER TWENTY-THREE

Roxy

Looking down, I huff out a sigh. I've been on the road for three hours. Apparently that's as much gas as Marco had in this thing. Easing over to the side of the road, I turn the bike off, hopping off.

I could keep walking, but where would I go? What was I thinking leaving like that? I should have at least run back to the house to get my phone and some money.

Maybe not the phone, but money would be helpful about now.

Standing with my hands on my head, I consider my options.

If I start walking now, maybe I can hitchhike far enough away, but without my ID there's no way to get a job. Well, not a legal one at least.

For a moment, my heart pangs. I hate that I'm leaving everyone else behind. They really have been quite good to me.

Shaking my thoughts away, I start to pace.

I could call Ross. He said he didn't want me to come back, but if I'm being honest with myself, that was never truly about me. Even making me leave, he still tried to keep in touch even if I refused contact. He has to care about me at least a little bit. Maybe he would send me some money to get away. Once I'm settled I could pay him back later.

Probably a terrible idea. Roman would've probably contacted him by now to tell him I'm on the run. Still the only other number I know by heart is Roman's and he is the one I'm running from.

I bite my lip.

Maybe I should go back. My heart is aching in my chest, but did I act irrationally? I mean, who jumps on a bike and high tails it like that?

Marco.

My chest spasms as I sob into my hand. My beautiful Marco. Fuck, I'm going to miss him. I might not have returned his feelings, but he became important to me. He was the lightness to Roman's dark. He was the kind ear when I needed to vent about whatever bullshit was going on. He was my best friend. Now he's gone.

Roman killed him.

Fuck.

I kneel down, sobbing into my knees as my whole body convulses. How am I going to reconcile the man I've come to love with the man who shot his best friend point blank? Does he even care? He didn't even look all that bothered by it. All he was worried about was me. About me leaving him.

Is he really that selfish?

Do I love someone as selfish as my mother? Only caring about themselves?

Logically, I know that Marco betrayed us. That should hurt me more than it does. Yes, I'm disappointed that went behind our backs, but he had good reason. They have his sister. What wouldn't I do for the people I love?

My mind starts to replay the events from the past few months. The attack outside the restaurant. The way Marco was insistent that he be the one who went on my first job with me to Zade's shop. Hell, maybe even when I thought someone was lurking outside the cabin. That all could have been Marco.

It makes sense now. Marco wanted to go to the shop because he was in on it. That's why Zade was there.

Then the attack. Roman said he was mad at himself for letting Marco talk him into giving me space. He even said it was Marco's idea to eat there that night. Did he know what was going to happen in that alley?

Reconciling the Marco I know and love with his admissions is heartbreaking.

Still, I'm not sure I can forgive Roman. How could he point a gun at someone he claims to love and pull the trigger? I meant what I said to him. If he can so easily kill a man he considered his brother for a good portion of his life, what would he do with a woman he has only known for a couple of months?

Startling from my thoughts, I look up to see a car roll to a stop next to me.

"Hey, are you okay?"

It's a woman's voice. Standing, I see a young woman who looks to be in her teens in the driver's seat with a similar in age woman in the passenger seat. The driver barely has her window rolled down. Only enough to talk to me.

The cross hanging on her neck glints in the sun. It reminds me of the cross Ross wears.

"Yeah. I ran out of gas. Do you have a phone I could borrow for a moment?"

The girl eyes me warily.

"Where is your phone?"

"Honestly, I'm a bit of a mess. I just witnessed my boyfriend do something terrible."

The driver's eyes soften with understanding. "I'm sorry to hear that. How about you climb in? I'll run you up the road to get some gas and bring you back and you can call someone on the way."

"Are you sure? I mean, I'm not going to hurt you, but I understand if you don't feel safe."

She gives me a smile. "Something in my gut told me to stop. I always trust my gut."

I hear the doors unlock. I go back to the bike, grabbing the keys before sliding back into the backseat of the car.

Once inside, the passenger turns around, holding out a phone.

"I'm Amber and this is Cheryl. Call whoever you need."

"Roxy"—I point to myself— "and thank you."

The phone is unlocked so I bring up the dial pad. I hesitate a moment.

I could call Roman. He would come get me in a heartbeat. I know he would, but I'm still too raw. I still don't know if I can trust him. I want to, but

I'm fucking broken from what he did.

Taking a deep breath, I let my mind clear, dialing whatever number feels natural.

When it rings out to voice mail, I chuckle when I hear his voice.

Of course he wouldn't answer on the first ring. That would be too easy.

I dial again with the same result. I keep dialing until finally on the sixth try, he answers.

"What." His gruff voice bites out the word as a statement rather than a question.

Just hearing his voice makes my heart catch.

I can't even help the sob that comes out next. Amber turns, giving me a sympathetic look.

"Ross, I need help. I fucked up."

I hear him let out a deep sigh. "Roxy, baby. What's wrong?"

I shake my head, unable to speak. When I hold out the phone to Amber, she takes it easily, pulling it to her ear.

I can hear her talking to Ross, but I can't focus.

I thought I was strong. That I could handle crew life. Maybe Ross knew me better than I know myself. Maybe that's why he wouldn't mark me. Maybe I'm not cut out for this life.

If killing your best friend is the right decision at any time, then I'm not sure I want to be in this life.

After several deep breaths, I calm. Amber turns, handing the phone back to me.

"Ross." My voice breaks.

I feel like the kid Roman always calls me.

"Hang in there. They are going to give you gas and some money. You take it and head this way. I already sent an escort. Get as far as you can, then call me and let me know where you end up. I got you."

"Thank you."

ROMAN

Ross/Soulless- I have her.

The text comes through and my heart stops. Without thinking about it I press the call button and bring the phone to my ear.

"Yeah?"

"She's there?"

"That's what I said."

"What has she said?" I ask, rubbing a hand over my face.

Ross pauses. "Look she hasn't said anything and I doubt she will. But even if she did what she tells me isn't your business," he says, making me groan. "If you care about her let her be. Trust me, she needs to work through whatever's bothering her. If she wants to talk to you she will."

"Okay," I say, hating how well he knows my woman.

"Now if you'll excuse me, I was in the middle of something," he says before hanging up.

I drop my cell down and brace my hands on my desk.

I miss her.

Does she miss me?

Is she happy to be back with Ross?

Did they have a thing?

A knock at my door pulls me from my thoughts and I look up and see Hannah standing there, shifting from side to side.

"Come in," I tell her as I drop down into my seat. "Did you get everything done?"

"Yeah, the funeral is planned," she says, biting her lip. "You should probably swing by tonight and see his mom. She kept mentioning you today."

I nod, closing my eyes bone tired. "Okay, I can do that."

"Have you gotten any sleep?"

"What do you think?" I ask, opening one eye.

"You know they would want you to take care of yourself," she chastises.

"Yeah, well they aren't here," I sneer, making Hannah flinch. I can't help but feel bad. "Sorry."

"No, don't be." She shakes her head. "Have you heard from her?"

"Her? No. Ross texted me and told me she made it to him though."

"I was hoping she would at least text me."

"Same here," I say under my breath.

"There you are," Blaze says from the doorway staring at Hannah. "When did you get here?"

"A few minutes ago." She shrugs.

"Why didn't you come find me in the shop?" he frowns.

"I figured you were busy and planned on stopping on my way out."

I watch the way they look at each other and shake my head. "Why aren't you two together again?" I blurt out, making them pause.

"It's not like that..." Hannah blushes.

"We're not done sowing our oats." Blaze winks, missing Hannah's flinch.

Idiot.

"Right... how about you guys take this out of my office. I have some paperwork to deal with."

"Okay, remember to stop by Marco's mother's house later," Hannah says as she stands.

"Drive safe," I say as she walks away.

I look down and take a deep breath knowing that it's going to get rough before things go back to normal.

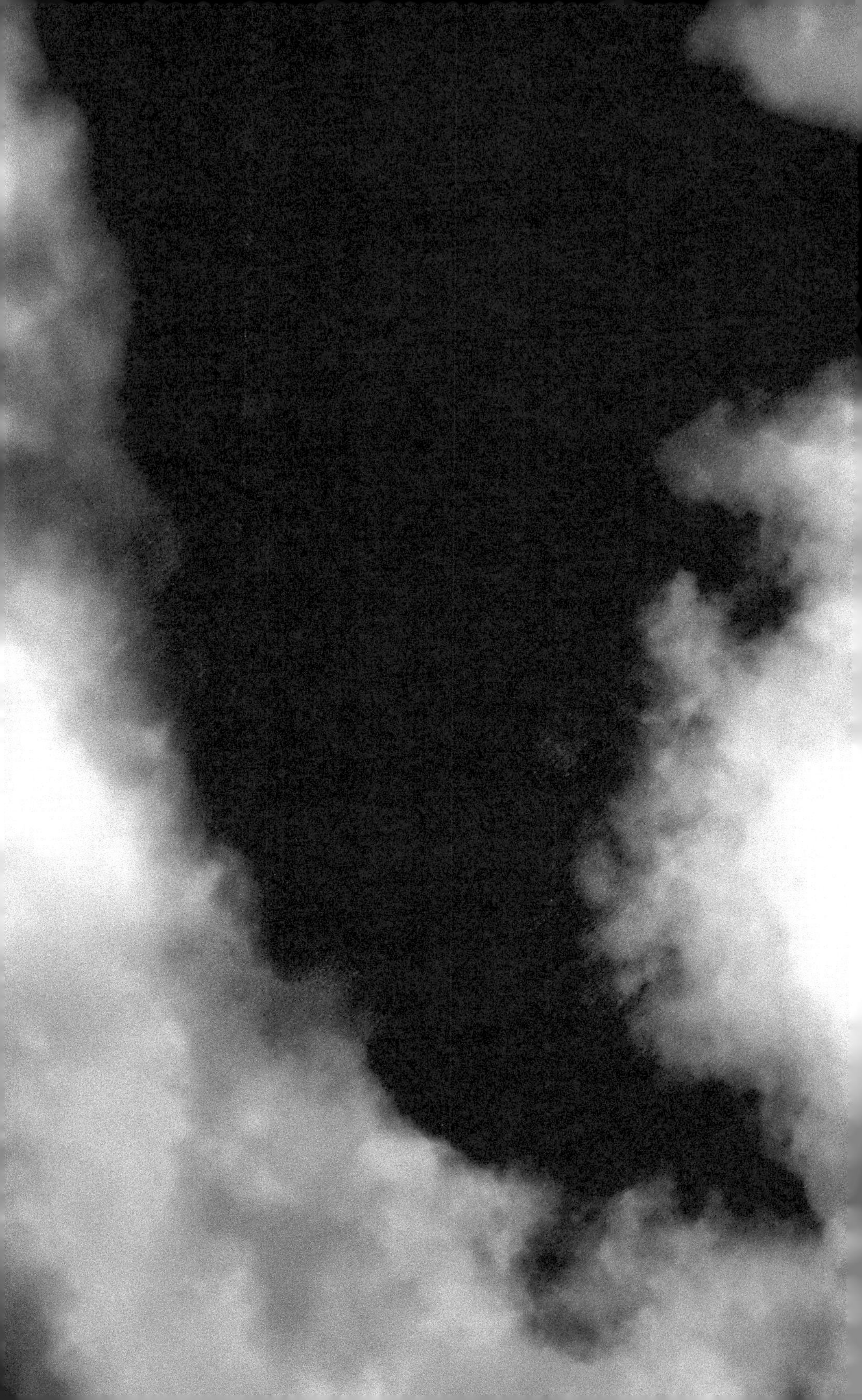

CHAPTER TWENTY-FOUR

Roxy

It's been three days. Three long days since my life imploded.

Ross was true to his word. I drove another two hours on the money the kind strangers offered before settling in a small town.

By the next morning, I had my own escort in the form of two of Ross's soldiers.

They wanted me to leave the bike, but I refused. It was Marco's bike and now it was going to be mine. Or maybe his sister's. That's if we get her back.

So they let me take the lead, driving all the way back to Riviera.

When Ross opened his door, arms open wide, I ran right to him, breaking down as soon as I felt his embrace around me.

I didn't realize how much I missed him. I tried to be tough. Pretend like my time here was nothing to me, but it was everything. They were my family as much as the Shadows were my family.

After I bawled my eyes out, he fed me and made me rest.

I knew I wouldn't get so lucky today. He'll want answers and I'm not sure I can provide them to him.

As much as I needed him, I also cannot betray my crew.

I feel like my life is a series of fuck-ups. One after another.

I don't stay in bed long. I need to get this over with. The more I lay here and think about it, the more I'm itching to get back home. I shouldn't have left. Not until I get Susie back.

That's what Marco wanted. It's what he asked Roman to promise before he died.

I'm not sure I trust Roman right now, but I have to believe he would want to rescue her. He might be an asshole, but he does have some morals.

I hope.

Heading out of the room, I make my way down the familiar hall to the kitchen I grew up in. Ross is where I expected.

I stop in the archway for a moment, lost in the countless memories.

Ross is sitting at the head of the kitchen table with a coffee mug in front of him as he reads the newspaper like he does every single day.

While I'm feeling the nostalgia, I don't feel quite at home like I used to. Sure, I miss Ross, but it's not what I want anymore.

"Are you going to stare all day or are you going to sit down and explain why some chick told me your boyfriend was caught cheating and you were having a breakdown?"

He turns the page of his paper before looking over the top quirking an eyebrow.

"What? She said that?"

"Is that not what you told her? Do I need to go to Chita and kick some punk kid's ass? I'll do it."

I let out a deep sigh. "Roman didn't cheat on me."

All of a sudden his humor disappears.

"Roman? Roman Carter?" He slams paper on the table causing his coffee to spill out of the mug.

I swallow hard. "You didn't know?"

"Know what? What the fuck have you gotten yourself mixed up in?"

"I thought for sure you'd have eyes on me somehow. Or at least that Roman would report back to you. He told me you called in a favor."

He shakes his head. "Roman Carter is the leader of the Shadows. He doesn't report to anyone just like I don't. Yes, I called and asked him to keep you out of trouble, but that was the extent of it. He wasn't reporting your every move to me. Since you blocked me and cut me out, I figured a clean cut was for the best."

I walk over to the table, taking a seat next to him.

"It's what I wanted. I wasn't ready to forgive you for sending me away."

He huffs. "I told you I did that for your own good."

"I know. I know that now. I don't think I really realized what it meant to be crew. Trust me, I do now."

"Jesus, Rox. What did you do?"

I hold out my arm, showing him my tattoo. He grabs my hand, pulling me closer as he studies the mark. Then he curses under his breath.

"Want to tell me how you ended up with Roman's mark?" he asks through a clenched jaw.

"He claimed me I guess? I'm not really sure. He said it was for my protection, but I feel like it has only put a bigger target on my back."

"You know what that mark means, right? That Roman will legitimately run through all the circles of hell to get to you. To protect you. He would take his own life before allowing you to take your last breath. You're telling me he did that and 'you guess he claimed you?' Fuck, he's letting the whole world know that you are the single most important person in his life," Ross rants.

I swallow hard. "He picked wrong. He should pick again. I'm not strong enough. I can't do this."

"Rox, you are one of the strongest women I know. You're fierce and loyal. You are the perfect choice. Trust me, that man does not regret it. I bet he regrets whatever he did to make you run though," he says, looking at me like I'm an idiot.

I shrug, not willing to give him that secret. Instead, I turn it on Ross, asking the burning questions that have plagued me.

"If I'm so great, why didn't you mark me. Why did you send me away?"

He lets go of my hand, leaning back in his chair to steeple his hands in front of his face. After a moment, he meets my eye, a pained look on his face.

"It's not that you weren't worthy. We would have been fucking lucky to have you in our ranks. You're a badass woman who can race like no one's business. That wasn't ever what it was about. It wasn't even necessarily about you."

"What was it about then?"

"I saw the stars in your eyes. You thought you had feelings for me. Strong feelings, but I knew I could never return them the same. I wanted to, but I couldn't. Even if I could, I already gave my mark to another," he says, shaking his head.

"What? Who?" I haven't seen him with a woman in a real long time.

He shakes his head. "A ghost from the past, but I promised her I would be a better person. I try to be every day. You deserved better than this life. To be honest, you remind me of her. That's why I didn't mark you. Not only because a lower level mark would have been an insult, but because I couldn't live with myself if something happened to you. That's why I sent you away. You got hurt and I couldn't bear to look at myself for allowing it to happen." He looks away with a pained look on his face. "It killed me watching your car roll. I thought for sure you were gone when I was running toward you."

"I'm here now though."

"So you are. I always told you I would be here for you and that still stands true. Even if you're a Shadow now. My loyalty will be with the Soulless first, but you are a priority too."

"Thank you. I'm not sure I'm even a Shadow anymore. He's probably glad I'm gone after the way I blew up at him. I physically hurt him to get away."

Ross smirks. "That's my girl. Trust me, that man wants you back. I'm surprised he hasn't knocked my door down to get to you yet."

"What do you mean?"

"He's already called me. He knows where you are, Rox. He wouldn't ever admit it to me, but I think he's giving you the space you so dramatically asked for. So do you want to tell me what happened? Since he didn't cheat, I suppose he can keep his balls."

I chuckle at the smile on his face. "I wish I could. Crew business. You know how it is."

"That I do. Listen, I know it can be rough, but trust him. Trust them. You obviously did enough to put that mark on your body. Sometimes Roman will have to be someone you don't like very much. He will do things you don't agree with. I've done them too. I shielded you from that to protect you, but you're in now. You will know it all. You need to decide if you can live with that knowing that you will be giving up the people who are your family if you can't. What's most important to you?"

I mull over his words. "My family."

"Okay then. How about I make you some breakfast before you head home?"

"That would be wonderful."

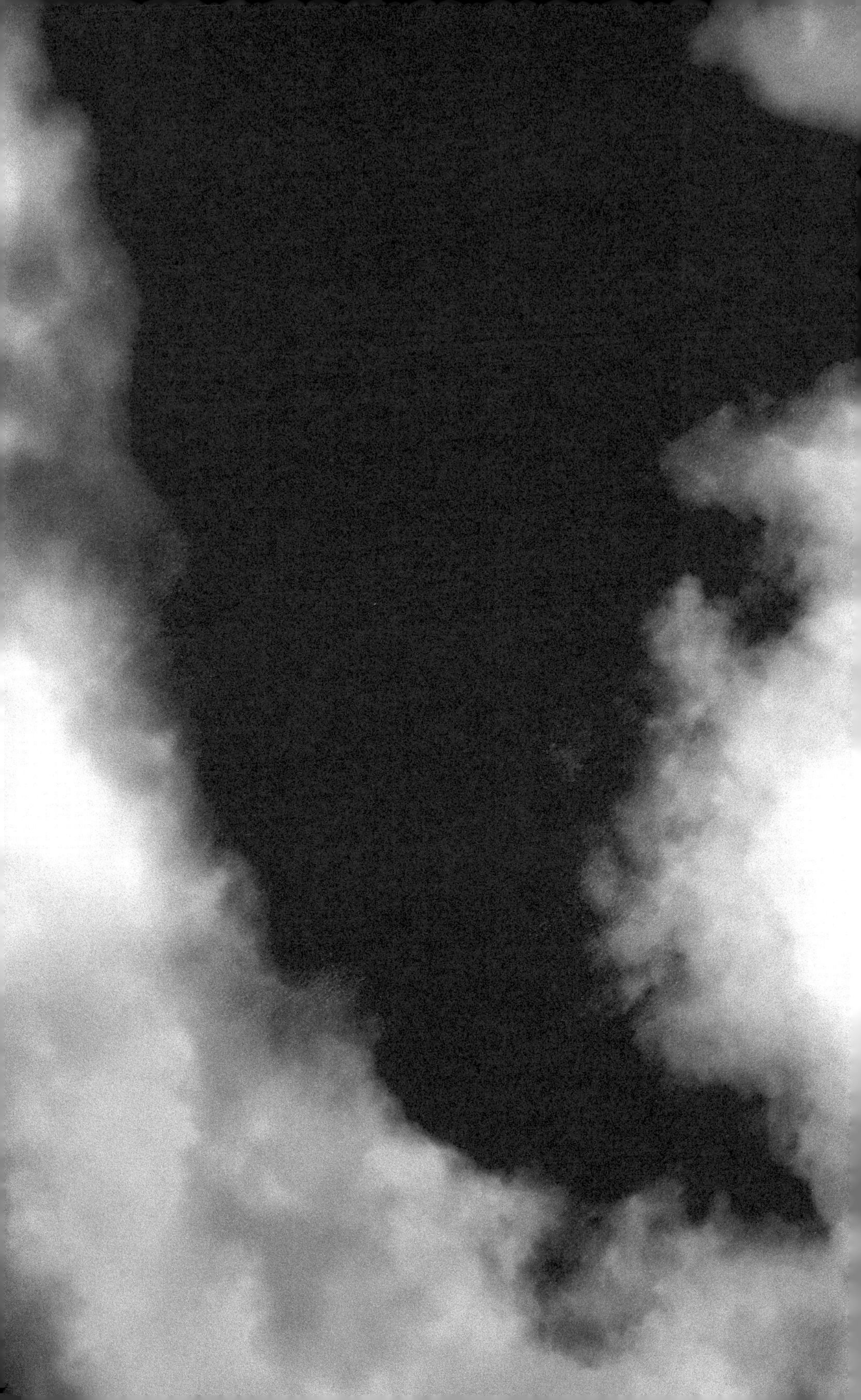

CHAPTER TWENTY-FIVE

Roxy

I don't know if it is luck or if he heard me coming, but as soon as I pull down the driveway, Roman is standing at the door waiting for me.

As soon as I climb off the motorcycle, he stalks toward me. I sidestep him, making my way to the house.

The last time we argued out here, I ended up in the river. I'd prefer not to repeat that experience. Even if it gave me my first kiss with him.

Thankfully, he lets me pass by him, following me into the house.

As soon as I make it to the kitchen, he grabs my arm, spinning me to face him.

I bow up, ready for a fight, but he surprises me. Instead of laying into me like I expected, he grips my hips to pick me up, setting me on the counter. He effortlessly slides between my legs, pressing against me as he leans his face into my neck, inhaling deeply.

"You left me," he growls.

"I know," I bite out, trying to find the anger I thought I would have when I saw him again.

It's not there though. Somewhere between running away, talking to Ross, and the ride back, my will to fight him has diminished. I'm not as angry as I am disappointed. I expected more from him.

"I only have one damn rule for you. We don't walk away from each other angry. Either we fight or we fuck, remember?"

I go to respond, but he cuts me off.

"No. I'm not ready to fight this out yet. You've been gone three fucking days. We are going to fuck this out then you can fight me as much as you fucking want. I don't fucking care if you hit me, scream at me, fuck shoot me if you really want to, but we will fight this out and then I'll fuck you all over again. Do you understand me?"

"Yes."

"Good."

Then his lips crash into mine. He's not soft or gentle nor is he passionate. Instead, he's frenzied. Like he's afraid this is the last time he will ever get to taste my lips. How could I ever think this man might leave me one day? He's desperate for me.

When did he go from the broody asshole to the man I'm in love with. The man who I trust to protect me until his very last breath.

My feelings flood me as I finally admit them to myself. I love him.

I love Roman Carter.

I might be a fucking fool for it, but I'm there.

"Fuck, baby. Don't cry. Please don't cry. I'll fix it. I promise I'll fix whatever it is. I'll do whatever you want. I can't handle your tears."

He repeats his words as he kisses my wet cheeks. I hadn't even realized I was crying. I thought we were going to hate fuck until the anger was contained, but instead, my heart is expanding. The emotions filling me so overwhelming, I'm unable to process them.

"Please, Rome. I need you."

He pulls back to look at me, his own eyes glassy like the thought of me being in pain is causing him pain as well. As if my sadness is his sadness.

"Anything, Rox. Anything you want and it's yours."

"You. I want you."

"You have me. I'm yours, baby. I've been yours since the second I laid eyes on you. You've owned my heart and soul. Every single decision I made from that point on was for you. Not the crew. Not myself, but for you."

My breath catches in my throat. All those times I thought he hated me.

The way he pushed me away or was an asshole to me. That was all a deflection from his true feelings?

"No more talking, Rome. We fuck this out then we can fight. Fuck me, Rome. I need you inside me now."

His eyes turn molten.

"Your wish is my command, baby. Lie back." He presses on me until I'm spread out on the counter.

Then he unbuttons my jeans, pulling my underwear and boots off with them. Then he kisses inside my ankle, alternating kisses from leg to leg until he reaches my center.

"Are you wet for me, Rox?"

My core clenches at his words. I'm always wet when he's around. It's like my body can't help but be primed and ready when he is within eyesight.

"Yes."

He licks up my slit, making me jolt in pleasure.

"Fuck," I breathe out.

"You're going to come on my tongue and then you're going to come on my cock. Understand?"

"Yes, sir," I try to mock, but I'm so horny it comes out more breathless than I expected.

"That's right. Later I might even spank this ass for leaving me, but for now. I need to taste you on my lips."

That's the last thing he says before he dives in. My eyes roll back as he assaults my clit with his tongue. It's like my body was made for him. He knows each and every button to press to push me higher. When he sticks two fingers inside me, curling them up, I about come off the counter from the sensations.

I've never felt as good as Roman makes me feel. Every second I'm with him, I realize I never will with anyone else either. As my climax hits me so hard I see stars, the only thought in my mind is of him. Roman.

Then I'm coming down, his lips pressing kisses up my stomach and breasts until he reaches my face.

"I fucking love you, Roxanne. More than I love my crew and more than I love myself."

I want to respond, but he thrusts into me, taking the words away with his mouth on mine.

The frenzied man from before is gone. In his wake, this loving man using each thrust to drive home his feelings for me. He maintains eye contact, his glazing over as the pleasure starts to fill him. He rocks his body against mine, making sure to rub against my clit each time. It's like a tiny burst of electricity each time.

Then, just as I'm about to come again, he leans down, biting into my neck, pushing me over the edge.

"Mine," he growls as he jerks inside me, filling me with his warmth.

It takes several minutes for me to come down, but when I do, I pull his face off my chest. He frowns, trying to move off of me, but I pull him into me even more.

"I love you too, Rome. I'm disappointed in what you did, but I still love you."

"You won't leave again?"

I consider his words. "No. We fight or we fuck, right? I won't run again."

"Good because it took everything I had not to come kidnap you back."

I scoff. "Like you could've found me."

He traces his fingers until it reaches the necklace he bought me. "I will always know where you're at as long as you always wear this."

My eyes narrow. "You put a tracker in my necklace? Seriously?"

"Haven't you figured it out yet, kid? I'll do anything to protect you. Even lie to you if I have to. You're my number one priority."

Well when he puts it that way, it's hard to stay mad at him.

"How about you don't lie to me no matter what?"

He nods. "So are we fighting yet, or can we fuck again?"

I chuckle, shaking my head. "Take me to bed, Roman."

Hours and several fucks later, I'm lying on Roman's chest, tracing the tattoo on his pec.

"What now?"

He laughs. "What do you mean? Are you ready to fight now?"

I prop myself on my hands on his chest to look up at him. "I'm not going to fight you. I told you. I'm disappointed in what you did but thinking over everything I can see why you did it. How much was Marco really involved in? Did he know about me being jumped? Did he know what I was walking into in that shop the first time?"

"He wrote me a letter. That's why I went to the park. He told me he would be there. He texted me and told me he left me a letter and that when I finished it he would be where we first met. I knew it was bad, but I didn't realize how bad. He was meant to go into that shop with Hannah. That's why he was adamant he go with you. Zade had promised not to hurt Hannah so he had hoped it would have extended to you too. Zade has been stealing car parts for months, trying to pin it on us. He wants to start a war and take over our turf, but I've kept the peace. I don't want war. So Zade went after Marco. He took Marco's sister knowing we couldn't retaliate without consequences. We might not be governed by a council or anything and we might not get along with other clubs, but when one is wronged, the rest will stand up for them. They will band together on principle. It's a stupid criminal code we abide by. So Zade wanted me to make the first move. Since Marco was in on it, they planned to kidnap Hannah and Marco, it wouldn't have actually been a move against me since Marco is one of us, but when I attacked to get them back, it would have been first blood. Then you showed up instead and alone, which Zade had no clue about. He didn't know who you were. He was legitimately hitting on you that day. When he figured out what happened, he sent Marco a video of them hurting his sister. Marco promised he wouldn't fail again. So that's when you got jumped. Marco had been telling them about how I react around you. They thought they could jump you, making me react since you didn't have a mark. I would have too, but you asked me not to. You put the crew above yourself. Then I marked you and Marco was jealous. So he went to them in a rage when he found out, making things worse. They put him on a timeline. He refused to abide by it, deciding to tell me the truth instead."

"So you killed him."

He bites his lip. "I made a decision that was the hardest one in my entire life. It was what was best for you and the crew. Marco knew that. He knew what I would have to do. He also knew he made the first mistake. When Zade took his sister, he should have told me."

"Why didn't he?"

Roman's eyes harden. "Because I would have gone to war over it, consequences be damned. Marco made a decision hoping he could get his sister back while protecting his family, but he couldn't."

"So what now?"

"Now? We get Susie back and make those mother fuckers pay for ever fucking with the Shadows."

EPILOGUE

Roxy

I can't stop the tears. Even knowing everything that happened, I still loved Marco. He had become one of my best friends. My heart is breaking for his family.

Looking past Roman, I see Marco's mother bawling her eyes out as she clutches onto her daughter Susie.

Susie is stoic. The guys rescued her three days ago and you can tell whatever she went through took a toll on her. Not a single tear has fallen down her face. It's almost as if she is a shell of a person.

That kills me even more. Marco did this for his sister, but she's not even living right now.

Roman squeezes my hand in his.

Looking up to him, he cups my face with his other hand.

"It's my turn to talk, baby."

I nod, watching as he walks to the front.

Marco was killed as a traitor, but Roman was insistent that he still speak today. We are all graveside as we say our final goodbyes.

When Roman gets to the front, he looks over at me.

Then he begins to speak.

"Marco was my best friend. As kids, we were inseparable. We always had each other's backs. He was a great kid, and he grew into an even better man. He always did everything he could for his family. His mother and his sister were the most important people in his life. I'm not here to grieve the loss of my friend. He wouldn't want that. Instead, I'm celebrating the life he had and making him this promise. I will watch out for his family as he would want. I know that one day, Marco and I will meet again. I cannot wait until that day, brother."

He kisses his fingers then holds them to the sky.

As he makes his way back toward me, a movement along the tree line catches my eye.

For a split second, I could swear I see Marco standing there, but when I blink it's gone.

It can't be. He's in the casket. I think.

Another voice argues, *It's a closed casket. Is he really in there?*

Roman didn't want Marco's mom to see the bullet hole, so he spun a tale of an accident so gnarly that they had to keep the casket closed. It's also why his mother told Roman to keep Marco's bike. The same bike he gave to me.

When Roman reaches my side again, he takes in my pale face.

"What's wrong, baby?"

"I could have sworn I saw Marco in the trees."

He glances over to where I look before looking back at me with sympathy in his eyes.

"We both know he died that night. In times of grief, we see things that aren't always there. Especially when it's something we want more than anything."

I nod, understanding what he is saying. Of course it was in my head.

As they lower the casket, all of a sudden a wail comes from beside us.

Glancing over, my eyes widen.

Susie is in Axel's arms as she sobs into his chest. He holds her, whispering in her ear.

"What's that about?" I ask Roman.

He leans down, pressing a kiss to my lips. "I don't know, but we should go."

Glancing over to the tree line one more time, I say a silent goodbye to the man I knew.

I'll miss you, Marco.

THE END.

THANK YOU!

Thank you for reading Redlined. We hope you loved this story as much as we do. Want more Shadow Crew Series? Check out, Friction now.

Want to stay up to date on our newest releases and access to exclusive content? Sign up for our newsletter now!

AUTHOR BIO

Cala Riley, better known as Cala and Riley, are a pair of friends with a deep-seated love of books and writing. Both Cala and Riley are happily married and each have children, Cala with the four-legged kind while Riley has a mixture of both two-legged and four. While they live apart, that does not affect their connection. They are the true definition of family. What started as an idea that quickly turned into a full-length book and a bond that will never end.

ACKNOWLEDGEMENTS

Husbands/Family- Thank you for loving us through the crazy and listening to us ramble.

Ashley Estep- Thank you for staying on us to make sure we stayed on schedule.

Louise O'Reilly- Thank you for being you.

Jenny Dicks- Thank you for all the swoons & ideas.

Nikki Pennington- For listening to our rambles and talking us off of ledges.

My Brothers Editor/ Elle- Thank you for being the most laid back editor and making the entire process painless.

Books n Moods- Thank you for everything that you do for us. From covers to formatting and just being a cheerleader in our corner.

Bloggers/Readers- Thank you for loving our stories as much as we do and spreading the word.

ALSO BY AUTHOR

Brighton Academy Series
Unbidden
Unpredictable
Undeniably
Unapologetically

Mafia Royalty Series
Mafia King
Mafia Underboss
Mafia Prince

The Syndicates Series
Matteo
Killian
Haruaki
Nikolai

Trailer Park Girls Duet
Mayhem
Harmony

Shadow Crew Series
Redlined
Friction
Shift
Finish Line

Standalone
One of Them Girls

WHERE TO FIND US

Facebook
Instagram
Tiktok
Bookbub
Goodreads
Amazon
Cala Riley's Boudoir of Sin
Website
Newsletter

Made in USA - Kendallville, IN
40375_9798485481506
07.08.2022 1304